GENESIS

DÉJÀ VU

The New Eden

DEXTER JAMES

Genesis Déjà vu – The New Eden

OTHER BOOKS BY DEXTER JAMES:

Genesis Déjà vu – The Beginning

Heist During the Rio Games

The Ultimate Conspiracy

Of Ghosts and Aliens

To

The Wonderful Jean

Contents

Preface..9

Chapter 1 - Stirring in the New Eden..............................11

Chapter 2 - Aboard the U.S.S. Augusta............................16

Chapter 3 - Realization of a Relapse...............................20

Chapter 4 - Potential for the Creation of Life...................24

Chapter 5 - Going About Their Chores 27

Chapter 6 - Thoughts of Rearing Stock.......................... 30

Chapter 7 - A Sad Day Onboard.......................................34

Chapter 8 - Life on the Island..40

Chapter 9 - Next Steps..43

Chapter 10 - Trip Planning to Nebraska.........................46

Chapter 11 - A Secret is Revealed..................................52

Chapter 12 - Funeral Arrangements Discussed...............57

Chapter 13 - The Devastation Returns.............................61

Chapter 14 - More Talk of Nebraska.......................66

Chapter 15 - New Visitors Have Arrived.........................69

Chapter 16 - Single Again..73

Chapter 17 - Nebraska Re-visited....................................77

Chapter 18 - Moving On...80

Chapter 19 - Contemplating Their Final Moments..........83

Chapter 20 - Funeral Arrangements to Be Made............85

Chapter 21 - Time to Leave the Capsule...........................90

Chapter 22 - A Surprising Decision..99
Chapter 23 - *From Out of This World*..*102*
Chapter 24 - The Funeral Party Sets Out....................................111
Chapter 25 - Life Without Tony...116
Chapter 26 - The Dreaded Nebraska Discussion.........................121
Chapter 27 - Socialising with the Bermuda Detachment......126
Chapter 28 - Surprising Revelations...130
Chapter 29 - Bermuda Breakfast Meeting..................................133
Chapter 30 - Arrival in Bermuda..137
Chapter 31 - Meet and Greet..140
Chapter 32 - Funeral of Admiral Stanford..................................144
Chapter 33 - Arrival in Norfolk..150
Chapter 34 - Search for Supplies..178
Chapter 35 - Fraternising with the Locals..................................160
Chapter 36 - Prepping the Plane...164
Chapter 37 - Awkward Overtures..170
Chapter 38 - The Trip to Nebraska...176
Chapter 39 - Meanwhile, Back on the Farm...............................182
Chapter 40 - Flight Departure..185
Chapter 41 - On Board the U.S.S. Augusta.................................189
Chapter 42 - Arrival in Clay...191
Chapter 43 - Relaxing on Earth..194
Chapter 44 - Reconnaissance in Clay..197
Chapter 45 - Foraging for Supplies...199
Chapter 46 - Trapped in Clay.. ...201

Chapter 47 - Alone on a Beach....................................203
Chapter 48 - Captured Like Pirates..............................206
Chapter 49 - Aboard the Jet..209
Chapter 50 – Confrontation..213
Chapter 51 - Hostage Negotiations...............................215
Chapter 52 - Animals Explained....................................219
Chapter 53 - Situation Defused.....................................226
Chapter 54 - Researching the Research Facility...........228
Chapter 55 - New Shipmate..232
Chapter 56 - Arrangements Agreed..............................236
Chapter 57 - Anxiously Waiting....................................240
Chapter 58 - Farm Hand Training.................................247
Chapter 59 - Finding a Plane..251
Chapter 60 - Arrival at Bermuda...................................254
Chapter 61 - Flying to Clay...257
Chapter 62 - Discussions at the Happy Mariner...........261
Chapter 63 - Hercules Arrival at Clay............................264
Chapter 64 - Augusta's Arrival at St. Santia..................268
Chapter 65 - Preparations Underway – North..............274
Chapter 66 - Preparations Underway – South.............283
Chapter 67 - In Search of Their Pilot............................286
Chapter 68 - On the Beach..291
Chapter 69 - Hercules Departure from Clay.................293
Chapter 70 - Hercules Arrival at St. Santia....................296
Chapter 71 - Awaiting the Return of the Hercules........301

Chapter 72 - Hercules Flight Back to Clay..............................304
Chapter 73 - Re-positioning Flight...307
Chapter 74 - In Search of Fuel..310
Chapter 75 – Concerns...314
Chapter 76 - Trip Back to Clay...316
Chapter 77 - Group Reunion...319
Chapter 78 - Medical Emergency..325
Chapter 79 - Incoming Patient..328
Chapter 80 - Sirens Approaching..331
Chapter 81 – Prognosis...334
Chapter 82 - Life Saving Attempts..337
Chapter 83 - An Accident on Bermuda.....................................341
Chapter 84 - A Life Saver on Bermuda.....................................345
Chapter 85 - Emergency Operation..349
Chapter 86 - Preparations for the Connecticut's Departure.351
Chapter 87 - Along the Coast of Florida...................................355
Chapter 88 - Gulf of Mexico the Time of the Devastation.....358
Chapter 89 - Returning to St. Santia...367
Chapter 90 - Preparing for Dual Operations............................370
Chapter 91 - Transplant Preparations......................................374
Chapter 92 – Transplant...378
Epilogue - Discussions about the Future...................................381

Preface

A meteorite had crashed into the Arctic, unleashing microbes that had taken the lives of all air-breathing creatures, it became to be generally known by the few survivors as the devastation. Throughout the world a few fortunate individuals had survived the catastrophe, submarine personnel, scuba divers, miners etc. but the only two, known, surviving couples left on earth, capable of breeding, had been on a diving holiday and they were marooned on the island of St. Santia in the Caribbean.

By setting up some automated telephones the two couples managed to contact Joan and John Hamax, an elderly couple in Maine, who had also survived the devastation because of an accident that necessitated them being in hospital wearing oxygen masks. The couple decided to make the trip from the mainland to the island of St. Santia and on route their vessel was detected by the submarine U.S.S. Augusta which was being accompanied by the U.S.S. Connecticut.

Many trials and tribulations had been encountered by all the survivors, not least of which was the fact that the two surviving, breeding couples, who had met in St. Santia as two men and two women; were actually gay. But life will find a way and the two couples did indeed produce children which coincided with the arrival on the island of the Hamaxs and the two submarines.

The submariners had made a commitment that they would visit Norfolk, U.S.A. on a regular basis in the event that sailors who had decided to leave the vessel after the devastation may someday wish to return. In addition, a small detachment of submariners felt that life would be better for them if they remained on the island of Bermuda.

Suddenly, overnight, the St. Santia community had grown and with the extra man-power, expertise and resources the submarines had brought, events would unfold that would once again change the lives of many of the survivors.

Chapter 1

Stirring in the New Eden

St. Santia

A lonely bird was scavenging for food along a deserted beach on St. Santia. The bird, a stilt, was totally oblivious of the events that had occurred prior to its hatching. The stilt is one of a few types of birds that are self-sufficient on emerging from the egg, if, that is, there was sufficient food in the immediate vicinity to sustain them. In the case of this particular bird, flies and maggots were plentiful as the insects fed on the carcasses of both humans and animals that littered the planet as a result of the devastation. The problem with procreation of the birds was the sparseness involved and the paucity of mates. Not all the birds survived their initial few days and died close to the broken shells of the eggs they had hatched from. There were those that would meet other birds and over the years, with no predators to diminish their numbers, flocks of birds would once more reappear in the skies.

……………………………………………………………

A few weeks had passed since the two submarines' arrival on St. Santia and both crews, as well as the new residents of the island were beginning to adopt to a new daily routine. The submariners were adjusting to an extended stay in dock and the families were dealing with two babies and two infants.

Maria had been woken by her recently born son and she was in the kitchen finishing up the nursing of her baby when she was joined by Joan Hamax. Maria Desouza, was looking down into her son's dark eyes that he had inherited from her. She pushed back her red hair that had grown long over the months since the devastation and stood up, to place her baby in his cot. Maria was not a tall girl, but she was grateful that her slim figure had returned since the birth of her son. She had originally flown in from Toronto and arrived on St. Santia for a diving holiday with her partner, Marlene. It was while they were underwater that the devastation had hit, a dive that had saved their lives.

"Good morning dear. How are you both?" Joan asked.

"Hi Joan, we're great thanks, but this little fellow was hungry." Maria replied. "Where are your two?" Maria was referring to the two babies Joan and her husband, John, had rescued from incubators in the hospital they had been sent to after a gas-fire accident. Joan Hamax was in her twilight years, grey hair with a kind face and the four of them had arrived at the house just as the birth of Maria's baby was happening.

"Still sleeping. They woke up earlier, I gave them a little snack and they went back to sleep." Joan answered. "Have you decided on a name for the little love yet?" Joan continued.

"You mean other than *'thing'*? You know, with all that has gone on over the last little while, naming our child has been the last thing on our minds." Maria said casually. "We had discussed names during my pregnancy but certainly had not settled on anything."

"Well there's definitely no rush. It isn't as though you are going to have to hurry down to obtain a birth certificate." Joan stated and they both laughed. At that moment Bob walked into the kitchen and wondered what the two ladies were both laughing at. Maria explained, and Bob pondered that for a moment.

"Well, government red-tape apart, we thought we had things pretty much covered for our survival but of course now we have nuclear capabilities and a whole source of expertise. One day, there was no future generation and now we have four new members. This is going to require some planning, both short and long term." Bob said with some seriousness as he sat down next to Maria at the counter. Bob Grayling, well-built and muscular, almost void of body fat with his blonde hair, blue eyed and tanned body he could have almost passed for a Californian beach bum, if it wasn't for his strong Boston accent.

"Wow, is it being so cheerful that keeps you going Bob." Maria offered with a smile. "But you're right, a lot of planning will be necessary, but this extra help takes a load off all of us. A few weeks ago, I worried about our future, with just the four of us and our limited skills; we were not equipped to handle any adverse situation. But since the Hamaxs turned up and the submarines' arrival we have been blessed with all sorts of expertise, I feel much more confident about the future now."

"You're probably hungry dear. Let me make you some breakfast." Joan said, as if food was the answer to everything. She patted Bob on the knee as she strolled towards the cooker to begin preparing some breakfast. As if on cue, John Hamax entered the kitchen, "did someone say breakfast?" John asked, "I'm starving." John Hamax, despite being a bit long in the tooth, was a spritely, slim, man, long limbed with fingers to match, generally soft spoken and gentle with it, kind, good-natured and always appeared upbeat. He had a full mane of grey hair, ice blue eyes with skin like leather as a result of years in open water during all seasons in his U.S. Coast Guard days. "You're always hungry, you're like a gannet." Joan told him. "But talking of planning, one of the things we must do, that is, John and I, is to look for a place to live. We can't stay here with you. You need your privacy."

"No, no." Maria replied, maybe a little too vociferously, so she continued in a much calmer tone. "I meant to say, this house is way big enough for all of us, you're more than welcome to stay here. Aren't they Bob?" Caught unawares, Bob certainly hadn't given the accommodation arrangements any thought at all, so he just replied totally agreeing with Maria. "Absolutely, no need to move out." Then in afterthought, "unless of course you want to, then we would understand of course."

"No, this is a nice place, plenty of room and we wouldn't have to worry about setting up another generator." John said, entering the fray.

"I don't know John; these young ones need their space." Joan countered.

"Well, look, it's time we sat down with the Admiral and the rest of the crew. I'm sure they will have some ideas about how everyone is going to move forward, so for now, you stay here and let's just see how it goes. Deal?" Maria asked.

"Deal." John replied. Joan nodded her head and continued preparing breakfast. But she was already hatching a plan to move out.

Chapter 2

Aboard the U.S.S. Augusta

St. Santia

The two submarines, the Augusta and the Connecticut had originally anchored off-shore, using porters to transport between the two submarines and the jetty. However, during the first week at anchor, Admiral Stanford had decided to utilize the high tide to dock the Augusta against the jetty on the island, just down from the current residents' houses. There was not enough depth for the submarine in a rough sea, but the Admiral felt it would be safe enough under the current conditions. Although radios had been issued to the residents on the island in the event of an emergency the Admiral felt it was better to be close at hand for the next little while.

Onboard both submarines the crews were going about their business with most of the crews in the galley enjoying their breakfasts. On the menu was a selection of dishes involving fresh eggs, courtesy of the residents of St. Santia. There were eggs that were scrambled, poached, boiled and even eggs Benedict. On the Augusta, the food had been prepared, as usual, by Peter DeVersa, one of the heroes of Janet and Mary's rescue from the group of mutineers from the Connecticut. Janet and Mary, together with Jason Hargreaves, were part of the group enjoying their meal and the topic of conversation was indeed their futures and suggestions were being bantered backward and forward. Janet, prior to her rescue with Mary from the clutches of some of the mutineers who fled the Connecticut, was the most despised person on board because of her obnoxious attitude. But since her terrifying incident, her rescue and her quick thinking to save the life of baby Augusta her relationship with the crew had traversed full circle. She was now holding court, leading the discussion on living arrangements and some of the tasks that would need to be carried out both short and long term. Her short dark hair and blue eyes covered by thick rimmed glasses gave her an intellectual look which made the seamen hang on her very word. Although she was attractive, the 'frumpy' old fashioned clothes she wore belied a great figure.

“Electricity is going to be one of the biggest problems,” Sparks, the Radio Operator, said entering the discussion. “The gas is not going to last forever, and the generators will wear out eventually. I think we need to establish alternate power very soon. We need to obtain as many solar panels on the island as possible and maybe develop wave power from the sea.”

“Even that's a short-term solution, they will all become unserviceable eventually.” Janet offered before continuing, “in about thirty to fifty years it will be just the next generation fending for themselves. I think what we need to do is document how to return to basics, almost caveman style. Without electricity or running tap water, we need to outline how they will have to grow their own food, make their own clothes and learn to raise the chickens." There was a lull in the conversation as the others in the group considered the wisdom of these words. Then Mary added her tuppence worth.

"Well, they will have one advantage, they will know how to make fire and candles for light." Mary offered. "But what about clothes? You can hardly make decent clothes out of chicken feathers!" Mary was Janet's friend and co-worker, they had been on board the Augusta at the time of the devastation researching Arctic plant life. Mary Briggs had reluctantly left the safety of the submarine with Janet when they had originally docked in Norfolk. But she had decided to stand by Janet. Mary was short, had mouse brown hair that had now grown down to her shoulders. Although she had a great figure, her feature was big brown eyes that melted just about any man that looked at them.

"Fortunately, they will be living in a climate where few clothes are required. Much like the Samoans before Europeans came along. They made tappa from the bark of a paper Mulberry tree." Jason Hargreaves stated, "now, I don't think that type of tree is indigenous to this island, but I am sure we could find something like it." Everyone looked at Jason, surprised that the ship's number 2 would possess such snippets of knowledge. Lieutenant Jason Hargreaves a tall, handsome, man with fair hair and dark blue eyes was usually quiet and unassuming. He and Mary had gotten extremely close since the mutineer incident and it was generally accepted by everyone onboard that they were a couple.

"But there is a better way." Janet said, and everyone turned to look at her. "The Samoans had an advantage, they had something we don't have." Janet paused as everyone looked at her, hanging on her every word, "they had pigs as well as chickens."

"Well that's unfortunate, we won't be able to find a pig anywhere anymore." Sparks interrupted and then said to no one in particular, "no barbequed ribs ever again. Shish."

"But there could be." Janet continued, undaunted. Again, all the attention was focused on her. "We have the ability to clone anything we want!"

Chapter 3

Realization of a Relapse

St. Santia, at the home of Maria and Bob

After breakfast was eaten with all the dishes washed and cleared away, Maria and Bob went outside to the patio to relax briefly before setting about their chores for the day ahead. Joan and John went back into the house to check on their young charges. For a moment or two Maria and Bob sat silently surveying their beautiful view of the island and watching the comings and goings of the crew on the U.S.S. Augusta. Then Joan and John reported back from their visit with their babies to report they were still sleeping. Coincidently, Tony and Marlene were leaving their house with baby Augusta and had begun to walk slowly over towards them. Everyone exchanged waves, well, all except the babies amongst them. Tony and Marlene joined the rest of the group in the shade under the awning attached to the house. Tony Dilenti, also from Boston, was originally Bob's partner, he had been prone to being overweight, chubby cheeks with brown eyes short brown hair fashioned in a college cut, but of course since their arrival on St Santia, he had lost a considerable amount of weight and his hair had grown to almost rock star length. Marlene LeCroix, another Canadian, would never have been considered slim but she too had slimmed down accentuating her well-proportioned figure. Her long sandy colored hair and green eyes with her now tanned face gave her model status beauty.

They exchanged pleasantries, Joan asked whether they had eaten breakfast yet, but Tony and Marlene assured them they had. After a little, more, light conversation Joan said to John, "come on old man, I want to go and see what the inside of a submarine looks like." She rose from her comfortable seat and indicated with her arm for John to follow suit. John merely rolled his eyes and did as he was told.

"Listen out for the little ones would you please?" Joan asked the group but more to Maria specifically.

"Don't worry. You enjoy." Maria said sincerely, Bob held up his hand in agreement and the elderly couple set off.

As Joan and John ambled down the gentle slope to the jetty where the U.S.S. Augusta was docked Marlene asked, "the submarine has been here for all these weeks and Joan suddenly wants to see the inside of one?"

"I think it's more of a subterfuge to discuss things with John. She had talked about moving out of the house this morning." Maria said.

"Really?" Marlene replied in surprise. "Surely the house is big enough for them to remain here."

"That's what I told her." Maria replied, "I think it would benefit all of us, but it's up to them if they wish to move out."

"Ironic isn't it?" Tony said with a depressing tone. The others turned to look at Tony.

"What's ironic Tony?" Bob asked. Tony paused as if the cogs of his brain were positioning themselves to reply correctly.

"Well, it has taken years for people like us to become an accepted part of the community. Same sex couples living together, openly and not being harassed for doing so. Now, in one foul swoop we have been thrust back into the closet and not one of those people," nodding towards the departing Hamaxs and the personnel on the two submarines, "are aware of our true persuasion. They just believe we are two happy loving couples bringing up baby like nothing is wrong."

Tony was sounding quite bitter and obviously Marlene was the most surprised out of the four adults. "I thought we are a happy couple Tony." Marlene said, looking down at Augusta rather than looking directly at Tony. It would be true to say that when the full realization of the devastation had first hit and the knowledge that they were the only known breeding pair of humans remaining on earth it was Tony who had been the last to accept their situation. He was the one who had been adamant about remaining together with Bob and just doing the business with the girls as and when necessary. But the others had accepted the situation and they thought that he too had resigned himself to a normal heterosexual lifestyle for the sake of the children they hoped to rear.

“Tony, what’s wrong?” Bob said. He didn’t want to stand and go to him, he had a feeling this was not the right time. “You’ve been able to accept our situation up until now. What has changed?” Tony said nothing for a few seconds. Then he suddenly stood up waved his arms and blurted out, “you’re right.” Tony made a poor attempt at a smile before continuing, “it’s just me, forget it. I think it’s just the trauma of almost losing Marlene to that idiot, Danny.” Marlene physically winced at the sound of Danny Martinez’s name. She had still not fully recovered from her near-death experiences during her abduction. After seeing Martinez smashed overboard by the yacht’s boom during the hurricane she thought she was going to die until her rescue by the crew of the U.S.S. Augusta.

“That’s more like it Tony.” Maria whooped, greatly relieved. But neither Bob nor Marlene felt everything was as it should be and there was no longer a great sense of confidence about the coming months.

Chapter 4

Potential for the Creation of Life

St. Santia, Aboard the U.S.S. Augusta

"Clone? Janet, you can't be serious." Mary said, completely taken aback by Janet's words.

"Why not? We have the equipment, the know-how and the necessary biological samples. Of course, we can do it." Janet replied confidently.

"But we have no surrogate mother Janet. All the hosts for supporting an embryo are dead!" Mary stressed.

"We don't need a host." Janet responded, enjoying this debate where she was countering every one of Mary's vocal obstacles.

"But that's impossible. How are –." Mary started to reply, then she realized where Janet was going with this train of thought. "Ectogenesis."

"Quite right Mary, ectogenesis." Janet smiled as she replied, knowing Mary was on the same wavelength. Which was more than could be said for the others in the group who were at their wits' end trying to keep up with the conversation.

"Ectogenesis?" Dr. Dennis Moore asked as he joined the group with a plate containing a full English breakfast so high in cholesterol it belied his slim appearance and his vocation. Although, he did keep himself fit, he could often be seen working out in the gym, his dark hair flopping as he strode his tall body on the treadmill.

“Janet, what exactly is ectogenesis?” Jason asked.

“It is the creation of an embryo in an artificial womb.” Janet replied.

“Is that even possible?” Manny, one of the submariners listening in on the debate, asked in utter disbelief.

“Not only is it possible, it has been achieved. But of course, it has not been openly pursued because of the moral and controversial stigmas attached to creating offspring on a mass scale.” Janet explained. “The stigmas revolve around the fact that you could use genetics to create what you want and that is where the moral issue enters in. But we are talking farm animals here and the preservation of life. I don’t think there is anyone amongst us who would have any moral objections.”

“But surely we don’t have the necessary laboratory on this island to achieve that do we?” Jason asked, looking first at Janet and then at Mary.

“No, we don’t. Not forgetting we would also need the appropriate animal tissue, eggs and sperm to even create an embryo let alone nurture it in an artificial womb.” Mary replied. “Janet where in

God's name do you expect to create all these animals on this island?"

"I didn't say we could do it all on this island." Janet replied with an air of superiority.

"But you said we had everything we need to carry out the research!" Jason countered.

Janet waited a couple of seconds while everyone in the group focused on her reply. "We do. But not here. However, everything we need is at the Clay Centre in Nebraska."

Chapter 5

Going About Their Chores

St. Santia, at the home of Maria and Bob

Baby Augusta was beginning to get decidedly antsy, so Marlene and Tony said their farewells and strolled back to their house to tend to her needs. Maria and Bob watched silently as the other trio walked away then Bob said with a sense of purpose, "well, this won't do. Things to do, places to go, people to see." He rose from his chair and said, "I think I will feed the chickens first and then visit the submarine to start planning."

"Planning. Planning what?" Maria asked.

"I don't know." Bob replied succinctly. "That's why we need to plan. Up until now, we just had ourselves to worry about and we were planning our livelihood day-by-day. Now we have future generations to consider and I certainly do not have the expertise to put in place everything that they are going to require to sustains themselves. They have doctors on board, scientists and all sorts of engineering know-how." Bob nodded his head towards the Augusta, "I'm just an ex-Bond Trader. A fat lot of good that's going to be in our New World." Bob's tone was beginning to sound a little bitter. Maria sensed it was the conversation with Tony that had spooked him.

“Hey, stop talking like that.” Maria admonished him. “You, alone have got us this far. Without you we probably wouldn’t have survived the first couple of months after the devastation. Don’t let Tony get to you, you of all people know he’s always had that moody, pessimistic, streak. Sure, the people on the Augusta have expertise but you are a father now. You have a responsibility to understand all the options for your son’s future. So, look upon it as an opportunity.”

Bob looked at Maria in total surprise. He had never heard her talk so philosophically. Maybe it was the maternal instinct that was bringing out the best in her. He just smiled.

“You know, you’re right.” Bob said slowly.

“I know I’m right, now, go feed the chickens and plan.” Maria said tauntingly. She rose and slapped him playfully on the arm as she went inside to change the baby’s diaper.

Bob walked the few hundred yards to the first chicken run they had built. It consisted of a shed with a hole cut in the bottom of the door for the chickens to come and go as they pleased. Inside the shed, roosts had been built to accommodate all the chickens and that’s where they went when the sun went down. The rest of the time, the chickens just scratched around, free-range, never really strutting too far from their home. Bob and Tony had discovered the chicken farm immediately after the devastation and eggs were hatching so rearing the chicks became a priority. Then they had set up four runs at various points on the island in an attempt to avoid disease wiping out their entire chicken population. Marlene had set about organizing the population of the chickens ensuring each clutch had a maximum of three roosters amongst thirty hens. The pecking order sorted itself out from there.

Every day, one of the group, usually Bob or Tony, would collect fresh eggs from the sheds but would leave some of the eggs for rearing. Any new males that were hatched were selected for cooking after a few months. The first chicken that had to be slaughtered was a traumatic time for Maria and at first, she threatened to refuse any part of the offering. Having got to know the poor bird, 'Claude', on a first name basis. Marlene, always the pragmatic one when it came to farming decisions, solved the problem by preparing a curry dish using both Claude and one of the chickens from their frozen cache. This satisfied Maria as she didn't know which chicken she was eating. All future slaughters had become less of an issue.

Chapter 6

Thoughts of Rearing Stock

St. Santia, Aboard the U.S.S. Augusta

"Nebraska?" Jason asked incredulously. "And how in God's name are you going to get there?"

Janet didn't say anything she merely turned her head slightly to look at the cook, DeVersa, who was innocently going about his business in the galley.

"You can't be serious!" Mary said but Janet merely smiled.

"I am sure DeVersa would be happy to fly me to Nebraska and we all know he is an excellent pilot." Janet said, referring to his exploits with the helicopter when saving Janet and Mary from the clutches of those ruthless mutineers. "Within months I should be able to breed enough farm stock to bring them back here as well as some for the boys on Bermuda." Referring to the members of the crews of both submarines who decided to set up a settlement in Bermuda rather than travel around the world in the submarines. The group all look astounded at Janet but they all knew well enough that she was serious and determined to see this through. To the point that if DeVersa was not prepared to fly her to Nebraska, she would get there by any means necessary and damn the risks. Her mind was made up.

"This is obviously a decision that requires preparation and is something we have to discuss in more detail with the Admiral." Jason said in an attempt to be diplomatic.

"Talking of the Admiral, where is he?" Dr. Moore asked with a fleck of egg yolk clinging to his lip, "he's usually up and about by now."

"Good question Dennis." Jason replied. "It's not like him to be this late in making an appearance, but it has been a trying few weeks and now that everything has settled down maybe he is just having a lie in."

"We should give him a little longer and then I will check in on him." Dr. Moore offered, which really meant 'when I have finished this feast I will go and see him'. "But I would like to hear more about how you intend to rear farm animals in the middle of Nebraska. Is that feasible? Any cultures and samples would no doubt be useless by now."

"You may be right Dennis but it's worth a shot." Janet countered, "I remember reading a paper on their facility. They had developed very sophisticated backup systems and their cooling systems were state of the art. It is possible that some samples would still be viable for development."

"Even after this length of time?" Jason asked.

“Even after this length of time.” Janet replied.

Mary merely looked at her with astonishment. Mary knew that no matter what objections she raised she would end up embroiled in this venture. The last adventure with Janet almost cost them their lives and here Janet was discussing the possibility of another trip halfway across the U.S. But before any further dialogue on the matter could be discussed, Dennis had finished his breakfast and rose from the table.

“Well, I think I will go and check in on the Admiral.” Dennis said.

“I’ll join you.” Jason said. They placed their used cutlery, plates and cups in the washing-up bin, gave a wave of thanks to DeVersa and his team before walking from the galley to the Admiral’s sleeping quarters.

On their way through the corridor Jason gave a quick look back to ensure they were not being followed before asking the doctor a question.

“So, what do you think of this ectogenesis idea Dennis? Is it viable?”

“Oh, sure it is. But I question the availability and condition of the staple ingredients necessary to create life.” Dennis replied. “Furthermore, as talented as Janet is, ectogenesis is a relatively new and specialized field. I am not sure even Janet has the necessary expertise to bring this off, but then again, you know Janet. Once she gets the bit between her teeth, she feels she can achieve anything." Before Jason could answer they had arrived at the Admiral's quarters and Dennis knocked gently on the door. There being no reply Dennis rapped on the door a little harder. They both cocked their heads against the door listening for any slight sound to indicate movement in the cabin but as none was forthcoming Dennis slowly turned the door-handle and opened the door.

"Admiral?" Dennis whispered as he entered the room. The bedside light was on, casting an eerie glow onto the peaceful face of the Admiral but he made no reply. Dennis walked closer to the Admiral's bed and after a few seconds he beckoned Jason over and said to him, "well Jason, I think you'd better start swatting up on ectogenesis. It's your responsibility now."

Chapter 7

A Sad Day Onboard

St. Santia, Aboard the U.S.S. Augusta

Joan and John continued slowly down the hill towards the Augusta. John was oblivious to the fact that the real reason for this walk was to get John away from the others so that Joan could discuss new living arrangements with him. Once they were out of ear shot of the two young couples sitting at the back of the house Joan resumed the discussion.

"John, I'm getting the impression that you don't want to move out! Do you?" Joan asked. John rolled his eyes once more as he began to realize what this side trip was really all about.

"To be honest Joan, I hadn't given it any thought." John replied.

"No. You never do." Joan said candidly.

"Jeez Joan, what is there to think about. The place is a mansion with plenty of room for everyone and we've only been here a few weeks. Why would I have given it any thought? But fine, if you want to move somewhere else we will. Not a problem. What's the big deal?" John demanded with not a little frustration.

"Well there's no need to take that sort of an attitude. I was only suggesting we should give the young ones some privacy that's all." Joan retorted.

They continued walking towards the jetty where the submarine was docked but silence reigned for a while, they had been married long enough to know how this argument was going. As they neared the submarine Joan was about to fire a parting shot, knowing John would have little time to reply before they boarded, but she was prevented from doing so by the sound of the submarine's emergency klaxon suddenly emitting from its inner decks. Sailors, who had been milling around the jetty having a relaxing morning smoke suddenly discarded their lit cigarettes into the sea, bounded onto the submarine and disappeared down into its lower decks. Others who had been lounging on the top deck immediately followed suit as they slid down the steps into the bowels of the submarine.

Joan put one hand to her mouth and reached for one of John's hands with the other. Obviously, an emergency of some kind was occurring, and John wondered if this was a good time to go aboard. He gently extricated his hand from Joan's, placated her by showing her the palms of his hands, "let me go and see what's happening." John said gently. Any thoughts on continuing their discussion regarding living arrangements had now dissipated and Joan meekly nodded her head in agreement.

John climbed onto the submarine then stepped slowly from the deck down the steps into the submarine. John had been on a submarine once before, many years ago when he was a young man in the Coast Guard. A U.S. submarine had been forced to make an emergency docking in Maine and he had been cordially invited on a tour of the vessel. That had been a World War II submarine in the Balao Class which was incomparable to the modern Augusta which was part of the nuclear Seawolf Class. Using his previous experience on a submarine as a benchmark John realized as soon as he reached the bottom of the steps it was almost as if he had taken a step into the future. Digital meters, computer screens colored buttons and switches littered the walls of the submarine. However, his amazement was cut short, amidst the hustle and bustle. The first person he encountered was a tearful Mary who came rushing into his arms.

“My dear, what’s wrong? What’s going on?” A querulous John gently asked Mary.

“Oh John, it’s the Admiral. He’s dead.” Mary blurted out before burying her face once more into John’s chest.

“The Admiral? Dead? But he was fine-” John began to say until he realized the futility of what he was saying. “Look, let me get Joan down here.” John said sympathetically as, not for the first time that morning, he gently pushed a woman away from him. He climbed back up the steps until his head reached above the deck, enough to see Joan waiting expectedly for him on the jetty. She saw him, and he made arm gestures for her to come on board. As Joan approached the gangplank John quickly told her the reason for the excitement and before she could respond with any emotion he took her hand and assisted her down the steep steps to the inside of the submarine. Joan immediately consoled Mary which gave John free range to go in search of Jason to find out exactly what had happened.

John followed the commotion to the Admiral's cabin but the closer he got the denser the crowd of seamen became, and his path was obstructed. But, respecting his years and his position as patriarch of the '*islanders*', the crew made way for him to join the officers and Janet in the Admiral's quarters. As he entered the cabin Dennis saw him and walked over to him.

"John, welcome aboard, albeit under such tragic circumstances but how did you find out so quickly?"

"Pure coincidence." John replied. "My wife needed an excuse to get away from the others to discuss something and we told them were going for a tour of your submarine but when we reached the jetty we heard the horns blaring. What happened?"

"Well John, normally the Admiral is an early riser. In fact, he hardly sleeps at all so by the time we had all finished breakfast and he was still a no-show Jason and I decided to come and look for him." Dennis said trying to smile, directing his gaze to the bed where the Admiral was lying covered by a sheet. "Anyway, when I opened the door, well, I'm an experienced enough doctor to recognize a dead person when I see one…." Dennis' voice trailed off as he recounted the events.

"I'm sure it was very distressing for you." John said placing a hand on the doctor's shoulder.

"I'm sure the Admiral would have been glad to have shown you around. Hardly any official secrets now." Dennis responded in a vain attempt to keep a stiff upper lip.

"So, next steps?" John asked.

"Yes indeed, next steps." Dennis said with complete uncertainty, so he turned to find Jason to attract his attention.

Jason walked over just as John asked Dennis, "will you be performing a post-mortem?"

Up until now, Dennis had been holding up extremely well but the thought of cutting up the Admiral to discover cause of death was the final straw for him. He shook his head and cried unabashedly.

"I don't think a post-mortem will be necessary," Jason immediately replied, indicating to one of the subalterns to fix the doctor a brandy and take care of him. Janet, who had become Dennis' companion during the last few months, put an arm around his shoulder and directed him to an easy chair to sit down before Jason turned back to John. "He merely died in his sleep." Jason added, "his time was up, he was tired and although he had his crew, he was lonely." John thought about that for a while.

"It was as if he had fulfilled his destiny." John said almost inaudibly, "fate had made him responsible for the crew of two submarines that were destined to arrive at this island that coincided with our appearance and the birth of a new generation." John then lowered his voice even more and looked directly into Jason's eyes, "now, I'm no believer in God or any other divine being for that matter, especially after what has happened to this planet during the last year or so. But, it has to make you wonder whether there is something out there guiding us."

Jason wanted to reply, 'yes there is, GPS and 21st century technology' but felt it would be inappropriate and unnecessary, so he said nothing.

Chapter 8

Life on the Island

St. Santia, at the home of Marlene and Tony

Marlene and Tony had returned to their own house, well at least it was theirs now, with the fidgety Augusta, so named because of her birth on board the submarine of the same name. Tony appeared to be in a sultry mood and had said nothing on their walk back and Marlene had been too preoccupied with her daughter to comment much on Tony's earlier little rant with the others. Once Augusta's diaper had been changed she settled down and after a while the baby soon fell asleep. Marlene returned the baby to her cot in the nursery, pulled the door to and was determined to confront Tony on his previous outburst.

It was Tony's day to check out the chickens on the other parts of the island, so he was gathering some refreshments to take with him for the ride on the Mini-Moke. He was just placing the vittles into a backpack when Marlene entered the kitchen. Tony had a feeling as to what was coming.

"Why are you not happy Tony?" Marlene calmly asked. Her calmness belied the emotions she was feeling, and Tony had hoped he could escape the house before this inevitable conversation could occur. Marlene was the toughest of the four of them mentally, emotionally and only Bob was stronger physically. This had always intimidated Tony somewhat, no more than right now.

"Why do you think Marlene?" Tony replied tersely.

"Tony, I thought you were over that!" Marlene replied surprisingly. "Yes, you're gay, I was a lesbian, but we had to put that aside -"

"Well the situation has changed, hasn't it?" Tony interrupted her, although Tony wouldn't look at Marlene. "We thought we were alone. We thought we were the only ones who could create a new generation but that is no longer true is it? And I don't have to live this lie anymore."

"So, you think that having one child is going to be enough. That's it, you've planted your seed and you can move on. Is that it?" Marlene replied, now getting quite upset and her voice reflected her rising anger.

"There are others now who can rise to the task, you can have your pick of men from two submarines, you don't need me anymore." Tony said, leaving Marlene aghast.

"What do you think I am Tony?" Marlene asked, looking menacingly at Tony. He still wouldn't return her gaze, but he could feel the imaginary daggers being thrown as Marlene continued. "I was faithful to Maria and I would be faithful to you, no matter how many submarines turned up but -. Oh, wait a minute." An ironic smile began to appear on Marlene's face as a sudden realization occurred to her. "It's not just me who can have the pick of men from two submarines is it?"

"Don't be ridiculous Marlene." Tony said, finally turning to confront the defiant Marlene. "I'm going to tend to the chickens."

Tony, picked up his backpack, turned on his heels and walked over to the back door to leave.

"So, when you move out, which you will, because I'm not going to. What about Auggie?" Marlene asked, referring to their daughter by the pet name they had given her. Marlene knew that would hit a nerve, Tony had already opened the door and for a second, he paused in the doorway, before continuing out, slamming the door in the process, leaving a sobbing Marlene seated at the kitchen table.

Chapter 9

Next Steps

St. Santia, On Board U.S.S. Augusta

There was nothing more John felt he could do on board the Augusta, so he decided to locate his wife and return to the house to inform the other inhabitants of the island. Jason also stirred into action, he was the Admiral now, the man, and nobody questioned the sudden promotion. The klaxon had stopped so he took the opportunity to broadcast the news to the submarine's crew, as if they didn't already know. He snatched at the microphone for the tannoy system and flicked on all the necessary switches.

"Ladies and gentlemen of the Augusta this is Jason Hargreaves." Jason said, taking great pains to not refer to the submarine's origins or his rank. This was part of the Admiral's direction, to be like a corporation not a navy belonging to any country, it didn't matter anymore. Although, everyone still referred to John Stanford as the Admiral. "It is with sad heart that I have to inform you that Admiral Stanford passed away in his sleep last night. I ask that now we continue with our mission as suggested by the Admiral. Let's make him proud. There will be a formal burial at sea and I will inform you all of the funeral arrangements as soon as they have been agreed. For now, let's go about our tasks just as the Admiral would have wanted us to."

Jason returned the microphone to its cradle, turned off the switches and took a deep breath. It was time to take charge, it was expected of him. He turned to face the group in the room, they too expected him to take charge and were quite prepared to do nothing until he told them to do something. The group that faced him consisted of the officers and bosun Giles who had transferred to the Augusta from the Connecticut because of his previous service with the Admiral.

“Giles!” Jason said.

“Sir?” Giles replied. Although it had been agreed that formal addressing of personnel in the tradition of the Navy was no longer necessary it was tough for someone like Giles to change his ways. He had started in the Navy long before some of the subalterns in the room had even been born.

“Send someone to tell Sparks to inform the Connecticut and the Bermuda detachment of the Admiral’s death. Also, tell Sheldrake to join us immediately.” Jason ordered. Sheldrake was the young Captain of the Connecticut as he had found himself unceremoniously placed in charge of the vessel by default. A mutiny that had occurred after the devastation had resulted in the deaths of all the senior officers, then, along with the mutineers, others left on arrival at the mainland, leaving him the senior officer standing.

“Sir.” Giles replied and was gone. As Giles left and all the crew drifted back to what they were doing prior to all the excitement

Janet took the opportunity to return Dennis to his cabin. Jason stole a look at the Admiral's immobile body under the sheet and decided this was neither the place nor the time to issue any further orders. So, he walked to the door of the cabin and indicated with a sweep of his arm that everyone should leave. Then, he quietly said to the group as they were leaving, "let's wait for Sheldrake to arrive and we will meet in the War Room to discuss what time we set sail for a funeral at sea."

Chapter 10

Trip Planning to Nebraska

St. Santia, On Board U.S.S. Augusta

Janet accompanied Dennis back to his cabin and sat him on his bed, he was still in a state of shock and disbelief. Janet suggested he should practice what he preached, which was to take a low dosage sedative and have a quick sleep.

"I can't. I have things to do. Surgery hours are soon, and the crew will be lining up. There are funeral arrangements to be made for the Admiral. No, I have to -." Dennis started to say and began to rise awkwardly from his bunk. Janet unceremoniously pushed him back down and curtly gave him a talking to.

"Dennis, there will be no malingerers amongst the crew to-day and if there is an emergency Mary and I are quite capable of dealing with it. In fact, we are more than capable. I am sure Jason will be planning the funeral arrangements with the other officers and he can consult with you later for your approval. For now, rest." Janet was adamant, and Dennis felt in no mood to argue.

"The pills, they are in that bag on the dresser." Dennis said pointing to his doctor's bag. Janet reached for the bag, rummaged through and found a pill-box marked 'tranquilizers'.

"These the ones?" Janet asked. Dennis read the label and nodded his head. The instructions on the bottle suggested one tablet. Janet opened the bottle, extracted one pill, replaced the top on the bottle and returned the bottle to the bag. She then half-filled a glass with water and passed both the pill and the water to Dennis. Dennis submissively took the pill, swallowed with a sip of the water and returned the glass to Janet. Dennis then laid back with his head on the pillow and closed his eyes. Janet sat with Dennis a few minutes and once she heard the rhythmic sound of his breathing she turned off the light and quietly left the room.

Mary had returned to the galley which is where Janet found her with most of the crew, silently drinking coffee lost in their own thoughts.

"How is Dennis?" Mary asked as Janet approached with a mug of coffee.

"He's sleeping, he'll be fine after a good sleep. I made him take a sedative." Janet said as she sat down at the table with Mary. "Where's Jason?" Janet asked, noticing that most of the other officers were present but not Jason. "Oh, he said he needed to start planning preparations. I'm sure he meant for the funeral, but he gave me the impression there was more to it than that." Mary replied.

"Maybe he is considering Nebraska." Janet said with a degree of seriousness.

"You have to be kidding Janet." Mary replied, surprised that Janet still wanted to pursue this endeavor, despite the morning's events.

“Absolutely not.” Janet replied, now dead serious. “I know it may sound callous, under the circumstances, but time is of the essence and we need to get there as soon as possible.” Before Mary could protest Janet turned and called over to the cook.

“Peter?” Janet shouted as she raised her arm to beckon DeVersa over. “Do you have a moment?” DeVersa had just begun to clear away the remnants of breakfast when he heard Janet call. He quickly washed his hands and was still wiping them dry as he waddled his short, portly frame over to the ladies at their table.

“What can I do for you?” He asked with a smile on his round face.

“I don’t know if you heard our conversation earlier but there’s a facility in Nebraska that could, possibly, be able to provide us with livestock.” Janet explained.

“No, I hear nothing when I’m working down here. Livestock? You mean like cows and pigs? Won’t they all be dead?” DeVersa was obviously confused.

“Yes, but there’s an experimental facility there that was creating animals from embryos. There may still be enough samples to continue the process. I think it’s worth a shot.” Janet told him.

“Oh, very Jurassic Parkish huh?” DeVersa jokingly replied.

“Well, not quite, but same sort of idea.” Mary said laughing with DeVersa.

“The burning question Peter, is would you be prepared to fly us there?” Janet asked, using his Christian name in an effort to persuade him. However, she didn't understand that Peter would go flying anywhere, anytime, at the drop of a hat.

"Be happy to. But obviously this is something that would have to be discussed at the next village hall meeting, wouldn't it?" DeVersa asked, based on the agreement between the crews as to where and when the submarine travels.

"Absolutely." Janet replied, "but I think the attraction of fresh beef and pork for the rest of their lives would be a huge incentive for them, don't you?"

"No kidding." DeVersa replied already thinking of a pair of succulent pork chops sizzling on a grill. To date, the meat on board had been rationed as their storage capacity was limited. They were able to replenish stocks from some still frozen storage facilities in Bermuda but even they were running low. Fortunately, they now had access to a new supply, courtesy of their friends on St. Santia who had kept some cold storage facilities going with generators. But they were not infinite, and stocks would be depleted or become inedible in the not too distant future. Fresh fruits and vegetables were not so much of a problem. They could make stops throughout the world and find enough plants running wild. Better yet, now they had a base, everything they need could be cultivated, there was certainly enough crew to maintain the crops. But the thought of fresh meat was tempting.

"So, you'll do it?" Janet asked excitedly.

“Yes, providing you can sell it to Jason and the crew. Cook can take over from me for a couple of days. I can help prepare the dinners ahead of time, he can handle the rest.” DeVersa said rolling his eyes, referring to his assistant, Amos Cook, whose position on the submarine just also happened to be a cook. Although, the problems DeVersa had experienced with the young happy-go-lucky seaman he had put down to the recruitment team having a joke because it certainly didn’t seem to be the boy’s calling.

“Great, thank you Peter.” Janet gushed enthusiastically putting her hand on top of his in thanks but before she could say anymore a whistle could be heard from outside indicating that the officers from the U.S.S. Connecticut were approaching.

Janet and Mary both stood up to go and greet the approaching porter but as she did, Janet gave a slight wince in pain.

“You O.K. Janet,” Mary said with some concern.

“Sure, must have been sitting wrong, that’s all.” Janet replied with a smile, then they walked outside the galley, heading towards the gangway, just as a resolute Jason was about to greet Sheldrake’s arrival.

“Jason, I know this isn’t the right time to discuss the subject, but you know what we were talking about this morning, Nebraska? Well DeVersa is quite happy to fly us there.” Janet told Jason. Although, because of the circumstances she had tempered her enthusiasm she was nonetheless shocked at Jason’s response.

"First of all, DeVersa has no right to discuss flying anyone, anywhere. Secondly, after your last aborted expedition, forget it. It's not going to happen."

Chapter 11

A Secret is Revealed

St. Santia, at the home of Marlene and Tony

Joan and John were walking morosely back up the hill from the Augusta, both caught up in their own emotions. Although they hadn't known the Admiral for very long they had known him long enough to realize they had lost a leader and a man of great experience. Something that would be sadly missed in this new world of theirs.

Just as they were passing Marlene and Tony's house, Joan's thoughts were interrupted when she saw Marlene quickly run into her house through the back door. It was as if she didn't want to see them right now, which was not like her at all, thought Joan.

"John, I'm just going to pop in to tell Marlene the sad news." Joan told her husband. "You go and tell the others."

"Sure thing." John replied succinctly.

Joan approached the rear door where she had seen Marlene rush in only moments earlier. She wrapped her knuckles on the wooden frame of the door a couple of times and called, "Marlene, is everything alright?" She heard a muffled response.

"Yes, yes, everything is fine, thank you Joan." Marlene said but her reply was interspersed with some poorly hidden sobs. Joan still wasn't sure whether Marlene was alone, so she was reluctant to go barging into the house in case Tony was still around.

"Can I come in?" Joan asked gingerly, "I have some rather sad news to share with you."

There was the sound of movement from just inside the house then Marlene appeared, eyes puffy and red, obviously, as a result of some recent crying.

"My dear, what's the problem?" Joan asked sympathetically and tenderly embraced the clearly grief-stricken young lady. Marlene didn't reply immediately, she just held onto Joan. For a few moments, they both stood in the kitchen holding each other, gently swaying as Marlene gradually recovered her composure. "What's the sad news?" Marlene asked, still clasped to Joan, resting her head on the older lady's shoulder.

"We just went down to the submarine, I'm afraid the Admiral died in his sleep." Joan replied gently. Marlene made an involuntary gasp; a hand went to her mouth and the tears began to flow once more. Joan waited a little while but felt it was time to get to the bottom of Marlene's anxiety. She gently broke the embrace and tenderly pushed Marlene away until she could look directly into her eyes.

"Now dear, what's the problem with you?" Joan asked softly. Her eyes were kind and her smile was motherly, this was something Joan had done a thousand times with her own daughters. At first, Marlene was reluctant to say anything, but Joan's demeanor persuaded her to open-up her heart to her. Marlene sat down at the kitchen table and began to explain the situation to Joan.

"Joan, all is not what it appears." Marlene began, looking down at her hands as she twiddled with one of Auggie's socks. "When the four of us arrived here for a vacation, before the devastation, we weren't the couples you see now. It was Bob and Tony, Maria and I who were the couples. We're gay Joan." Marlene stopped talking and looked up at Joan for a negative reaction, but none was forthcoming, so she continued.

"It was the phone call with your husband, John, that made us realize we could well be the last surviving men and women who could produce a new generation. So, to cut to the chase, we made a commitment to swap partners. Bad choice of words, but you know what I mean." Joan merely nodded. "Well, Bob and Maria got on like a house on fire, while Tony and me, well we just got on. More like a poorly arranged marriage really. I thought the incident with Danny, when he abducted me, and the Augusta rescued me was a turning point. I thought Tony genuinely loved me and we were really going to be happy together."

"He was ecstatic when you were coming up the beach with baby Augusta." Joan recalled. "Yes, he was," Marlene agreed, "but I think it was his pride that was restored more than being happy for my return."

"But he must have been pleased about the baby!" Joan said.

“Sure, but that was just for show.’ Marlene smiled cynically. “Tony had felt bad that on the night of my kidnapping he had been so drunk that he passed out on the beach, which gave Danny his opportunity to get away.”

“Yes, but Danny was after a woman, any woman.” Joan replied and then stopped for a second, “well almost any woman, I’m sure I wouldn’t have been suitable.” Which made Marlene laugh a little. “I think if Tony had been sober, it would have still occurred some other time and it could just have easily have been Maria who was taken.”

“But he had to get clear away from the island before the submarines arrived. Otherwise he would have been caught out as one of the mutinous crowd that had left the Connecticut.” Marlene pointed out.

“Yes, he was a desperate man alright. Which is why, I think that night he would have made a move of some kind on either you or Maria, regardless.” Joan countered. “but we’re getting away from the point here dear. What has gone wrong between the two of you?”

“Well, the arrival of the submarines has changed everything. Tony doesn’t seem to think he has to live this charade anymore as there are plenty of men available to provide their sperm for the cause as it were.” At this, Marlene began to cry again. “How do you think that makes me feel Joan?”

“There, there.” Joan said as she went around to where Marlene was sitting to console her once more. It was at that moment Maria entered the kitchen.

Chapter 12

Funeral Arrangements Discussed

St. Santia, Aboard the U.S.S. Augusta

Raymond Sheldrake was welcomed aboard the Augusta and immediately escorted to the War Room. The news of Admiral Stanford's death had obviously come as a great shock to both Sheldrake and the entire crew of the Connecticut. Although Sheldrake, like most of the crew of the Connecticut, had not met the Admiral until they had docked in Norfolk after the devastation it was still regarded as a loss to one of their own. Sheldrake was accompanied to the meeting with two other officers from the Connecticut. In addition to the Connecticut's representatives there were Jason and three other officers from the Augusta attending the meeting.

Raymond and Jason shook hands and the former expressed his sympathies for the loss, which Jason duly acknowledged. Then it was down to business, discussing the funeral arrangements.

"Raymond, given that one submarine and necessary crew, as per the Admiral's wishes, should always remain at the island the only questions are where the Admiral's body should be committed to the deep and who shall be attending the service." Jason stated.

"Agreed." Raymond said.

"I've been giving this some thought and my suggestion is this," Jason began, "the Augusta, with those personnel who request to attend the funeral will set sail at first light tomorrow. It will rendezvous at Bermuda to allow those from the island who do not wish to attend the funeral to pay their respects and take aboard those who do wish to attend the funeral. We will then proceed to Norfolk and once we are in American waters we will carry out the funeral rites." Jason looked first at Raymond and then the other attending staff for any objections. There being none, Jason continued, "on completion of the funeral we will take the opportunity to sail to Norfolk and verify there are no lost souls looking for a safe-haven. We will stay at the naval yards for a couple of nights to see if there has been any sign of activity and pick up supplies before returning to Bermuda to drop off our passengers before arriving back here. Any questions?" There being none, Jason continued once more. "So, during the Augusta's trip, the Connecticut will remain on St. Santia and once the Augusta has returned, Raymond, you can cut loose for a trip with the Connecticut and any volunteers. Any questions?" Jason looked around the War Room at the other attendees.

"So, it is just the guest list that needs to be finalized." Jason said. "First of all, I don't believe there is anyone from the original Augusta crew who will not be attending. The Bermuda detachment has six members from the original Augusta crew." Jason continued, "now, I have not included any other crew members from the Connecticut. So, let's discuss that. Are there any of the original Connecticut crew that will be wishing to attend?" Jason asked.

"I was considering attending but I believe Giles could represent the Connecticut even though he is now on your boat." Raymond replied. "Other than that, I don't believe we will be upsetting protocol if no other crew members attend." Raymond said as he looked at his officers, who were all shaking their heads.

"Fine, but if all the original Augusta crew will be attending, will that leave you vulnerable in any essential positions Raymond?" Jason asked. He was referring to the role balancing they had to accomplish when crew members jumped ship after the devastation. Some positions were exposed, and they had to carry out transfers of personnel between the two submarines to ensure they could be adequately and safely operated. Raymond conferred with his contingent before replying.

"Jason, obviously, the temporary loss of some personnel would leave us wanting in certain areas but there should be no impact if we remain in dock. We suggest that after your departure, we could use your berth and remain here. We should be fine." Raymond said.

"Excellent. What we could do is switch berths this evening and then after dinner, ferry the Augusta people aboard so that we will be in a position to leave at first light. Probably arrive in Bermuda at about ten the next morning. Sound like a plan?" Jason asked. Everyone nodded their heads in agreement.

"Lewis, would you be so kind as to tell Sparks to get onto Bermuda and tell them we will be arriving to pick up personnel the day after tomorrow." Jason asked Lewis, the Augusta's Communications Officer.

"On it." Lewis replied. As Lewis went to the radio room with his instructions Jason offered drinks to the Connecticut crew and spoke briefly with each one of them. By now, it was past lunch time, so all the officers took their leave to visit the galley while Jason took the opportunity to find Giles and update him. The morning had been busy, and he had not had the time to stop to speak with the wizened old seaman. The Admiral had a special affinity with Bosun Giles and Jason spoke with him at great length, reminiscing and swapping stories.

As the meeting in the War Room was winding down, Lewis reached the Radio Room. "Yo, Sparks." Lewis said as he greeted the young radio operator sitting at the desk. "We're off in the morning and we should be arriving in Hamilton at approximately 10:00 A.M. the day after tomorrow. Can you let the Bermuda lot know that please?"

"Good timing Lewis my man." Sparks replied with a concerned look on his face as he just finished writing on a message pad and handed the completed note to Lewis. "They've just called, they have an emergency, they want us there as soon as possible."

Chapter 13

The Devastation Returns

Bermuda

The news of Admiral Stanford's death had been broadcast to the Bermuda detachment by Sparks, aboard the Augusta. The receiver of the call was David Sexton, one of the fifteen men from the two submarines who, for various reasons, had decided to permanently remain on the island of Bermuda. David was a tall, slim, athletic looking young man who in fact had been a very good basketball player but was just not that tall, neither that exceptional. So, he decided to join the navy and when the opportunity came to remain on Bermuda he jumped at it, choosing to be constantly mobile rather than being restricted to a submarine. Of the fifteen who chose to remain in Bermuda, there had been nine from the Connecticut and Dave was one of the six from the Augusta. Most of the men had decided to live around the Hamilton area but a few had moved to the beach just outside of the capitol. However, with the help of some generators, solar panels and wind turbines they all had electricity, so they managed to communicate by rechargeable, hand-held CB radios. There were emergency procedures in place that in the event that no communique had been received by an individual the others would immediately investigate. This was also true between Bermuda and the submarines. Even if there was nothing to report, a call was made from one of the submarines every day at noon. If no reply had been received, subsequent attempts were made on the hour for 24 hours. Failure to hear from Bermuda at that point would result in one of the submarines being dispatched to investigate further, while still attempting to make connection.

That day David managed to contact all but two of the new residents on the island, the no-shows were Moose and Dutch. They were probably sleeping off another night of heavy drinking, as was their wont. David would probably wait until the noon call from the Augusta, he was responsible for the call to-day, as he was most days, then he would try and reach the men again. If, unsuccessful, he would grab one of the others to accompany him on a search for the errant matelots.

Because of the nature of the news all the men who had been contacted descended on the restaurant that had unofficially been designated as their meeting room, which was aptly named 'The Happy Mariner'. The restaurant was housed in a very old building and had originally been a public house, allegedly, frequented by pirates and other infamous characters. The bar section of the establishment was in fact the original pub and it suited the new guests nicely. Stocks of the more popular spirits had been replenished from other local bars in the area and after selecting a drink of their choice the most senior submariner in terms of time in the service, Gregory 'Provo' Marshal, suggested a toast. Provo was so called because he was somewhat of a barrack room lawyer and of course his obvious surname.

“To Admiral Stanford. A gentleman and the finest Admiral I have ever had the pleasure to serve under.” Provo said with all relevant sincerity as he raised his glass. The other men in the room stood, raised their glasses and echoed Provo’s words, ‘Admiral Stanford’. They then sat down and decided a wake was as good an idea for a drinking session as any.
“Not wanting to put a damper on things,” David added, “but before you guys get too far into this I need to remind you, there has been no word from Moose and Dutch. I’ll give them another hour then I’m going to need someone to come with me to check out their whereabouts.” David’s announcement and his penchant for the rules was met with groans of derision.
“They’re probably out there fishing and getting drunk, again.” Moxley said, pointing in the direction of the ocean. His comment was met by grunts of agreement and nodding of heads from most of the men but one of them did offer to help.
“I’ll just have one more drink and if you still need to go searching I’ll come with you.” Alex Laarson said. Alex was one of the youngest and shortest of the men that had been onboard the Connecticut, his sense of humor, jokes and willingness to help had endeared him to the rest of the crew.
“Thanks.” Said David and began another attempt to contact the missing men. It was getting close to noon, so David went back to the transmitting room which had been set up in the old police headquarters.

After the daily call to the Augusta, David made another unsuccessful attempt at raising the missing men. David returned to the bar, Alex, as promised, had only had one more drink and was ready to accompany David to the beach area where Moose and Dutch usually hung out. They took off on their electric scooters and within ten minutes they were at the condos where the rowdy couple lived. They parked their scooters and were just about to walk into the condos' entrance when Alex noticed a boat about 500 yards off shore and he brought it to David's attention. Visibility was not great, it was one of those cloudy days where the sky met the horizon and it was difficult to differentiate one from the other. David walked back to his scooter to retrieve his binoculars and focused them on the boat out at sea. Sure enough, it was Moose and Dutch sitting and drinking in a high-tech fishing boat with what looked to be about eight rods working the waters. They probably hadn't taken their CB radios with them, or if they had, they hadn't turned them on, which accounted for their inability to reply. David reached for the air-horn he always carried in the event of an emergency and was about to press the button to catch the two men's attention when a strange thing happened. A heated, smoking object came hurtling out of the sky to splash into the sea not more than a few hundred yards from the fishing boat. It created a steaming plume of water that rose high above the waves. For a few moments, the impact caused a wake that bobbed the fishing boat around like a cork in a maelstrom. The two men in the boat were not wearing life preservers and were forced to hang on for dear life, which was no mean feat after a morning's drinking on the high seas. Alex and David just stared at each other in total fear, their initial reaction was that this was yet another meteorite about to unleash even more of the deadly microbes.

Chapter 14

More Talk of Nebraska

St. Santia, Aboard the U.S.S. Augusta

Janet and Mary had remained in the galley for most of the morning, helping, where they could, to console the Augusta's crew, still stricken with grief regarding the death of their beloved Admiral. Lunch was well on its way when the officers from the Connecticut entered the galley, obviously, the meeting with Jason was over and Janet was eager to hear about the itinerary to try and finagle a trip to Nebraska, despite what Jason had said earlier.

Once the officers had selected their food they brought their trays over to the table that Janet and Mary were occupying. Why wouldn't they? They were the only two females onboard, even though they were both spoken for.

"Janet, Mary." Raymond said in greeting as he sat down next to Mary, a little too close for her comfort.

"Hi Raymond," Janet said with a smile and she nodded to the other two officers as they sat down. Mary made an excuse to go and get a coffee. "So, what's happening?" Janet asked.

"Well, the plan is that this old tub will be going to Bermuda and then on to Norfolk while we will stay on the Connecticut and hold the fort while you are away." Raymond replied and as if to confirm his statement Jason's voice came over the P.A. system informing the crew of the decisions that had just been made during the meeting.

“Well it’s a sad circumstance that is forcing us to carry out this trip, but life goes on.” Janet said cryptically as she was already planning what she was going to propose to Jason, but she would need the added persuasive powers of Mary. “Talk to you soon.” She said with a smile to the men as she rose from the table and beckoned Mary to join her. Mary had already filled a couple of coffee cups, so she picked them up and followed Janet out of the galley.

Janet didn’t say anything to Mary until she arrived at Mary’s cabin, she waited for Mary to enter with the coffees before closing the door conspiratively behind her.

“I’ve been thinking, I figure that once we arrive in Norfolk, Peter could find a plane and have us in Nebraska within a few hours.” Janet said, continuing with her scheme.

“But you heard what Jason said, there’s no way he is going to let us do this.” Mary replied, fully convinced she wasn’t going to do it either based on the last trip she had made with Janet.

“He can’t stop us. If Peter is prepared to fly us to the Clay Center, then I’m going. Now are you in or not?” Janet asked.

“I can’t Jane, not after the last time.” Mary replied. “I just can’t.”

“Can’t or won’t Mary?” Janet asked officiously. “Mankind’s future is at stake here and you can help it survive.”

"Jane, we have fish, fruit, vegetables, chickens and eggs. We have more than enough to survive. We don't need to risk our lives going on a wild goose chase." Mary pleaded.

"It's not a wild goose chase, they would be tame." Janet said in a desperate attempt to lighten the situation and bring Mary on board.

"Janet this is all a game to you, isn't it?" Mary said frustrated with her ex-boss' flippant approach to the problem.

"No, it's poultry not game Mary. If the goose is tame, it would be poultry, a wild goose would be game." Janet said with all seriousness.

"Oooooh, you." Mary replied. "You're not funny." Although Mary had calmed down somewhat. "Anyway, how are you going to convince DeVersa to fly you to Nebraska if Jason is against the plan?" Mary asked and then continued, "if Jason says no way, DeVersa won't go!"

"Well we will just have to persuade him to let us make the trip, won't we?" Janet said connivingly.

"What do you mean us and we, Janet?" Mary stated confidently. But before she could answer there was a knock at the door. When Janet opened the door, she was surprised to see Jason standing there.

"Oh, we were just talking about you." Janet said casually, but before she could continue Jason interrupted her.

"If it is about Nebraska you can forget it. We have a bigger emergency on our hands."

Chapter 15

New Visitors Have Arrived

Bermuda

David and Alex were running to their scooters and starting them up to return to the bar to get everyone to don their breathing apparatus. Emergency procedures had been set up so that in the event of a return of the microbes, emergency breathing equipment was readily available in all of their homes and at places they regularly frequent like their favorite bars. It is also likely Moose and Dutch had scuba gear on the boat so if they were thinking quickly enough, once the boat had stopped its chaotic motion they may be able to get to their breathing equipment.

Alex was about to speed away when he saw the object rise back up about six feet from the sea and then settle back down with another splash, only to float around in its own turbulence. The rays of the afternoon sun were glinting off the object which suggested to David that it wasn't a rock-like formation. Once more he reached for his binoculars to inspect the object in a little more detail. David was having a problem focusing on the module as the waves forced it to reel up and down; and from side to side. As the commotion of the water slowly subsided David could see both Moose and Dutch, now standing unassisted, and they were also looking at the strange object. David switched his focus to the boat and he could see Dutch moving to the boat's console while Moose quickly began to reel in the fishing rods. David could vaguely hear the powerful outboard engines roar into life and Dutch deftly negotiated the boat slowly towards the object in the water.

By the time Dutch arrived within a boat length of the object Moose had stowed away all the fishing poles on the upper deck and was now attempting to attach a line to the still bobbing object. Despite how many drinks Moose had consumed he was still a good sailor and was now in his element messing around on the sea. The object had a circular transom around it so once Moose had his line secured he nimbly moved from the boat to the object for a closer inspection. Moose was a big man, hence his name, and he had put on a little weight since his new life-style in Bermuda but despite this, he was still reasonably fit with all the sea going activities he and Dutch enjoyed.

From David's standpoint, there appeared to be what looked like windows or small port-holes in the floating object. Moose was leaning over one of the windows with his hand across his forehead to investigate the craft. Suddenly he stood up as though he was anticipating something to happen, which it did. A door slowly opened revealing a hatch and David could distinguish an arm reaching from it. Moose grabbed the arm and a person, dressed in an astronaut's suit climbed unsteadily from what now David was believing to be a space capsule. Moose, with Dutch's help assisted the astronaut onto the boat but by now the waves had turned the tied-up boat and capsule around so David's sightline was obstructed. He decided to use his air horn in an attempt to catch their attention. He waited until the boat had swung around once more and pressed on the button of the horn. Dutch immediately heard it and rose an arm in acknowledgement. David responded by pointing east, indicating the bar which had a dock beside it. Dutch raised his arm again indicating that he understood. Then he decided to reach into the cockpit and turn on the boat's radio.

"Dutch here copy." Dutch said.

"David, here. Meet you at the clubhouse." David said.

"Copy that." Dutch said and put the microphone down as he went to assist Moose once more, but to do what David couldn't tell because the boat had swung around again obstructing his view.

David and Alex scooted back to the bar and as they approached, in the distance, they could see the boat returning with its additional passengers. David blew the air-horn once more to attract the attention of the men in the clubhouse. It had the desired effect as they all came outside, some with drinks in hand, to see what the commotion was all about. They then saw the boat approaching the dock, which was no big deal, they knew it was Moose and Dutch until one of the men said, "there's someone else in the boat." Slowly, the men, now joined by David and Alex reached the dock and awaited the arrival of the boat. One of the men had a line ready to toss to the crew and another was getting ready to secure the bow. But they nearly fell off the dock in surprise as the boat approached, they could clearly see seated in the stern a man, a woman and a baby.

Chapter 16

Single Again

St. Santia, at the home of Marlene and Tony

Maria had immediately gone to Marlene's house after learning the news of the Admiral's death from John. Naturally, Maria thought that was the reason for Marlene's current emotional state, after all, it was the crew of his submarine that had saved both her life and that of her baby, Augusta. Then, she began to understand it was a little more than that as Marlene explained the situation to her.

"That means Tony has been giving this some thought since the appearance of the submarines and his little tantrum this morning isn't going to be an isolated occurrence." Maria said, almost talking to herself.

"He's just been going along with the arrangement because there was no alternative, but now, as far as he is concerned, the charade is over." Marlene replied, while Maria bit her lip, suddenly concerned that Bob's attitude may also change. As if Marlene could sense what her friend was thinking she continued. "I think Tony wants to make a clean break from all of us." Then turning to face Maria, she said, "getting back together with Bob is not an option, I'm sure of it Maria."

"Of course, it isn't dear," Joan said, patting Maria on the knee as if that was confirmation enough.

"Sorry Joan, this is a complicated situation. I didn't mean to get you all embroiled in our sexual orientation problems." Marlene said apologetically. "You're not used to this sort of thing I'm sure."

"You're not so unique my dear, it's just the situation you are in that forces you to be something you are not." Joan casually replied. "It's more in the open to-day of course. In my day homosexual people were around but it was kept under wraps, or 'in the closet' as you say."

"And now we have to shove it right back in the closet." Marlene said bitterly.

"People are what they are dear," Joan told Marlene sympathetically, "and you have to make choices. In your case, circumstances have forced you to make a choice and now they are forcing you to make another decision." Both Marlene and Maria were now listening very attentively to the older lady's wisdom. "Unfortunately, the options available to you for meeting the person to satisfy your sexual orientation in this new world are somewhat limited. I know it is hard dear, it may have been too difficult for Tony to change his spots, but you have proven you can adapt. Now, you must do it again."

"It's easy for you to sat that," Marlene retaliated between sobs, "you're considered normal with a husband and you had three kids."

"Yes dear, had." Joan replied and paused while a tear formed in her eye, Marlene instantly regretted her remark but then Joan continued unperturbed. "I know you think I don't understand what you're going through, but let me tell you something, I grew up in a small town in Maine where everyone knew everyone else, their problems and their goings-ons. Nobody had any secrets in that town. One of my best friends from kindergarten right up through to high school and even after at nurses' training college was Trisha. Everything was fine until we started going through adolescence, that was when we realized Trisha was different, she discovered she was a lesbian. Of course, she didn't come on to any of us, she respected what we were and what we wanted, and we remained great friends. As we got older she was forced to take trips to the city to find what she was looking for, but you couldn't take the small-town gal out of her. So, she'd come back and of course the jibing would start, especially with the boys in the town. I'm sure you've heard it all, what they would do to her to make her feel like a real woman." Both Marlene and Maria nodded their heads in agreement remembering their own bad experiences during their younger days.

"Her two older brothers used to protect her as best they could, but they weren't always around. When they were, you knew it wasn't going to end well." Joan said squirming as she thought back to some of the fights she witnessed in the bars and clubs. "She had trouble getting a job locally due to the stigma attached to her, then there were the verbal barbs, they were constant. So, after about ten years of this she decided enough was enough, she needed to escape it all. Trisha was forced to move away to the big city, permanently. In those days, if you knew where to look, she could find the type of people she was yearning for. Unfortunately, she couldn't hack it in the city either so at 25 years old she committed suicide."

"Wow that's so sad Joan." Marlene said.

"That must have been upsetting for you Joan." Maria said almost crying in empathy with Joan.

"It was a lot harder for John," Joan stated matter-of-factly, "it was his younger sister."

Chapter 17

Nebraska Re-visited

St. Santia, Aboard the U.S.S. Augusta

"My goodness, what's wrong Jason?" Mary asked with some concern, she had never seen Jason so harried.

"You're not going to believe this." Jason said shaking his head, "Bermuda has reported the landing of a space capsule in the sea, just off the island. A couple of the guys were out there fishing, so they motored over to the capsule and they have brought two astronauts back to the island, a man, a woman and get this," Jason paused for a second, hardly being able to believe it himself, "a baby, that was born in space."

"You're joking with us Jason." Mary said not believing her boyfriend.

"Not at all." Jason said in all honesty. "As yet, I don't have any details, but I expect they will fill us in when we arrive in Bermuda. Hopefully they will be comfortable in Bermuda for a couple of days with the Connecticut crew members while we go onto Norfolk and we will bring them back here on our return. I wouldn't have thought being cooped in a submarine would be too stressful for them if they have returned from space in a small space capsule.

"That's incredible Jason, yet another baby to add to the next generation of children." Janet said.

"Precisely. Now that's where you two will come in," Jason began to say, getting to the point as to why he has paid them a visit, "I think it would be best if you could be available to the new family for as much as possible. Now, I know you would like to attend the funeral service, so I am considering changing the itinerary a little. What we could do is sail into American waters, carry out the service then return to Bermuda to drop you both off while we continue onto Norfolk, as planned. I am sure the lady would appreciate some female company amongst that group of drunken seamen."

Jason's change of plan was met with a stony silence. Mary looked uncomfortably at the deck while Janet's demeanor was tense, and her jaw was resolute.

"What's wrong? I thought – Oh no. Wait a minute." Jason suddenly clued into what was going on. "You're still not harboring thoughts of going to Nebraska are you Janet?"

"We have to Jason. Think of the implications if we could rear livestock." Janet replied.

"Think of the implications if you meet up with a band of renegades like you did last time you went off on a foolhardy trip." Jason shouted at Janet, "only last time, you dragged Mary along on your pathetic journey, well that is not going to be repeated."

"Jason, you don't have to shout." Mary reprimanded him, "and as much as I love you Jason, I agree with Janet, I believe this is something we can achieve. We just need to talk about this, calmly and collectively to come up with an appropriate schedule."

"Mary, I'm surprised you are going along with this I can't-" Jason started to reply, still shouting until Mary interrupted him.
"Jason. This has been a terrible day for you. We appreciate that, and we are not helping." Mary said, holding up the palms of her hands to signal Jason to stop talking. "But this is important, we need to discuss this rationally. Let Janet and I talk to some of the crew, we will come up with a plan and we can go over it with you on our way to Bermuda. Now is not the time. O.K?" Jason, still seething with anger, said nothing, he just turned on his heel and left the two ladies standing there in Mary's cabin. For a few seconds neither of the women moved, then Mary slowly and carefully closed the cabin door. She had hated questioning Jason's authority and hoped that this did not infringe on their relationship.
"Thank you for your support Mary, I know how difficult that must have been. I didn't think you were going to back me up." Janet said gratefully.
"That's O.K. Janet, but I didn't do it for you." Mary stated.

Chapter 18

Moving On

St. Santia at the home of Marlene and Tony

"My point is dear, you have proven you can adapt. Poor Trisha was unable to." Joan said before continuing, "you also have an understanding support group to help you through this. Even if your past was revealed to the others you would not have to suffer all the shame and humiliation that existed in Trisha's days. We now have four babies on the island, whether you wish to have more with someone else it's your decision and yours alone." Joan then looked in horror at what her latest remark must have sounded like. "Oh, my goodness, that sounded terrible, I'm not suggesting for a minute that you are going to tout yourself around the crew, mind you, there are some handsome looking hunks on those submarines." Joan managed to get the girls laughing again, then for a few moments the three ladies just sat around the table enveloped in their own thoughts. Suddenly, the silence was broken by the familiar sounds of a baby awaking from a sleep demanding attention. Augusta had decided she had slept for long enough.

"Would you like me to see to her dear?" Joan asked Marlene.

"No, I can do it, she probably wants a feed." Marlene replied, reluctantly rising from the table.

"Well, best I be getting back to the house." Joan said, "John will think I have eloped with one of those hunks from the submarine." The other girls smiled, and Maria also decided to stand and was about to leave but decided to remain.
"You know Joan, I'm really sorry about the crass remark I made." Marlene said ashamedly, "I really feel bad about it."
"Don't worry about it. I'm not the only one who have lost loved ones Marlene." Joan replied with a forgiving smile.
"I'll catch you up Joan." Maria said.
"No problem, dear. See you up there." With a wave, Joan was out the door and gone.

Both Marlene and Maria went to see to Augusta. With some cooing and oohing Marlene lifted the diminutive child from the cot and prepared to breast-feed her. While Marlene was nursing her baby, Maria broached what she thought was now a delicate subject and she felt she had to tread carefully.
"Marlene, I love you dearly, you know that." Maria was standing in front of Marlene, not being able to make eye contact with her so she was looking down at her toes, twiddling in the flip-flops on her feet, "but what Joan said about adapting, I've adapted Marlene, I'm with Bob now and that's not going to change."
"I know that." Marlene replied softly, "I never gave it a thought, I'll be alright." Which was a huge relief to Maria who felt that Marlene might consider this as an opportunity to resume their relationship. Then on a lighter note Marlene added, "look on the bright side,

maybe we can invite all the sailors over for a party. We could have a '*Bachelorette*' theme."

"Who for? You or Tony?" Maria said and they both burst out laughing.

It was just at that very moment Tony walked into the house.

Chapter 19

Contemplating Their Final Moments

Above the Earth, Aboard the Space Station

Amy Lovett and her baby daughter were looking through the porthole of the International Space Station at planet earth. The baby, Mir, named after the original space station, had been born on the International Space Station as part of a secret American Russian study on human reproduction in space. Amy was holding her baby daughter and talking to her. With tears in her eyes she said softly to her, "Mir, my baby, look, that's where we came from. That's mummy and daddy's home. We were hoping to take you there someday but I'm afraid we can't." Ivan was gently holding his daughter's small fingers while she gurgled and smiled at the beautiful blue orb orbiting some 200 miles away.

In addition to Amy, Ivan and Mir there was Petr Yenin who had arrived at the ISS with Boris Denekin some nine months earlier. Petr, a Russian cosmonaut, was an engineer and it was his job to keep this puppy on the correct orbit and not let it get drawn into earth's gravitational pull. Boris was an obstetrician and had arrived to be on hand for the birth, even though both Amy and Ivan were doctors. The baby was born about three months after the devastation and they knew their lives together would be limited. It had in fact been too much for Boris, he had held up well until Mir's birth, then, after waiting a few days to ensure everyone was healthy he took a cyanide pill to end his life. In a note that he left, one of the reasons he cited was to provide the survivors with an extra few weeks provisions in the outside chance help would somehow arrive. Moreover, he was deeply upset about the loss of his wife and his own three children. He didn't think surviving an extra few months would ever take away that grief. He wished them well and hoped his sacrifice would at least provide them with a few extra weeks with their baby.

Behind them, Petr had now arrived in the room, it was time. Amy, with Mir in her arms, turned away from the window and accompanied by Ivan they faced Petr and the inevitable. Petr had carefully placed four small red boxes on the table between them and they remained there, in the gravity-free environment, secured by a strap. Each box contained a vial of lethal cyanide. There was no food left on the space station, oxygen was running critically low, the generator was only days away from ceasing operations and soon the place would turn into a gigantic freezer. The original schedule, was for Amy, Mir and her father, Ivan, to return to earth twelve weeks after the baby's birth, Mir was now six months old and today was the day she was scheduled to die.

Chapter 20

Funeral Arrangements to Be Made

St. Santia, Aboard the U.S.S. Augusta

"So, what's your great plan Janet?" Mary asked, still upset for what she had just said to Jason.

"Well, we know, DeVersa is prepared to fly us to Nebraska." Janet replied undaunted, "I have no idea where the nearest airport is, but I'll leave those details to him. I'm sure we can locate transport to the Clay Centre when we arrive there."

"What about security?" Mary asked very concerned, "are you going to ask Grover to come along?"

"Yes, if he is prepared to come along, I will let him arrange whatever help he needs." Janet suggested, quite enthused now that she had another project to keep her mind occupied.

"What if he is not prepared to participate?" Mary asked.

"I'm still going Mary." Janet replied resolutely.

"Janet, that would be madness." Mary said with frustration at her friend's obstinacy. "And how long are you going to be staying there? If Grover doesn't go, you're on your own. You know that don't you?"

"I'll stay for as long as it takes." Janet replied, now realizing that Mary was not prepared to make the trip.

“What about supplies?” Mary asked trying to place further obstacles in Janet’s way. “Anything there will be either dead, putrid or inedible.”

“I will take some food, a generator and other necessities and hopefully DeVersa can keep me supplied on a monthly basis. A few eggs, bread, just the staples.” Janet casually countered. “I expect I can find a vehicle to drive to a town and supplement my requirements with canned and packaged goods, I’ll survive.”

“But Janet, it’s going to be the middle of winter there right now.” Mary was pleading with her, “can’t you at least wait until spring?”

“The longer we leave it, the less chance we have of nurturing any cells, you know that.” Janet replied and with that she rose to leave. “I’m going to speak to Grover to see if he’s interested. Are you coming?”

Janet strode purposefully along the corridor, down some steps to the bow of the submarine that housed the small, yet functional gym. Grover was a man of routine. A five-mile run every morning, except Sundays, shower, breakfast then wait to be assigned to a work detail, usually one that required heavy labor. Then lunch and another work detail before hitting the gym. To-day was an exception because of the events that had unfolded so Janet fully expected Grover to be working out, she wasn’t wrong. Mary dutifully followed her like a doting puppy, not for the first time, as she entered the gym.

"Janet, Mary, hi!" A sweating Grover said as he returned the bar he had been bench pressing back to its resting place.

"That looks heavy," Mary casually said, stating the obvious.

"500lb, I needed a tough one to-day." Grover replied. "You two coming to work out?"

"Hardly, we've come to talk to you." Janet replied, noticing for the first time, in the confines of the small gym, just how big Grover was. Grover was wearing tight black shorts, a white vest, that exposed his almost perfect torso and as Janet looked up at his 6' 5" frame to see the beads of perspiration trickling down his handsome face she was amazed she hadn't noticed this before.

"What would you like to talk to me about?" Grover replied, quite surprised as the two women had never really said much to him despite his rescue of them from the clutches of mutinying sailors. He reached for a small white towel to mop his brow and waited for Janet's response.

"Grover, what is your first name, or do you prefer Grover?" Janet asked politely.

"It's Stefan but only my mother called me that. I prefer Grover." Grover replied.

"Oh, Stefan, that's a nice name. I can't understand why you don't like it."

"My name was originally Stefan Groveliski, my father was Polish, went to California in the sixties to buy into the body building scene. He was on the fringes of fame but never quite made it, so, he left us to return to Poland, never heard from him again. So, my mother had to work hard, sometimes two jobs to make ends meet. Well, with a name like 'Grovel' 'iski'," Grover said purposefully splitting the name into two words, "she decided to change it to Grover. Unfortunately, she died when I was just 17 so being all alone, I decided to join the navy." Grover merely smiled and shrugged as if to say, 'well, that's it, that's all you get.'

"Oh, what a sad story," Mary said.

"Well, Stefan," Janet said, trying to get back on track. "Do we have a mission for you?"

"Yea?" Grover asked with some interest, "doing what? Fishing polar bears out of the sea again?" Grover said laughing, referring to the last time Janet demanded a task to be carried out by Grover, immediately after the devastation.

"No, no, no." Janet said also laughing. "No, this is something more up your alley, more like the mall rescue mission where you saved us. Except, you will just be joining us for protection, hopefully, you will not have cause to fire your weapon."

"Tell me more." Grover said as he sat down on a black vinyl work-out bench.

Janet proceeded to tell him her plan and once the facility was secure, she fully expected him and his team, whoever they may be, to return with DeVersa to Norfolk and ultimately the Augusta. However, Grover, had other ideas.

"I can't speak for others who may choose to accompany me on this 'mission'," Grover moved his fingers up and down to indicate quotes, "but I am quite prepared to stay on to offer continued protection. Just in case there are any wandering survivors in the area. You must realize the sight and sound of any type of flying object would attract unwanted attention."

Chapter 21

Time to Leave the Capsule

Above the Earth, Aboard the Space Station

Surprisingly, Petr produced a sophisticated piece of webbing he had been holding behind him.

“I am hoping that this contraption that I have made will fit the baby as you travel back to earth.” Petr said. Amy and Ivan looked strangely at the man, thinking he had succumbed to cosmic cabin fever.

“I have been working on the emergency space capsule.” Petr continued, “it needed some modifications to accommodate the three of you, but I still couldn’t find room for the little one. So, I have adapted this seat belt for you, Amy. It is designed to fit around your shoulders to secure Mir during your re-entry into the earth’s atmosphere. In that little capsule, it is going to get very bumpy and without this,” Petr said as he held up the belt, “you may not be able to keep hold of her.”

“What are you talking about Petr?” Ivan asked.

“You are heading back to earth, aboard the Soyuz.” Petr replied enthusiastically.

“But how? There’s nobody on earth to control the capsule.” Amy asked imploringly.

“On earth no, but I can operate the Soyuz from here.” Petr replied.

"That's impossible! It is an emergency escape craft that was not designed to be controlled from here. Only from a base on earth."

"I have made a few modifications, trust me, I can control the Soyuz from here. The only slight deviation is that it will land in the water not on land."

"Will that be a problem?" Amy said, her thoughts reacting like a yo-yo to this latest news.

"Shouldn't be. The Soyuz is airtight and designed to land in the desert so landing in water, shouldn't be a problem." Petr replied confidently.

"Well, why couldn't we land in the desert as it was designed to do?" Ivan asked.

"Because a landing in a Russian desert may be so far from help you may just as well stay here. Same could be true of any other desert. So, I have programmed the capsule to land off Bermuda where the water is deep, and the Gulf Stream should take you to the island. The capsule is capable of floating as are your space suits. You will also have a week's supply of food that I have saved from my rations." Petr said proudly.

"But this is a huge risk Petr." Amy said unconvinced.

"No Amy, the risk is staying here." Petr replied with a serious expression on his face. "If necessary, you will still have your cyanide capsules. I don't see a risk. Only a chance at life." Petr said.

"But what about you Petr?" Amy asked. It suddenly occurred to her that the Soyuz was a two-man craft and he could not join them.

"Someone has to control the capsule from here." Petr said. "I'm the only one who can do that."

"Petr!" Amy said almost inaudibly.

"Oh, and I have designed this little space suit for Amy." Petr said, reaching behind him for a mini suit that would fit the baby, albeit with a full-size helmet. "Sorry, couldn't do anything about the helmet." Petr laughed.

For the last few months Petr had been almost inaccessible, Amy and Ivan thought their pending demise caused by the devastation was the reason. Well, it had been, but for all the right reasons. Petr had been quietly making, programming, modifying and planning the necessary preparations for their ultimate survival.

"But Petr, we can't leave you here to die alone." Amy said, the tears now rolling down her beautiful cheeks.

"Of course you can." Petr replied with authority. "I am a trained Russian cosmonaut. I was employed knowing full well the dangers and the high risk that dying on the job was a strong possibility. You are not fully-trained cosmonauts, you are doctors conducting an experiment."

"Petr, I appreciate what you have done but I won't leave." Ivan said sincerely. "Amy and Mir must leave but I will remain with you."

"Very gracious of you Ivan." Petr replied. "If it was just you, you Siberian reprobate, well, I would agree, we could die together. But you are not alone, you are a father of possibly the only child in the universe. Mir is going to need her father. We don't know what, if any life, is on earth. You could at least build a family. You would be like Adam and Eve, Ivan and Amy. No, you both must go with Mir."

"But to die here alone Petr, I can't let you do it." Amy pleaded once more.

"Amy, fate has brought me her. Had I have remained on earth I would already be dead by now. I have enjoyed these extra months doing what I have been trained to do. What is more, I believe there is a reason for my presence here." Petr paused as he thought carefully about his next few words. "That reason is to provide you with the gift of life and that is a gift you must accept." There was a silence in the room, except for Mir's constant cooing. Amy and Ivan looked at each other and both shook their heads. Amy reached for two of the boxes containing the cyanide capsules.

"By all means, take the cyanide with you," Petr said as Amy took the boxes of cyanide, "in the unlikely event that things start to go wrong on your return to earth you still have that option. But think about this, if all goes well, the other option is a life for your baby in a new world."

Amy hesitated before opening the box containing the suicide pill.

"And remember this," Petr said with all seriousness, "I happen to be the commander of this vessel and I am ordering you into the Soyuz.

You must leave now." Petr then turned around to a locker behind him and pointed to two space suits.

Reluctantly, Amy and Ivan sidled over to the locker and began to dress into the Sokol space suits that Petr had prepared for them. Meanwhile, Petr began dressing Mir in her new designer suit. Petr had become a loving '*uncle*' to Mir so she was enjoying the attention she was receiving from him. Once they were dressed in their suits, Amy and Ivan walked ungainly over to the Soyuz where Petr was waiting with Mir. Petr passed Mir to Amy while he and Ivan gave each other a good old-fashioned, Russian, bear-hug. Then Amy passed Mir to Ivan and Amy gave Petr a long, loving, hug. The last embrace was saved for Mir, who was still giggling at Petr's antics, this was the one he knew would be difficult, it was. Amy administered a light sedative for the anxious young baby, she would soon be asleep as they travelled through the rigours of re-entry into the earth's atmosphere, unaware of the cramped living space she would be in. Finally, it was time to put on their helmets, which did not go down at all well with the baby.

Petr was till holding Mir as her parents entered the space capsule, Amy and Ivan attached their electrical cables to the right of their suits, Petr felt it was his responsibility to connect Mir's suit. The air and oxygen hoses were connected, then the modified webbing restraint for Mir was placed around Amy's shoulders before finally the seat belts were clicked in place. Petr, almost reluctantly, passed Mir to her mother and once she was sitting securely on Amy's lap, her restraints were secured. Mir was still not happy with her new clothes, so Amy jokingly said, "this is our first trip together as a family and we are not going to have a crying baby the whole way."

"Well it will only be for 3.5 hours. She'll survive." Petr said, upsetting Amy once more at the poor choice of words, as innocent as they were.

Petr did one final check to ensure the cables, wires and hoses were all properly connected to the three passengers. Satisfied that all was well, Petr wasted no time on a prolonged farewell he merely said, "Bon Voyage," then he closed and secured the hatch. Seconds later, they could hear Petr's voice in their helmets' radios.

"Preparing to undock the capsule," Petr said, and the passengers could feel the hooks and latches that secured the capsule to the Space Station begin to open. With the hooks open the Soyuz spacecraft was now physically separated and it began to travel at a speed of four inches per second. Amy subconsciously felt for the boxes containing the cyanide pills that were stored in a zipped pocket of her suit. One pill for her and one for Mir. Nothing further happened for another six minutes until Petr came on air again.

"Preparing a short separation burn." Petr said. The capsule was now approximately 66 feet from the Space Station as the passengers felt the thrusters turn on for some fifteen seconds. For almost an hour the capsule travelled silently through space. There were no communications from Petr, Mir was sleeping peacefully, Amy and

Ivan said nothing. They were approximately twelve miles from the Space Station when Petr spoke to them for the final time.
"Preparing to position the capsule for the deorbit burn." Petr said matter-of-factly then after a short pause he added almost inaudibly, "farewell." This time his voice was chocked with emotion as with this final act there was little more he could contribute; his task was done. The engines fired for just over four minutes as the capsule prepared for its re-entry into the earth's atmosphere, the most critical phase of the trip. The passengers could feel the unoccupied Orbital Module separate from their Descent Module and at approximately 400,000 feet from earth the capsule began to buffet as it re-entered the earth's atmosphere.

To Amy and Ivan, it felt like somebody was hammering the capsule with a sledgehammer and to endorse their thoughts, every few seconds there were loud bangs emanating from outside. Fiery plasma was streaking outside of the window, which was now getting dark as the outside layer of the pane was burning. To make matters worse, as bulky as their space suits were, the passengers were beginning to feel the heat permeating through the heat-resistant material. By now, Amy had unzipped the compartment in her suit that contained the cyanide pills and just as she thought she couldn't take any more the capsule's descent was suddenly jolted. Parachutes were automatically deployed that reduced the speed of the capsule from the speed of sound to 262 feet per second. Then, not only did the speed of descent reduce as a second parachute was deployed but the passengers could feel the orientation of the capsule being slowly re-positioned. Amy couldn't see too much from the window, but they were obviously now close to the earth's surface and she was still very concerned that they were travelling too fast. At that moment, she felt engines fire that slowed their descent even further and then they plummeted into the sea amidst the sound of hissing and gurgling water.

After splashdown the capsule was only underwater a mere matter of seconds but to the passengers it felt like an eternity before it bobbed back to the surface. For a full minute, Amy and Ivan sat perfectly still, gathering their thoughts and verifying that they had successfully made the trip. Without a word being spoken, they both began to simultaneously remove their helmets.

"You O.K.?" Ivan asked.

"Yes, fine." Amy replied.

"How's Mir?" Ivan asked, quite concerned as Amy began to remove the baby's oversized helmet.

"She's still sleeping, she's O.K. too." Amy replied as a small tear ran down her cheek, relieved that their baby had survived the hectic trip.

Now that the most difficult part of the journey was over, their concern was what were they going to find back on earth? As if to answer that question a face suddenly appeared peering into the darkened window. Ivan reached over to release the hatch cover and the person on the outside opened the door fully. Pleasantries were exchanged, and the passengers began to undo their assortment of attachments and restraints. Amy and Ivan were now smiling and laughing with relief as they floated in the Atlantic talking to their would-be rescuer.

Meanwhile, in space, in the gravity free environment of the Space Station, Petr was also floating and had anyone have been there to witness it they would have seen a slight, satisfying smile on his now cold lips.

Chapter 22

A Surprising Decision

St. Santia, at the home of Marlene and Tony

With Tony's return a silence descended on the room, even baby Augusta stopped feeding temporarily. Maria thought this was a good opportunity to take her leave.

"I better get back," Maria said to Marlene, "don't forget to tell Tony the news." Maria put a hand on Marlene's shoulder and lovingly squeezed it before leaving the house. Once Maria had left Tony, walked over to the sink to pour himself a glass of water.

"If it's about the Admiral, I know. I saw one of the crew, he told me." Tony said between gulps of water. Tony was looking out of the window and he still had his back to Marlene.

"So, I guess Maria knows about us." Tony said quietly.

"Joan does too." Marlene said, just as quietly.

"Well, that's just great. Why don't we get the submarine to just broadcast the news to everyone?" Tony replied angrily as he slammed his empty glass down on the kitchen counter. This sudden noise disturbed baby Augusta and gave cause for her to let out a frightened yell.

"Now look what you've down you, selfish bastard." Marlene shouted at him angrily. She rose to leave the room with baby Augusta, but Tony held up his hands.

"No, don't go. Please, I'm sorry." Tony said quickly. "I'm really sorry, I've handled this badly."

"No kidding!" Marlene replied tersely.

"Since everyone has turned up I've been confused." Tony said. He had his hands on the sides of head which he was shaking from side to side as if he was saying 'no'. "I was prepared for us to live together and rear children. I get that, but now…." Tony's voice trailed off.

"Now what?" Marlene asked. "What's changed? You are a father now, you have a responsibility to Augusta."

"I know, I know. But I don't have the responsibility to live this kind of life anymore." Tony blurted out. "There are others who can assume that mantle, the future human race doesn't need me, you don't need me."

"But what about Augusta, she needs you?" Marlene asked incredulously.

"Augusta? Right now, she doesn't even know of my existence. She was born on that boat with all those sailors around her, they still come and see her. I'm not her father." Tony said with a pathetic sort of pity in his voice.

"Who the hell do you think is her father then?" Marlene was now shouting, causing Augusta to let out another yell of distress.

"That's not what I meant, and you know it Marlene." Tony responded angrily but then began to calm down. "Of course, I'm her father, biologically, but I don't think I can live this life and be a proper father to her."

"So, what do you plan on doing?" Marlene asked, also in a calmer tone.

"I think it would be best if I made a clean break. Now!" Tony said.

"So, are you going to move out and leave me on my own?" Marlene asked.

"You won't be on your own Marlene. Maria is close, so is Joan." Tony replied, "You could always let the Hamaxs move in here."

"I don't think so, they need their privacy too." Marlene explained.

"How long do you think it will be before there is a line-up of crew members knocking on your door, once they know you are available?" Tony said flippantly. Marlene didn't reply, her temper was beginning to get the best of her, Tony sensed it, he had crossed the line.

"Look, as I said, I'm not doing a very good job of this," Tony said, trying to pacify the situation. "We need a couple of days apart to get our thoughts together."

"Is that the '*Royal We*' Tony?" Marlene said bitterly. "I think it is you who need a couple of days, don't you?"

"Whatever Marlene." Tony replied tetchily, "anyway, I think it's best if I leave, so I have decided to travel on the Augusta to represent us at Admiral Stanford's funeral."

Chapter 23

From Out of This World

Bermuda

The arrival of the astronauts was just what the small community of sailors on Bermuda needed as it galvanized them into action. Some of them had fallen into a daily routine of foraging throughout the city of Hamilton for alcohol and then returning to the Happy Mariner pub to drink it. Others, went fishing to supply everyone with fresh fish, some were scuba-divers and they were in their element in the clear Atlantic waters around the island. It was a man's world for sure, no one to give orders, enough food and drink to last the small detachment of men for the rest of their lives together with sunshine, sea and boats. What else do you need? But having no real purpose to do anything other than simply lazing around was beginning to tell on most of the men, especially the younger ones. They needed a reason to get up in the morning, something to strive for, that was the natural order of things.

To David, this lack of purpose and not having a person to share his life with; was eating at him. To some extent, that is why he became the person responsible for the regular calls to the Augusta, but he was beginning to believe that even they were becoming superfluous to requirements. David felt that the reason most of the Bermuda detachment had decided to remain here was to die and the sooner the better. No, they weren't suicidal, they just had no desire to live, there was no real reason to. Other than the crew, they had no friends or family left alive, no future generations to support. Of course, they were now aware of the children on St. Santia, but they hadn't seen them, and they meant nothing to them; out of sight out of mind. But seeing this couple with a young child had a poignant effect on them, well almost all of them.

David was by no means the senior member of the detachment, on the Connecticut he had just been an able-seaman, but at this moment he was the only one who was completely sober, so he took charge of the situation.

"Lacy, Smee, can you go and clear a space in the pub and get some food going for these people please?" David asked. Without hesitation, the two men ran from the dock towards the Happy Mariner, happy to do as they were requested. Lacy and Smee were both originally from the Connecticut and were a couple. Although their relationship never fully flourished onboard they recognized their attraction for each other and when the opportunity came to remain on Bermuda, they took it eagerly. On the Connecticut, Lacy had been a torpedo specialist, not something that was in much demand, post devastation. Smee, however, had been a cook and still enjoyed conjuring up dishes for the men of the detachment who preferred real food to a liquid diet, despite their lack of appreciation. Of course, Smee wasn't his real name, that would be, Lionel Barton. But being a plump man, from all that tasting of the food he cooked, his grey unkempt hair and round spectacles maintained a resemblance to Smee from the Peter Pan movies, or at least that's what his compatriots thought, the name stuck.

On the jetty, the sailors secured the boat then began to assist the passengers from the vessel. First to disembark the boat was the female astronaut, she was carrying the still sleeping baby. The lady introduced herself as Amy and mentioned the baby's name was Mir. Despite the cumbersome spacesuit she was wearing and the sweat pouring from her brow, it was obvious to the sailors that this was one beautiful woman. She needed a little assistance to stand and walk off the jetty, so she was helped by a sailor on either side of her who gently supported her weight until they got to the dock. After all, because of the nature of the experiment they had participated in and the tragic events that occurred afterwards, Amy and Ivan had spent more time in space than any other individuals in the history of the space program. This was the first time in 460 days that they had experienced gravity, not to mention the hectic journey back to earth. David decided to bark out another request.

"Danby, can you get the truck down here, I don't think they will make the walk to the bar." Danby was another member of the Connecticut crew who had decided to remain on Bermuda. Danby had been in the navy almost twenty years and as he was approaching middle-age he enjoyed the solitude he could get on the island.

"You got it." Danby replied, and he went rushing off, meanwhile, Amy had been plonked down on a public bench overlooking the ocean. Still sweating profusely, she asked the men who had escorted her there to help her out of her space suit. While Amy waited for Ivan to join them she extricated Mir from her safety harness and as Ivan arrived she handed the small, still sleeping, bundle to him. Amy knew she could trust the sailors around her, but it was that maternal instinct to not hand over her baby to complete strangers, even though, during the boat-ride, Moose had provided a brief explanation as to who the men were and how they had arrived in Bermuda.

With Mir taken care of, Amy instructed the men as they gently undid all the straps, zippers and buttons until she was able to wrestle herself out of the outer suit to reveal her Liquid Cooling and Ventilation Garment that just accentuated her voluptuous figure. However, the bump of her astronaut's diaper that was used for the re-entry left her a little embarrassed, but Amy was more concerned about Mir's well-being. With David's assistance, Amy now concentrated on removing the modified suit from Mir which brought a tear to her eye. She suddenly realised that they were safe but Petr, with nobody to adjust the space-station's orbit, was probably, by now hurtling towards earth inside the crashing, dismantling, burning capsule.

As Mir was being seen to, a couple of the men were assisting Ivan in extricating him from his suit. In the background, they could hear the roar of an engine as Danby fired up the Range Rover, he then began driving it towards the dock to escort the new arrivals to the pub. Further assistance was required from the sailors to seat the guests onto the back seat of the SUV and just before Danby set off David shouted to him, “don’t drive like a maniac Danby, you’ve got delicate cargo in there.” Danby’s reaction was to shoot his arm out of the open driver’s side window and present a sign that would have been considered a chargeable offence had he have still been in the navy. Nevertheless, Danby did indeed take care on his return trip, while all the others used scooters, bikes or Shanks’ Pony to follow him back.

Once the truck had stopped outside the pub the men that had followed behind on scooters were falling over themselves to assist the trio out of the SUV. Inside the pub Lacy had done a great job, in the short time that had been available to him, to clear, sweep and clean an area in the dining room where the new arrivals could sit comfortably on a well-padded bench seat. He directed the men to sit the trio in the space he had cleared like an experienced maître d’hôtel while the smell of Smee’s culinary concoctions were beginning to emanate from the kitchen.

Once the trio was settled, the two adults were asked if they wanted a drink.

“Vodka and a big glass of water.” Ivan said with a wide smile on his face.

“Coke for me.” Amy replied smiling.

“Are you sure that’s not a big glass of vodka too?” Moxley jokingly asked. Somehow, Moxley had become the recognized barman in the pub, which was a little like putting a fox in charge of the chickens. But, nevertheless, he did do a good job of maintaining stocks of the more popular spirits being requested by his clientele. Which shouldn't have been too surprising as he had been the quartermaster onboard the Connecticut.

"Maybe later." Ivan replied. The others in the room, who had returned to their original seats, lifted their glasses in accolade of Ivan's comment.

During all this, David realized that a shower, clothes and a place to stay would be an immediate concern for the new guests. The condos, where most of the men lived, had been cleared of bodies and trash, was a likely candidate, but so was the very place they were in right now. The pub was also an hotel and only Moxley was living here, it would be perfect, providing Moxley would agree. As for clothes, he called Lacy over and asked him to visit some of the local stores and return with an assortment of new clothes. He was a little unsure how to obtain measurements, especially from Amy, but it was of little consequence, Lacy had taken one look at her and had sized her up accurately, even down to her bra size.

While Lacy went away to forage for clothes, the food was served, and the astronauts were ravenously enjoying some fine cooked food in sharp contrast to the packaged, vitamin enriched sustenance that they had been living on for what seemed an eternity. Mir had now emerged from her stupor and was enthralled by the entourage of strange men in front of her. She had drunk a whole glass of water and she was now tucking into a piece of chicken, gazing from one man to the next. The men in front of her represented a strange collection of manhood. Some were dressed in t-shirts and shorts while others chose to cling to their navy dungarees. The variety and combinations of hirsute was also a sight to behold. Untrimmed beards, long hair, shaven heads, naturally balding heads and even a few clean-shaven faces, Mir looked at them all, fascinated. She also gave a little smile if one of the men acknowledged her when she was looking at him.

Amy and Ivan swapped stories with the crew as to how they all came to arrive in Bermuda. Amy explained the secret experiment that Ivan and she were participating in while the men shared stories of the devastation here on earth.

"So, when all is said and done," Danby began to say, "the experiment was a waste of time because no data is ever going to be analyzed."

"Oh, I wouldn't go that far," Amy replied indignantly, "we do have Mir to show for it."

Danby, was one of the youngest members of the detachment and he instantly realized what a faux pas he had just made and blushed at Amy's reply, "of course, sorry, didn't mean –," he was silenced by a friendly smack across the back of his head by one of the others, he didn't know who.

"I would like to make a toast to Petr, the astronaut who sacrificed his life to save the lives of our new friends." Provo said. The other men from the detachment responded with a raising of their glasses and a simultaneous 'Petr'.

"Technically, Petr, like myself, being a Russian, was actually, a cosmonaut, Amy however, an American is an astronaut." Petr pointed out to the others. For a moment, there was silence in the room, no one really didn't know how to respond to this clarification. Was Ivan being pedantic, patriotic or awkward? Then the silence was broken.

"That's why you like vodka then." Danby peeped up and everyone burst out laughing.

During the conversation the group was having with the trio David spoke with Moxley, broaching the subject of letting Amy and Ivan remain in the hotel. Surprisingly enough, he agreed wholeheartedly, which amazed David because up until now he had been very protective of the site he had chosen for his new home.

"I expect it will only be for a couple of days because I am sure they will want to go onto St. Santia to be with the other families." David stated.

"I'm sure you're right Dave my lad," Moxley replied. "They can have the Empire suite, that's just down the corridor from me. I'll go and make sure everything is ship-shape and see if I can find a baby's cot."

"Thanks, Moxley," David replied. Just at that moment Lacy returned.

“Got all the clothes in the car. Where do you want me to take them to?” Lacy asked.

“The good news is, Moxley is letting them stay here so you can take them up to the Empire room.”

“Really?” Lacy replied looking quite surprised. “I’ve never been upstairs in this place, which room is that?” Lacy replied.

“Just follow Moxley, he’s going up there right now!” David replied. He watched as Lacy chased after the newly assigned hotel manager before he went over to the group to announce the arrangements.

“Sorry to interrupt.” David said, addressing the new arrivals, again meeting the expected derisory comments from his compatriots. “But we have prepared a room for you, with a bath and laid out what we hope are appropriate clothes for you.”

“That’s very nice of you David, but I’m quite happy with my current arrangements thank you.” Moose jokingly replied.

“Wait a minute Moose. You haven’t asked what color dress he has picked out for you.” Dutch shouted. The other men all laughed, mocking Moose’s heterosexual persuasion. David smiled with everyone else, but he was also proud of his efforts to help and accommodate the new visitors. However, the only ones who were not smiling were Amy and Ivan. They merely looked at each other uncomfortably for a few seconds. Then Amy meekly asked, “would it be possible for Ivan and me to get separate rooms please?”

Chapter 24

The Funeral Party Sets Out

The Atlantic Ocean

As dawn arrived over the island of St. Santia, the U.S.S. Augusta slipped silently beneath the waves as it headed for Bermuda. For the first time in his career, Jason Hargreaves was in command of a U.S. navy, nuclear submarine. It was a position he had always coveted, but certainly not under the circumstances that had presented themselves over the last few months. The crew were going about their business in the same professional manner as they had done prior to the devastation. That was the agreement that had been put forward by the Admiral and had been accepted by the crew. In summary, the deal supported the idea of a corporation with the Admiral and now Jason, as the CEO. It was agreed that a vote would be taken as to any new destination the crew would like to travel to. In fact, prior to the discovery of the inhabitants on St. Santia the Augusta was on route to Brazil. Under the agreement, the crew members are free to come and go as they pleased, which is why many left in Norfolk and a small detachment remained on Bermuda. However, a schedule had been posted of when one of the two submarines would pay a visit which would provide those who had left with an opportunity to return to the vessel. But one thing was made abundantly clear, for the safety and the security of both the crew and the submarine it was imperative that when under power, all naval personnel strictly followed orders to the letter, as if they were still in the navy.

Satisfied that everything was going to plan, and all personnel were properly attending to their duties, Jason decided to pay a visit to the galley for breakfast. The seating area was sparsely occupied and fortunately, the girls, Janet and Mary, were not in attendance. Jason was still not ready to discuss extracurricular activities with them. However, Jason was pleased to see Dennis up and about sitting with Giles. They were both laughing, had obviously finished their breakfasts and were enjoying a cup of coffee. Jason picked up a tray and selected his choices from the tureens of fine food. He exchanged greetings with DeVersa but was grateful the proposed trip to Nebraska wasn't mentioned. Naturally, he went to sit with the two senior, naval men, just as Giles was finishing relating a story regarding the Admiral which brought more laughter to the pair of them. Between laughs Dennis explained what was going on, as if Jason couldn't guess.

"Giles here is telling me some tales about the Admiral during his younger days. He was quite the rebel-rouser." Dennis said, looking fully recovered from the shock of the Admiral's death.

"He was that." Giles said, endorsing it with a smile and a shake of his head.

"I'm sure he was." Jason said as he began to tuck into his breakfast.

Jason continued to listen to the two men exchanging stories while he finished eating. At first, he thought it was good therapy for them, mainly because it was part of the closure process on the death of a very good friend. Then, the more he listened the more he realized it was good for him too, after all, the Admiral had been his mentor as well as a friend. But once Jason had finished his coffee his persona as commander of the vessel returned.

"Well, I had better get back to the bridge." Jason said as he rose. "By the way Giles, how are the funeral arrangements coming along?" The previous day, Jason had asked Giles to make the necessary arrangements for the Admiral's funeral. As Giles had participated in more ship's funerals than every crew member combined it was logical to assign the task of preparing the arrangements to him, to which he readily agreed.

"All done sir." Giles replied, still refusing to relinquish the naval tradition of calling an officer 'sir'. "Put a draft copy of the schedule on your desk for approval. A broadcast need to go out regarding the time of the funeral and to remind the crew to wear dress whites. Of course, we won't know the actual timing until after we leave Bermuda. But it's all there on the draft. Sir."

"Thank you bosun." Jason replied, reciprocating the use of rank. "I'll go through it and finalize the details with you before we leave Bermuda."

"Look at the poor man's hands Jason." Dennis said. "Show him Giles." As Giles brought his hands up from under the table Dennis pointed to Giles' fingers that were mostly wrapped in bandages.

"My God Giles. What happened?" Jasion asked, reverting to a first name basis as genuine concern got the better of him.

"Bloody sail-cloth, sir." Giles replied. "Nowadays, modern body bags are typically used for our lost comrades. I felt that the Admiral would have wanted a more traditional send-off, so I used sail-cloth. There is nobody else on the boat who can sew sail-cloth, so I did it myself. Trouble is, I am not quite as dexterous as I used to be, so this is the result." Giles said with a quick laugh while holding up his fingers. "But not to worry, Doc here patched me up and it was well worth it, it was the right thing to do sir." Giles smiled proudly.

"Thank you, Giles, thank you very much." Jason said with sincerity. "I will go and review your arrangements right now." Jason gathered his now empty breakfast things onto his tray and left the table.

Jason placed his tray, dirty dishes and utensils in the cleaning area and proceeded back to his cabin to review Giles' funeral arrangements and catch up on other paperwork, which had of course greatly diminished since the devastation. Nonetheless, provision orders, requisition requests and equipment status reports still needed attention. Jason read through Giles' report, the man hadn't missed a thing, no surprise that the Admiral rated him so highly.

So, by now, Jason was in good spirits, despite the reason for the trip, and he was just about to process his last piece of paperwork when there was a knock at his door.

“Come in.” Jason said. His elated spirits fell like an out of control elevator as the door opened and there stood Janet and Mary. It was Janet who spoke first.

“We need to discuss the Nebraska trip.”

Chapter 25

Life Without Tony

St. Santia, the residents' homes

As dawn broke on what was once the home of Tony and Marlene, baby Augusta decided she needed to be fed. Marlene, still in a sleepy stupor, responded almost zombie-like to the cries of her baby. Marlene picked up her little bundle of love and went over to sit on the comfortable divan, strategically placed by the window that provided such a spectacular view of the bay. With Augusta feeding contently, Marlene was slowly coming to a state of full wakefulness. She suddenly realized that this was the first time in her life that she had ever spent a night, anywhere, without another adult. At first, she didn't know if she should feel frightened, worried or in any way concerned for her well-being. She looked down at her daughter, as Augusta suckled at her breast, Marlene felt ambivalent at the prospect of living alone and facing the future with only her little girl. But the more Marlene began to think about her situation she realized, she had a support group and plenty of help if she needed it, what was there to worry about? It was not as if she had any bills to pay, food was plentiful, and the weather was great. No, things were good, Marlene thought, trying to put a positive spin on her predicament. Although, she was hardly thinking that way when Tony had packed a bag and left the house the previous afternoon.

No more words had been spoken between them as Tony left the kitchen and went upstairs to pack his bag for the trip on the submarine. He even left through the front door of the house, so he could avoid saying goodbye. Marlene just sat there, she had felt totally rejected and left unsure as to what to do. Circumstances had made them a couple, an arranged marriage by default. Marlene had learnt that many arranged marriages are successful, love grows through mutual respect and common goals. In fact, Marlene had been quite happy playing house with Tony and awaiting the birth of their first child. She had accepted the situation but as it turned out, despite his apparent approval, Tony had merely tolerated the arrangement because he had no other choice.

Augusta eventually fell asleep, so Marlene placed her in her cot and took the opportunity to shower and get dressed. She made herself a coffee and returned to the kitchen table to contemplate what she should do next. Marlene wasn't sure how long she had sat there, with the tears slowly forming tracks down her cheeks, but once more, the sounds of baby Augusta waking from her nap shook her out of her reverie. Marlene decided she would go for a walk and visit her neighbors. So, she went to the sink, splashed some cold water on her face and dried the water away from her cheeks. Marlene then turned her attention to Augusta.

"Let's go and see auntie Joan and auntie Maria shall we my little darlin'?" Marlene asked her daughter. The question was received by Augusta with some shaking of the arms and some extra cooing.
"Yeeea, that's right." Marlene responded as she picked the baby up and sat her in the baby carrier she was wearing.

Marlene strode purposefully up the slight hill on the path that led towards Maria and Bob's house. She could see John sitting outside, he waved, and she could just make out the words "company's coming" as he shouted to someone inside the house. Marlene waved back just as Joan, Maria and Bob all suddenly appeared on the patio, almost as if they were expecting her. When she arrived, a little breathless from the jaunt up the hill Joan asked,
"Cup of tea dear?"
"Oh, I'd love one please." Marlene replied, trying to act normal as though nothing significant had happened. Joan disappeared inside while the others made small talk with her. Joan then re-appeared with a beautifully patterned cup and saucer of the finest bone china containing the requested tea and a plate full of chocolate digestive biscuits on a matching plate. One of the beauties of being on a British held island was enjoying some of those confectionaries that are indigenous only to that country. Unfortunately, it would only be a matter of time before the last of the goodies were consumed, which was all the more surprising to Marlene that they had been offered to-day.
"There you are dear." Joan said.

"Bob, you were going to take me to visit the chickens on the other side of the island." John suddenly said.
"I was?" Bob replied looking quite perplexed. Then he saw a conspiratory wink from John, so he added, "oh yes, I was, wasn't I? Now is as good a time as any I guess." With that, Bob and John left the group to go for a drive in the Mini-Moke, leaving the trio of ladies to talk girl-talk, but not before each of them reached over and took a couple of the cookies. Joan responded with a mock slap of the wrist to the greedy gannets.

As the men were leaving, Joan took Augusta from Marlene and began saying all those things that older ladies say to babies. Marlene took a cookie and dunked it into her tea before taking a bite of the now melted chocolate and crunchy biscuit.
"Well, he's gone." Marlene said between mouthfuls of biscuits.
"We saw him leave with a bag." Maria said. "Where's he going?"
"He's gone on the Augusta. He's attending the funeral. He said he would be representing us." Marlene answered as she nonchalantly licked an errant blob of chocolate from the side of her mouth.
"What?" Maria said in surprise. "He's representing us? Whose idea was that?"
"It was all his. I think it was just a made-up excuse." Marlene replied, he didn't know where to go or what to do so that buys him a few days, that's all."

"So, when he comes back, where's he going to go?" Joan asked during a temporary intermission of her silly, motherly questions to Augusta. Marlene said nothing for a few seconds then she replied, "To be honest, I don't give a damn what he does." Then Marlene added, defiantly, "but he's not coming back to live in my house."

Chapter 26

The Dreaded Nebraska Discussion

In the Atlantic, Aboard the U.S.S. Augusta

Jason sat back in his chair as the two women entered the cramped space of his cabin and shut the door behind them. Now that he was in command of the vessel he was entitled to move into the Admiral's quarters, but he didn't think that would be appropriate, at this time. He would make that transition sometime after their return to St. Santia. Jason had not been looking forward to this meeting, which he knew had been inevitable. He remembered the unpleasant experiences the Admiral went through prior to the devastation because of how demanding Janet had been during the ladies' tenure as civilian researchers on the submarine. For the most part, the Admiral would say nothing, he would merely sit and listen before making any decision, which for the most part, would be final. Although circumstances were wildly different now, especially with Mary being Jason's companion, Jason decided he was going to take much the same approach. Consequently, he was fully prepared to let the ladies, specifically Janet, do all the talking, which she proceeded to do.

"Good morning Jason," Janet said politely with one of her nicest smiles.

"Good morning to you Janet, Mary." Jason responded in kind, nodding first to Janet and then Mary.

"Hi." Mary said sheepishly. Mary was still feeling uncomfortable about this confrontation and being stuck on the fence. Although she felt Janet was right, she also understood Jason's reluctance to agree to the trip based on their last escapade. She had not been with Jason at all for the last couple of days but that had nothing to do with this disagreement, he had been busy. He was, after all, now responsible for the submarine and its crew since the Admiral's death.

"I'll cut to the chase." Janet begun. "We have been speaking to both DeVersa and Grover about this trip and we think we have come up with a plan that, hopefully, you will find acceptable."

"I'm listening." Jason replied stoically.

"Once we have docked in Norfolk, DeVersa will prepare for our trip to Nebraska by seeking out a suitable aircraft." Janet said.

"Wait a minute!" Jason interrupted, already overruling his determination for a self-imposed silence. "DeVersa is an ex-helicopter pilot, he can't fly a plane!"

"That's what we thought," Janet replied smiling. "He told us that the helicopter we used last time does not have the range, even with the extra fuel tanks. That's when he said we would need a plane, seems that our Peter can fly just about anything."

"But he told me he was just a helicopter pilot." Jason replied incredulously.

"And that he is. However, a plane wasn't appropriate for your mission, but he knew a chopper would be." Janet replied. "So, he just told you he was a helicopter pilot, which got your attention." Jason had to admit, remembering back, it certainly made him stop and listen to DeVersa at the time.

"So," Janet continued, "he will find the appropriate aircraft and he estimates it will be a seven-hour flight, give or take, depending on the type of plane he can find."

"What about fuel?" Jason asked. "My understanding is that fuel breaks down over time, it may have already decomposed to an unusable level."

"Myth." Janet replied emphatically. "We spoke to DeVersa about that too. Sure, there is some degradation to the fuel, viscosity stuff like that, he said, but it would take years to be completely useless." As usual, Janet had carried out her research and appeared to have all the objections covered.

"What about protection?" Jason asked, concerned for the welfare of the two ladies, especially Mary, "there could be marauding groups at bay, much like the mutineers you met earlier in the year. The sound of a plane would be sure to attract them." At the thought of those unpleasant memories an involuntary shudder went through Mary's body, a movement that didn't go unnoticed by Jason.

"Our thinking is that the chances of any survivors remaining in the Nebraska area is pretty remote. One would think that any people left alive would have moved south. Why would you want to try and survive a winter in a hostile environment like Nebraska when you could be in Florida or California?" Janet reasoned.

"But what if they haven't moved on?" Jason asked. "Why did people live there before the devastation? Not everyone likes permanent sunshine."

"Well, just in case, accompanying us will be Grover," Janet replied, "he has put the same support group together that rescued us in the mall, except for you of course, you will need to remain with the submarine."

"They have all agreed to join you on this escapade, have they?" Jason asked, knowing full well that one of the support group, Jon Graneski, had remained on Bermuda and they could not have possibly contacted him yet.

"No, not all of them, we will be talking to Graneski as soon as we see him in Bermuda." Janet replied with some frustration, knowing that Jason was all too aware that Jon had not been spoken too. "But Hernandez, Stenich and Lewes are all in and even if Graneski declines, Grover feel we would still have enough protection."

"So, what is the proposed timing of all this?" Jason asked, eager to see how this was going to play out.

"Well, we looked at the itinerary you provisionally published, even though we don't know the exact times and duration until we leave Bermuda, we think it can accommodate our trip." Janet replied.

"We aim to please." Jason said sarcastically.

"For the purposes of our schedule we can consider our arrival in Norfolk as Day 1. DeVersa, with the help of Grover's team as protection, will seek out and make ready an appropriate aircraft." Janet was looking down at some notes, "Mary and I will gather some supplies and a generator with some fuel, enough for a week, ready to be loaded on the plane. Day 2, the group will fly to the Clay Centre and establish a base. Day 3, find some transport and locate places where we will be able to forage for more provisions, then on Day 4, the plane returns bringing back the men."

"You say bringing back the men." Jason said slowly, and he began to sit forward as the full realization of what Janet had just said sunk in.

"Yes," Janet said matter-of-factly, now looking up from her notes to stare directly at Jason. "Mary and I will remain at the Clay Centre."

Chapter 27

Socialising with the Bermuda Detachment

Bermuda

Amy's little bombshell silenced the clientele of the Happy Mariner, which was not an easy feat. Did she want a room apart from Ivan because they had been cooped up on the space station for so long or was it because they were no longer an item? For the heterosexuals amongst the group, which were most of them, this was an encouraging sign.

"I'll just go and inform Moxley," David said, once he too had recovered from the surprising revelation. He quickly left the room to impart the request to Moxley.

During David's departure from the restaurant area, the conversation resumed between the astronaut, the cosmonaut and the matelots, although Ivan was doing most of the talking on behalf of the space travelers, Amy was relatively quiet. Although, her withdrawal could be related to shyness in the presences of so many men or her preoccupation with Mir's welfare, either way, it was food for thought for the sailors. After approximately ten minutes, David returned to inform the new arrivals that their rooms were prepared whenever they were ready.

"Amy, there's even a little cot for Mir in your room." David added proudly.

"Oh great." Amy said enthusiastically, as if she wanted to get away at the first available opportunity. "I just want to finally get out of this jump-suit. If you will excuse me, I hope you all understand." There were murmurs of assent from all the men as Amy gingerly rose to leave. She stood with Mir in her arms but almost immediately her legs began to buckle. Fortunately, Moose was siting close by and with lightening reflexes that belied his size he had hold of Amy's elbow providing her support. Amy grabbed his hand and to Moose the pleasure of her touch felt almost like an electric shock.

"Here, let me help you to your room." Moose said softly.

"Thank you, I think I might need it." Amy responded.

"Will you be O.K. Amy?" Ivan asked, but he made no attempt to get up now that Moose was on the case.

"Fine thanks Ivan." Amy replied, still holding onto both Mir and Moose. "I just need to lie down and take a good, hot soak in a bath." The group watched as Moose helped the stumbling Amy out of the room and as soon as they could be heard going up the stairs Ivan said in a voice, slightly above conversational decibels.

"More vodka, that's what we need!" The group responded accordingly and in Moxley's absence David went behind the bar to get everyone's orders.

Moxley and Lacey returned to relieve David and he joined the rest of the group around the tables in the bar. Ivan was still the center of attention as he explained all about life on the space station and the experiment he and Amy had participated in. In fairness, he discussed the details as a scientific experiment, not as some of the men would have wished as a pornographic depiction of sex in space. He was also very cognizant of Amy's dignity and did not divulge any intimate details. As he was relating the objectives of the research, Moose returned to join in the conversation having escorted Amy and Mir to their room.

"Everything alright with Amy?" Ivan said with some concern, his Russian accent beginning to come through with the consumption of a couple of vodkas.

"Seems to be." Moose replied indifferently, but with surprising directness he asked, "but why the separate room?"

"Because she still needs her space." Dutch replied, laughing at his own pun. His laugh was infectious, and the rest of the group joined in the laughter, even Ivan had to smile.

"I was just telling the others," Ivan began to explain to Moose, "us being together and having the baby was the result of a secret experiment being conducted by the American and Russian space agencies. Amy and I were selected from among several candidates, the prerequisite of course was that we were prepared to do the deed, as it were, in space."

"So, you are not, technically husband and wife?" Dutch asked.

"God no." Ivan replied emphatically, "we had both agreed that once the experiment was over, we would return to earth and resume our lives in our own respective countries. Obviously, I would be permitted to see Mir on a regular basis, but Amy and I would not remain together. The devastation, as you call the catastrophe, has not changed that."

That significant piece of information had got Moose thinking, when Amy inevitably leaves the island to travel to St. Santia, perhaps he will be joining her.

Chapter 28

Surprising Revelations

In the Atlantic, Aboard the U.S.S. Augusta

"Mary, is this true?" Jason asked.

"Mary agrees –," Janet began to reply but was rudely interrupted by Jason.

"I wasn't talking to you Janet."

"Jason, you have to remember I am a scientist." Mary began sheepishly. "I know you are upset by this decision, but a supply of livestock would be vital to the survival of future generations of people."

"Mary, we have chickens, eggs and fish, humans can survive without red meat, that has been proven, I don't have to be a scientist to know that." Jason countered.

"True," Janet re-entered the fray, "but it's not just meat. We could have horses for riding, dray horses for working, leather for clothes and a variety of other uses. If there is even a remote opportunity to providing these essentials we must pursue it."

Jason understood the wisdom behind the trip, but his memory of the womens' last excursion was still haunting him. He calmed a little.

"How long will all this take?" Jason asked, looking down at a blotter on his desk, unable to meet Mary's eyes.

"As long as it takes." Janet replied, returning to the more pedantic, difficult days Jason recalled prior to the devastation.
"That's not an answer Janet. How long?" Jason replied, not prepared to be as accommodating as the Admiral was.
"I'm hoping we will know within six months whether our experiments will be successful or not." Janet replied.
"So, you will be jeopardizing other crew members to supply and support the two of you while you are out in the sticks for this hair-brained scheme that may not even be successful!" Jason stated, raising his voice in tune with his temper that was beginning to boil.
"Such is the life of a scientist." Janet replied casually, as if that explained the situation. It didn't, Jason merely shook his head. Technically, he had no control over the women and if any of the crew wanted to leave the boat, for any reason, that was their decision. The agreement that Admiral Sandford had made with the crew to touch base with Norfolk on a regular basis applied to the women just as much as the crew, regardless of their reasons for their comings and goings.
"Fine, do what you have to do." Jason conceded, "Mary, may I have a word please, in private." He directed his last words to Janet and it was her invitation to leave.

After Janet had left, for a few moments there was silence as if both Mary and Jason were unsure as to how to continue with the conversation.

“Mary, please, sit down.” Jason said, pointing to one of the vacant chairs in front of his small desk, his voice was calm now, almost soothing. Mary sat down and leant on the desk so that their faces were now quite close together. “Mary, look, I’m sorry, this is difficult for me. I’m having trouble finding the right words to say.”

“Just say what you feel Jason.” Mary replied, looking intently into Jason’s eyes.

“Mary, you know I’m very fond of you. If anything was to happen to you I could never forgive myself for letting you go on this trip.” Jason said, returning her loving gaze and reaching out to hold her hands.

“I know Jason and the feeling is mutual, you know that. But I have to go with her and help her, I hate to say it, but she’s right.” Mary said almost apologetically.

“But why do you have to go?” Jason questioned. “She could do this on her own, she is more than capable.”

“Jason, believe it or not, I am also a good scientist and I am more knowledgeable in certain areas of biological testing than Janet and my expertise would be invaluable to her research.”

“But she could still accomplish her goals without you Mary. So why do you have to go?” Jason was pleading, holding Mary’s hands even tighter.

“Because she’s my friend.” Mary simply replied.

“And I guess I’m not.” Jason said softly and slowly pulled his hands away from Mary’s. The conversation was over.

Chapter 29

Bermuda Breakfast Meeting

Bermuda

After a good night's sleep, Amy awoke feeling much better. Getting acquainted to a gravity filled planet once more had not been as difficult as she had expected. Mir, too, seemed to have adjusted well as she had slept right through the night. Which was surprising because this was her first experience of gravity and until now you could count on one hand the number of times she had slept through the night. Amy left Mir playing in her cot while she went to have a long hot shower. Between the long hot soak in the bath the previous day and this shower it felt luxurious compared to the cylindrical shower stalls she had used in space where she had to catch the floating water droplets to get washed.

Amy slowly dried herself off while she scanned the wide selection of creams, perfumes, make-up and lotions that Lacy had procured for her. Amy was impressed with his acumen and chose, what would have been prior to the devastation, an expensive skin lotion to rub onto her long, beautifully shaped legs and arms. She then sprayed an equally expensive perfume into the air and walked into the cloud of scented mist capturing the droplets on her fair skin.

Nothing had been mentioned about breakfast, so Amy was a little unsure as to what to do, but Mir needed feeding. So, once they were both dressed she carried Mir quietly down the stairs with the intent of finding something to eat in the kitchen. She needn't have worried, although the Happy Mariner was no longer a functioning hotel, you would never have known it. David directed her to a table by the window, resplendent with a high-chair for Mir who had already started her flirting with the men. A smartly dressed Moose, clean-shaven, his hair cut and neatly combed presented Amy with the day's menu as she was assisted to her seat by David.

"Wow, Moose, look at you. You clean up good." Amy said and meaning it. She took the menu that was offered to her, "a printed menu with our names on it. You have computers too?"

"Computers we have, but unfortunately no internet." David stated.

"Oh, of course not." Amy replied. Just then, Lacy, walked over with a pitcher of water.

"Madam, would you care for a glass of water, orange, grapefruit or apple juice, tea coffee?" Lacy offered.

"Wow, I wasn't expecting this. I thought it would be dried fruit and water." Amy exclaimed.

"Would Mir care for a cookie?" Lacy asked Amy. He was showing the plain biscuit to Amy out of Mir's sight so if Amy had said 'no' the baby would have been none the wiser.

"Sure, she'll love that." Amy replied, "oh and by the way thank you for everything. The clothes, the stuff in the room, just great. Thanks."

"My pleasure." Lacy merely replied.

When Amy had entered the room, David had sensed the intoxicating perfume she had put on, while she looked stunning in a red vest and a thigh-hugging, colorful sarong. Damn, Lacy was good, David thought, his selection and sizing of clothing was spot on, even down to Mir's little pink jump-suit.

"To drink madam?" Lacy brought the conversation back to the task at hand.

"Water would be nice and an orange juice please." Amy responded to Lacy's question, then sheepishly added almost questioningly, "and a coffee too please! If I may."

"No problem." Lacy replied with a smile.

"And do you have milk for Mir?" Amy asked, not sure of the milk situation on the island.

"We can arrange that." David replied. "Would that be in a regular glass or a sippy cup?" Lacy turned to Mir and asked her.

"You have a sippy cup too?" Amy asked laughing. "Sure, you'd love a sippy cup wouldn't you Mir?" Mir merely smiled and banged her hands on the table of the high-chair, crumbling her cookie into a hundred pieces, to everyone's amusement.

Lacy left with David to prepare the beverages which provided Moose with the opportunity to step forward and began idle chatter with Amy. Moose's new persona and his presence here at this early hour was not part of his usual routine, Amy realized this, based on the conversations amongst the men the previous day. Moose was in fact a handsome man, but the last thing Amy wanted right now was any involvement, she knew she had to tread carefully. Fortunately, any moves Moose was intending to make was interrupted by the noisy entrance into the bar of two of the other Bermuda residents whose ribald remarks addressed at Moose made the situation only too obvious.

"Up early this morning aren't you Moose?" Graneski asked and continued conspiratively, "why's that then?"

"That's not Moose. It can't be." Smitty said jokingly, "Moose has a beard and long hair – wait a minute!" he said looking closer at Moose who was standing beside Amy's table towering over Smitty, "look, it is Moose." Smitty and Graneski were now both laughing at Moose's expense. Even Amy and Mir joined in the amusement but as David and Lacy returned with the drink orders Moose was seething and became determined to exact revenge on the two men that marred this opportunity to begin his quest for Amy.

Chapter 30

Arrival in Bermuda

Bermuda

At 9:30 in the morning the Augusta surfaced just under two miles from the coast of Bermuda. Once it was within one mile of the island Giles blew a welcoming signal on the klaxon. The sound of the submarine's approach was clearly heard by the island's inhabitants. But it was quite superfluous as by now the entire Bermuda contingent had congregated in the 'Happy Mariner' in anticipation of the submarine's arrival. As soon as it had surfaced. David wasn't sure whether it was Amy's presence or the pending arrival of the submarine, but all the men were smartly dressed and for the first time since their arrival on the island every one of them, was clean-shaven with meticulously cut hair, at least of those who chose to have hair.

As the crew of the Augusta began its maneuvers to position the submarine parallel with the dock some of the men from the 'Happy Mariner' went to assist with the securing of the lines and to greet their comrades. Once secure, the men on land manipulated into position the cumbersome gangway that forged the gap between the submarine and the dock. As they were carrying out this task a gravely, authoritative shout suddenly rang out from the submarine's conning tower.

“Put yer backs into it you lazy land lubbers. That’s the hardest you have had to work for a dog’s age!” It was a familiar voice to many of the men as they looked up to see a beaming Giles glaring down at them. All the men laughed and gave salutary responses to the veteran, none of which would have been appropriate had any of the women been present.

Once Giles was satisfied the submarine was secure he informed Jason who had now joined him in the conning tower. Jason in turn, gave the ‘System Shutdown’ order and waved to the men on the dock while he waited for the completion of his order. Jason, at his position in the conning tower, could hear the giant turbines of the submarine slowing down and the responses of other crew members relaying status.

“System shutdown complete sir.” Lewis reported.

“Boat is secure, crew may stand down.” Jason broadcast to an eagerly awaiting crew. Not only were they keen to greet their ex-comrades in arms, but they couldn’t wait to meet with the recent new arrivals. Especially, Amy, to see if she was as beautiful as the Bermuda lot had said she was, if what had been communicated to Sparks could be believed. They almost climbed over themselves in their haste as they poured out of both the forward and aft hatches. Jason and Giles took a more sedate approach as they exited the submarine from the conning tower, waiting for the other hordes to run down the gangway. The crew had been given strict instructions regarding drinking, any crew member who was the worse for drink would not be permitted back on board. As tempting as it might be, this was just an overnight stop, more time had been scheduled on the return trip to indulge in a little partying.

Jason was delaying his departure from the submarine as he was waiting for Dennis to meet with him. Jason had spoken to the doctor thinking it would be a nice gesture if the senior officers on the vessel went to greet the space travelers together. Jason had hoped they would be accompanied by Janet and Mary, but he had not seen or heard from them since their last conversation in his cabin. By the time the last of the crew went down the gangway Janet and Mary emerged through the forward hatch. They had been politely assisted by their new partners in crime, Grover and DeVersa.

Chapter 31

Meet and Greet

Bermuda

At just about the same time Mary and Janet reached the gangplank Dennis emerged from the conning tower.

"Good morning ladies, gentlemen." Dennis said cheerfully, and salutations were politely exchanged, fortunately sparing any uncomfortable greeting that Jason had feared he would have with Mary.

"If you will excuse me, I'll seek out Graneski to bring him up to speed." Grover said, as he proceeded down the gangway. He had denoted the tension between Jason and the ladies and felt he needed to leave them to it.

"I'll join you." DeVersa said. The two men sidling down the ramp depicting an almost cartoon like picture, the tall, burly Grover followed by the diminutive, chubby DeVersa, but the remaining members of the group were not laughing. Dennis was aware of the conversation that had transpired between Jason and the ladies; and the conflict that had resulted, but it was not his position to interfere. He was cognizant of Jason's disapproval of the trip but also understood Mary's reasons for going, so he attempted to diffuse the situation.

"I understand there's some people here on the island who have only recently dropped in. We're off to meet them, would you ladies care to join us?" Dennis asked.

"Very funny Dennis," Janet replied with a smile, "sure why not. I hear they tell stories that are out of this world." Dennis crooked his left arm and Janet linked her right arm through it as they proceeded to leave the submarine. Jason smiled at Mary and following Dennis' lead crooked his arm for Mary. She paused, looked directly into Jason's eyes then returned his smile, linked arms with him and they walked happily towards the Happy Mariner to meet the new guests.

A patio area had been set up outside the bar and the usual banter was being exchanged between the residents and the incoming visitors, not least of which was the pristine appearances of the locals. Amy, Ivan and Mir were holding court on the patio and the Augusta's crew was being introduced to them as they arrived. Moxley and Smee had prepared some appetizers and were distributing them among the tables while Lacy was bringing out pitchers of beer, shots of alcohol and sodas. The residents had found from experience that the commercial beer on the island was no longer fit to drink. In the heat, the contents in the kegs were no longer potable although some of the cans and bottles that had been stored in cellars had not all gone stale, but they were hit or miss. But, being the entrepreneur that he was, Moxley had begun making his own brand of beer from kits and the various stores of cereals he had found on the island. He had even printed up his own labels under the 'Happy Mariner' logo. This was the beer that was now being enjoyed by the clientele on the patio.

As Jason and the rest of his group walked onto the patio the crew moved to allow a path to be formed for the foursome to meet the new guests. Sailors who were sitting with the guests offered their seats to the officers and their ladies, which they politely accepted. Although, Moose, who had been firmly ensconced next to Amy, was extremely reluctant to relinquish his prime location, but he felt this was not the time to create a scene, so he moved away.

Pleasantries were exchanged and of course, with their medical backgrounds the group, with the exception of Jason, were equally intrigued with each other's tales and naturally, excited about Janet and Mary's new project in Nebraska. Mir, by now, was thrilled to see that other women existed beside her mother, but she was also being passed around all the new arrivals laughing and gurgling as if she was the object of a *'pass the parcel'* game.

Introductions were also being made for Tony's benefit, of course he knew the crews of the Augusta and the Connecticut that had sailed on to St. Santia but not the personnel left in the Bermuda detachment. He was being introduced as one of the fathers of the next generation and details of his arrival, survival and life on the island were in almost just as much demand as the space crew. Tony accepted a drink from Lacy and they began chatting with David until Moxley called him over for some assistance.

Meanwhile, Grover and DeVersa saw Graneski standing on the inside of the patio and they made a bee-line towards him.
"So, you old Polack, how are you doing here?" Grover asked, he felt being a second generation Pole he could say that, "do you miss us yet?" They shook hands.
"Hi," DeVersa said and also shook hands in greeting.
"Ah, you know!" Graneski replied sulkily, "not quite working out how I expected."
"We may have something that will cheer you up." Grover suggested, "let's take a little walk." Grover and DeVersa escorted Graneski out of earshot of the jovial crowd to discuss with him the opportunity to join their expedition.

The subtle exit of the trio from the crowd on the patio was a move that did not go unnoticed by Moose who had not forgotten Graneski's barbs earlier that morning. But at that moment Moose had other priorities as he noticed Jason slip away from Amy's table. Jason had decided that the conversation in his group had naturally turned to medical issues and he felt he had nothing to offer to the discussion, so he decided to mingle with the others to casually remind them about the drinking rules of the day. Of course, in doing so, this vacated the seat next to Amy, which Moose gratefully regained, much to the discomfort of Amy who knew only too well what his intentions were.

Chapter 32

Funeral of Admiral Stanford

In the Atlantic, Aboard the U.S.S. Augusta

Right on schedule, the U.S.S. Augusta departed Bermuda at dawn with a full complement of crew plus a few additional passengers that would be attending the Admiral's funeral. Jason was pleased to report that all crew members were checked as they had boarded the submarine the previous evening, but nobody had violated the restrictions imposed regarding the '*too much drinking*' rule, although there were a couple of border line cases. After supervising their departure and satisfied that everything was in hand on the bridge Jason went to the galley for breakfast. In one section of the galley, Grover was reviewing procedures with his security team, Jason was glad to see that Graneski had decided to participate in the exercise. At the galley, DeVersa was, as usual serving and checking the food so Jason took the opportunity to ask him about the trip.

"Do you have an appropriate airfield picked out yet Peter?" Jason asked the cook with a casual air of indifference that he didn't feel.

"Sure, the Central Nebraska Regional Airport is only an hour away from the research center, but you know?" DeVersa paused in his cleaning and checking as he looked at Jason. "The roads up there as so straight and traffic is so light that I'm going to make a pass close to the facility to see if we can land right there."

"What if the roads have fallen into disrepair?" Jason asked, now a little concerned.

"No guarantee the airstrip will be any better." DeVersa replied nonchalantly. "Don't worry sir, I'm too experienced to take any chances." DeVersa added, trying to put Jason's mind at ease.

"But won't you have to get refueled?" Asked Jason.

"Sure, but I will have more than enough fuel to get me to the airport, refuel and make the return leg." DeVersa replied as though he had it all worked out, which he had. This gave Jason a little more confidence until DeVersa added, "depending on what plane I can find."

Giles was sitting on his own at one of the tables, so Jason decided to join him.

"Morning Giles, everything prepared?" Jason asked.

"Yes sir, if it isn't, it's too damn late now." Giles replied stoically.

"I saw your work with the sailcloth, great job." Jason said, having seen the shroud Giles had painstakingly sewn for the Admiral. Until late last night the Admiral's head was still visible for those members of the Bermuda detachment who wished to pay their respects. Once they had all passed through, Giles completed the total wrap of the Admiral.

"Yes, finished the shroud last night but it is not quite regulation." Giles replied. Jason was poised to place a forkful of food into his mouth but was forced to pause at the statement.

"Really? Why's that?" Jason asked, surprised at Giles' lack of conformity.

"Well if you really want to know while you are eating your breakfast I can tell you." Giles replied with a smile.

"Yes Giles, I really want to know." Jason replied.

"Well, sir traditionally, a large needle is usually pushed right through the nose of the deceased." Giles replied. Jason physically winced at the thought of such an action.

"My God, what possible reason is there for doing that?" Jason asked, but the conversation was not enough to put him off his food, he still continued to eat his breakfast.

"It's the law of the sea sir." Giles answered. "You're supposed to put the last stitch through the nose and if that doesn't wake him up, you pretty much know he's dead."

"That's a bit macabre in this day and age, isn't it?" Jason asked incredulously, "wait a minute, you didn't, did you?"

"Yes, it is a bit ghoulish," Giles laughed, "and no, I didn't. I think we can trust the good doctor to inform us whether someone is dead or not."

"That's a relief." Jason replied with a sigh.

"What, the fact we can trust our doctor or the fact I didn't do the deed with the needle?" Giles said. Jason smiled at the question.

"Have you prepared the service?" Giles asked.

"Yes, pretty much, some of the wording I need to finalize but for the most part, it's done." Jason said.

"Not that I'm telling you your job sir," Giles began to say, "but I've been through too many of these and you can overthink it. Short and simple because half the crew are not listening, and the other half want it over as soon as possible."

"I will take that under-advisement Giles, thank you." Jason responded, "now I had better get back and finish that service and remind the troops to wear their whites."

At 11:00 A.M. the submarine arrived in U.S. waters and Jason gave the order to surface. Just before noon, the designated firing squad, consisting of Grover, Graneski and Lewes stood on the deck of the U.S.S. Augusta with the six shroud bearers that also included Dennis. In the absence of any specialized bugler Sparks had volunteered to play Taps.

"Pass the word, all hands bury the dead" Jason broadcast to the boat's crew and passengers. "Stop all engines." As this was happening, Giles brought the colors to half-mast.

Jason patiently waited while the boat's assembly neatly lined up along the deck. It was an eerie feeling, nobody was speaking, so all that could be heard was the sound of the wind whistling through the submarine's superstructure and the waves lapping against the hull. Fortunately, although brisk, the weather was co-operating, a fairly, mild sea, beautiful blue sky and a light breeze.

Once everyone was assembled, Giles brought the crew, neatly dressed in Naval Whites, to attention before moving to

Parade Rest, standing with their heads bowed. Attention turned to Jason to read the scripture.

"God is our refuge and strength, a very present help in trouble. Therefore, will we not fear, though the earth do change, and though the mountains be shaken into the heart of the seas. For this God is our God forever and ever. He will be our guide even unto death."

There was a brief silence before Jason said, "there will now begin a minute's silence during which you may make your own prayers." At the end of the imposed silence Jason continued with the committal of the Admiral's body.

"Unto Almighty God we commend the soul of our brother departed, and we commit his body to the deep." Jason paused as the funeral party tilted the board that the Admiral's body was lying on and his remains were released into the sea. Jason continued, "in sure and certain hope of the resurrection unto eternal life, through our Lord, Jesus Christ, Amen."

Giles brought the crew to attention and they saluted to the committal of the Admiral. Jason continued with the Benediction, "the Lord bless thee and keep thee, the Lord make His face to shine upon thee and be gracious unto thee, the Lord life up the light of His countenance upon thee and give thee peace. Amen."

"Amen." The assembly replied in unison. Giles then indicated to the firing squad to step forward to issue three volleys into the air above the submarine. On completion, Sparks took a pace forward and began to play a very acceptable renditioning of Taps. While

Sparks was playing, Dennis and other members of the funeral party encased the flag. As the last note of Taps was played, the engines were fired up and the previous course was resumed. It capped off a perfect service that left many in tears and provided the ultimate send-off for a great man, Admiral Stanford.

Chapter 33

Arrival in Norfolk

Naval Yards, Norfolk, Virginia

Jason was using his binoculars to search for any signs of life on the quay as the submarine approached the dock at the Naval Yards in Norfolk, Virginia. He was wearing a heavy-duty, navy issue, duffle coat to protect himself against the cold weather. Fortunately, there was a beautiful blue sky and all the indications, based on their limited resources, were that there was no precipitation in the immediate forecast. He had honestly thought that by now some of the men that had left during their last visit would return to seek comradeship. If any of them had met others he would have thought that would be even more of a reason to return to the submarine and all its resources. Alternatively, maybe loneliness and the lack of human interaction had driven them to simply give up.

Jason's search was interrupted by DeVersa arriving at the base of the conning tower, champing at the bit to go ashore to find an aircraft.

"I trust you have sorted out breakfast and lunch before you leave!" Jason jokingly said.

"All in hand sir, Cook's on it." DeVersa replied.

"Prepare to dock." Jason said into the boat's broadcast system. Immediately, crew exited both the forward and aft hatches and were preparing to tie lines and grab hawsers to secure the vessel. Jason watched as the crew expertly wrapped lines around the cleats on the dock, then they dragged the heavy hawsers onto the submarine and secured them to the cleats on the deck. Jason received a 'thumbs up' from the team on the bow and then looked back to see that the stern team had successfully completed their task and they reciprocated. He raised his arm in acknowledgement and in turn, they began to secure the gangway.

"System shut down." Jason ordered and continued to watch the crew on the ground go about their duties.

"System shutdown complete sir." Lewis reported.

"Boat is secure, crew may stand down." Jason broadcasted, but unlike their arrival in Bermuda the mad exodus of sailors did not materialize, except of course for DeVersa, who Jason could now see waddling down the gangway. Although, Jason was surprised to see he was on his own.

"DeVersa are you going off alone?" Jason called out to him.

"Yes Sir, but I did receive a radio from Sparks," DeVersa shouted back, holding up a CB radio, "and I told him of my expected route."

"Even so, I would prefer a buddy system, just in case." Jason replied.

"I can go with him sir!" It was Sean Huxley, a young man from Ohio, he was calling from the starboard bow where he had been walking back from helping with the hawser. Sean was a young, happy-go-lucky type, quite prepared to do anything, he had been on his very first posting on the Augusta when the devastation had hit. DeVersa didn't say anything but he resignedly beckoned him with his arm and the young ensign eagerly ran towards the gangway.

"Don't take any crap from him Sean." Giles shouted out from the conning tower, he had just joined Jason to supervise the crew as they secured the submarine. DeVersa merely flung out his arm in response to Giles remark and everyone smiled.

Next in line to leave the submarine was Grover and his fledgling security team.

"Where are you lot off to?" Jason asked with a surprised look on his face.

"Sir, to find provisions for the trip and at the same time we can spend the morning practicing some maneuvers. That was a luxury we didn't have on our last trip." Grover replied, in his element now he was leading a group of wannabee Navy Seals.

"Good thinking Grover. There should be a depot here with a stockpile of dried food. We could do with some onboard for emergency rations. See what you can find that may be of use to us too." Jason told them.

"Will do." Grover replied.

"By the way, do you have radios with you?" Giles asked.

"Sure do," Grover replied, turning so that Giles and Jason could see his radio attached to the combat gear on his left breast. The other members of the team followed their leader and presented their radios in the same manner. “Sparks has our channel,” Grover added.

“Glad to see you guys are so well prepared.” Jason said and added, “take care.”

“We will,” the members of the team replied, almost in unison.

By now DeVersa and his newly found companion had reached one of the vehicles parked near the quay, it could well have been the same Jeep that had been used for the trip to the helipad last time DeVersa was there. DeVersa climbed into the driver’s seat and having started the engine was now giving it a few revs to satisfy himself the engine was still healthy. Meanwhile, Grover and his team were walking along the quay in a reverse ‘V’ formation with Grover at the head. Their weapons were at the ready and under Grover’s supervision they were constantly on the look-out for anything suspicious. They reached the pool of vehicles that DeVersa was just driving away from and they too, selected jeeps to carry out their reconnoitering and their quest for stores.

DeVersa had decided to drive to Norfolk International Airport, he felt at that location there should be a wide selection of appropriate planes to choose from. Preferably, he could find one in a hangar that had not been exposed to the elements since the devastation. DeVersa knew from experience that he could typically complete the drive to the airport in under fifteen minutes, but not knowing what obstacles to expect on the roads he wasn’t sure how long this trip would take. In that they were fortunate, the southbound I564, that basically serviced the Naval Yards, was relatively hindrance free and what few stalled cars were present were easily avoidable. So, much to DeVersa's delight the trip to the gates of the airport took no more than the quarter of an hour. However, poor Sean was not feeling quite so happy. Surprisingly, this was Sean's first experience with the aftermath of the devastation and he found the sight of all the badly decomposed bodies very disturbing. To date, Sean had not been exposed to the carnage that existed beyond the Naval Yards. When the Augusta docked earlier in the year there were very few bodies on the quay and they had been cleared by a detail sent by Admiral Stanford prior to any of the crew leaving the vessel. Likewise, Bermuda and of course, by the time they had arrived in St. Santia that was pristine. DeVersa was sympathetic and he helped the young matelot through the ordeal so by the time they had arrived at DeVersa's planned destination the young man felt a little better, albeit very pale-faced.

DeVersa was aware of a private charter company that operated on the south-east corner of the airfield, he'd had dealings with them in the past when very senior officers needed transporting to Washington. They couldn't make the three-hour plus drive, bless their hearts or heaven forbid, take a commercial flight, so DeVersa would arrange a charter on their behalf, they didn't care, Uncle Sam was paying for it. Consequently, DeVersa was hoping that there would be something at the facility that could accommodate the group's needs for a trip to Nebraska. As they headed towards the hangar there were numerous, suitable jets sitting on the apron but DeVersa headed straight for the hangar, hoping not all the available planes were outside. The doors to the hangar were not completely shut but were closed enough to have protected any aircraft inside from the elements. DeVersa parked outside the hangar and turned off the jeep's ignition. Both DeVersa and Huxley exited the vehicle at the same time and DeVersa led the way.

There were a few decomposed bodies lying around inside the hangar, but Huxley tried not to look at them and just waited for DeVersa to issue instructions. Suddenly, DeVersa shouted. "Eureka! Over there." DeVersa pointed to an aircraft in the front corner of the hangar. "She's perfect."

"Nice looking plane Pete. What is it?" Huxley asked as he followed DeVersa, who was now walking very quickly towards the aircraft.

"That, my friend, is a Cessna Citation X." DeVersa replied eagerly, "one of the finest small passenger jets ever made. We could make the Nebraska trip there and back without having to worry about refueling."

"We? Does that mean I can come too?" Huxley asked excitedly.

"Sure, I may need some help in the cockpit. You can be my co-pilot." DeVersa replied. "Just got to hope there's enough juice in the battery to power up this baby." By now, Huxley wasn't listening, he was too busy admiring the plane he would be helping to fly, he didn't have the heart to tell DeVersa that he'd never even been on a plane before.

Chapter 34

Search for Supplies

Naval Yards, Norfolk, Virginia

Grover was in the lead jeep with Lewes driving, while Graneski was driving with Hernandez and Stenich in his jeep. Grover had spoken to DeVersa onboard the submarine during the previous days in terms of the best stores to procure and more importantly, where the appropriate warehouse was. Every unit, ship or barrack seem to have an individual who knows all the ins and outs of military life, how to get things done, who to talk to and where to get deals. Onboard the U.S.S. Augusta that person was DeVersa.

Following DeVersa's instructions, Grover led the team around a myriad of roads until they came to what, based on DeVersa's description, looked like the correct place. The main doors were closed but Grover exited the jeep, strode to a Judas door and tried opening it. The door was unlocked and although it opened easily Grover didn't immediately enter, he waited for the rest of the team to arrive. He honestly didn't believe there was any real danger, but he thought this would be a wonderful opportunity for his inexperienced team to train for the real thing. First, Grover extracted a high-intensity flashlight from his equipment belt, then, on one knee he quickly shone the beam of light from one side of the dark warehouse to the other. Seeing no movement of any kind he repeated the process, only more slowly this time. Satisfied that the place appeared to be devoid of any people, he felt they could proceed to enter the building. He turned to his team.

“O.K., we’ll proceed in the same V formation and if you see anything shout out the position using the clock method we went through, I will be at 12:00. If somebody shouts, we all halt and crouch. Got that?” Grover said and waited for a reply. He was met with a chorus of ‘got it’ from the other four members of the team.

“You’ll all need flashlights on and the safety catches of your rifles on. Check!” Grover said and looked at each member of his team to confirm and even verified each of their guns as a ‘belt and braces’ check. Pleased, that they had all carried out their orders he instructed, “O.K., let’s go!”

The improvised team entered the dark, cavernous warehouse and taking Grover’s lead began scanning the inside with their flashlights. The only daylight to be seen was coming through the office windows on the one side of the building and it cast eerie shadows from the crates and boxes that had been stored in the facility. Grover proceeded slowly, he felt that if there were any strangers in the Naval Yards, this is where they would be hanging out. Although, he wouldn’t expect them to be hostile he knew time can do strange things to people’s psyche, especially if they had been on their own for a significant length of time, so he was taking no chances.

As Grover entered an alley that had been created by two lines of storage crates he could see an open area ahead and he indicated to the rest of the group to halt. Grover stepped stealthily forward until he arrived at the end of the alley. He crouched down on one knee and used a flexible periscope to reconnoiter. There was obvious evidence that someone or some people had been here but there was no sign of anyone there now. Food boxes were strewn all over the floor, some empty, some with rations still inside them. A small, propane cooker was in the center of the area with some camping pots. Judging by the dried contents of the pans it had been some considerable time since anyone had decided to do any washing up. There didn't appear to be any other exit points in the area, so he felt comfortable that the place was secure. Grover rose to his full height and shouted, "clear" and ushered the others forward. As the others began to rummage through the shelves for appropriate supplies, Grover couldn't help but wonder who had been here and where were they now?

Chapter 35

Fraternising with the Locals

St. Santia, Aboard the U.S.S. Connecticut

According to the Gregorian calendar that the inhabitants were still adopting, to-day was a Sunday, so Sheldrake thought it would be a great idea to have an outdoor meal with the '*locals*' in an attempt to get to know them a little better and to understand their needs. To date, Sheldrake had stayed mainly in the background as the Admiral and Hargreaves had monopolized the liaising, this would be a perfect opportunity to take the initiative and fraternize. Sheldrake approached the galley staff to see if they would be prepared to put together an adequate repast at such short notice and he was pleasantly surprised at their agreement and enthusiasm to accommodate him. He placed Bosun Walters in charge of informing the ship's company and organizing the appropriate seating accommodations on shore. Meanwhile, Sheldrake would visit the houses to invite the occupants to the banquet and take the opportunity to see if there was any immediate assistance he could offer.

As Sheldrake walked off the jetty he looked towards the two houses that housed the three families, the only living residents on St. Santia. Although he had been introduced to the three families at the initial banquet that had been held when the two submarines first arrived he had been too busy organizing efforts to properly get to know any of them since. He was approaching the first of the houses when he could faintly hear laughter and voices coming from the rear of the other home. He decided not to knock and proceeded to the source of the noises originating from the other house. He turned the corner of the house to see Bob playing on the patio with the two young children brought to St. Santia by Joan and John Hamax. Surrounding him, seated round the patio and laughing at the trio's antics were John, Joan, Marlene, Maria and the two young babies. Everyone was there, and it was Joan who first saw Sheldrake's arrival.

"Raymond, what are you doing here?" Joan said, quite concerned. "Is everything alright?"

"Absolutely. I hope I am not intruding." Sheldrake replied, removing his naval cap. Like most of the officers, he still had not yet got out of the habit of wearing his uniform.

"No, no, of course not, come and sit down." Maria said as she pulled up a chair. "Can I get you a coffee?"

"No thank you." Sheldrake replied as he sat down on the offered chair. "I see everyone is relaxing this morning, good to see."

"We try to keep Sunday as a day of rest and getting together." Bob explained. "Not for any religious reasons, I might add, but just to recharge the batteries and take a break from the usual chores."

"Good thinking. And good timing." Sheldrake replied, and the group looked at him somewhat surprised. "As we only have a skeleton crew and just yourselves to worry about I'd like to invite you all to a luncheon this afternoon down by the beach."

"Oh, that would be lovely Raymond," Joan replied. "We had only just begun to discuss what we would be doing for meals to-day. Now that's settled." This was followed by a consensus of agreement in the way of smiles and nodding of heads. Then, everyone's attention was drawn to Edward, one of the children Joan and John had rescued from the hospital in Maine. He had tripped on the patio stones and banged his knee, nothing serious but enough to draw tears from the little fellow. Maria was closest, so she picked him up and made it better for him.

"We have to be extra careful here with this next generation." John said watching as Edward, wiped his tears away and resumed playing with his step-sister, Amilia. "Only four so far, but there may be more soon!" John added with a glint in his eye as he smiled at Bob.

"Oh, indeed there will." Sheldrake said and not for the first time that morning the group once more looked questioningly at him. Only this time it was with more of consternation than surprise, as if he was trying to infiltrate on their private lives.

"Oh, sorry, you haven't heard, have you?" Sheldrake asked, suddenly realizing that the news from Bermuda had not yet been imparted to the islanders. The group looked at him, now with another questioning look.

"Heard what?" Bob asked.

"Yesterday, Bermuda announced that a space module had splashed down, just off the island and there were three occupants onboard." Sheldrake paused for effect and looked around at each of the four adults. "Yes, a man, a woman and a six-month old baby."

Chapter 36

Prepping the Plane

Norfolk International Airport

There was a set of steps leading up to the open doorway of the Cessna. DeVersa was hoping it was because the plane had been fueled and was being prepared for take-off just before the devastation hit. DeVersa climbed the steps and opened the door to the plane, he was pleased to see it was immaculate inside and was a standard model with available seating for twelve people. That would provide enough seating for the ladies, Grover's team and some additional cargo. He moved forward to the cockpit and located the pilot's checklist and maintenance records. DeVersa reviewed the logs and was relieved to see that the last entry was the day before the devastation, so all maintenance checks were up to date for that time. The litmus test, however, was the charging condition of the battery so, he reviewed the checklist to begin turning on the appropriate switches to check the voltage. As he did so, he was relieved to see the needle of the voltage indicator immediately turn to positive. Happy to see all systems appeared to be 'go', he switched off and proceeded to leave the plane with the pilot's checklist to prepare to open the hangar doors.

Huxley was still admiring the plane when he saw his new captain coming down the steps.

"Everything O.K. Captain." Huxley asked.

“So far so good,” replied DeVersa, “let’s hope we can open these hangar doors between us.” DeVersa strode over to the doors to inspect them and was relieved to see they were of the bi-fold variety and although it would take some effort, it looked as though the two of them would be able to push the doors to their fully open positions.

“Come on then, earn your stripes. Put yer back into it.” DeVersa said as he began to push against one of the doors. At first, DeVersa didn’t think the door was going to budge but once young Huxley added his youthful exuberance to the endeavor the door slowly began to move along in its track. Once the movement had started, the door began to slip back relatively easily. They then turned their attention to the other door and repeated the process.

With the doors open DeVersa wanted to complete a more thorough walk-around of the plane. Using the pilot’s checklist, DeVersa then made a quick visual check of the outside of the plane before verifying that the fuel tanks were indeed full and with the correct type of aviation fuel. Satisfied that all the rudders and alerions were functioning correctly he made one more check to ensure there was adequate clearance for the plane to exit the hangar without having to use a push-back tractor to tow it. That in itself would have been a problem as the only tractors DeVersa could see were outside and the likelihood of any of them having a charged battery would be remote. Fortunately, there appeared to be plenty of room on his starboard side and a few feet on his port wing, so he wasn't expecting a problem, but just to be safe, he would instruct Huxley to guide him out.

"Excellent, so here's what's going to happen." DeVersa said to Huxley who was hanging on his every word, "I'm going to start this puppy up and move her out of the hangar and onto the apron."

"Where's the apron?" Replied Huxley, much to DeVersa's chagrin, but then he realized the poor boy was a young submariner, what would he know of flying terms?

"We're standing on it." DeVersa replied. Huxley looked down as if there was some magical platform before realizing it was just an aeronautical term.

"Gotcha Captain." Huxley replied enthusiastically.

"Now, this is where you come in. I want you to stand back over there," DeVersa said and he pointed to a spot about fifty metres away, level with the end of the port wing on the Cessna. "There are potentially, only two signals I want from you, 'clear' and 'turn right'.

So, hold your right arm up with your arm crooked from the elbow and your left arm down by your side."

"Gotcha." Huxley replied.

"Well, do it then!" DeVersa said.

"Oh, you want me to do it now?" Huxley asked with DeVersa wondering what he had got himself into. However, he had trained rookies before and this was nothing unusual or even as bad as he had seen with some of the young, sprogs he had taught in the past.

“Yes, I want you to do it now.” DeVersa countered politely. Huxley accommodated him and with a couple of slight corrections that DeVersa made he was happy with what he saw.

“So, that is the ‘All Clear’ sign. If the wings are going to clear the sides of the hangar you keep that pose until I am clear of the hangar. O.K.?”

“Gotcha Captain. But what if it isn’t?” Huxley asked.

“I’m glad you asked me that my boy. In which case, all you have to do is keep your right arm in the same position but stick out your left arm like so.” DeVersa positioned his arm pointing diagonally downwards, which Huxley immediately imitated to perfection.

“Now you are telling me to ‘Turn Right’ but hopefully that won’t be necessary because I think there is enough clearance.” DeVersa said. “O.K. Let’s try a few dry runs.”

After a few test calls of the two instructions DeVersa was satisfied that Huxley could manage the signals.

“If all else fails, just jump up and down in the air shouting and waving your arms. O.K.?” DeVersa added, then indicated to Huxley to walk over to his assigned spot on the apron. They were both satisfied it was the correct angle to watch for clearance so DeVersa walked back to the plane, removed the chocks from the wheels and climbed up the forward set of steps. He brought up the steps and closed the door then entered the cockpit. He retrieved the pilot’s checklist from his pocket and began following the list of instructions to fire up the jets and taxi the plane out of the hangar.

Once all the instructions had been successfully adhered to, he was ready to fire the engines. The moment of truth, he pressed the firing button and the beautiful sound of the whine from two Rolls-Royce engines began to fill the hangar. DeVersa checked all the instruments one more time, satisfied that everything was showing green he looked towards Huxley who was standing in position showing the 'All Clear' signal. DeVersa gave one more check of the instruments, looked to the port side to get a feel for the clearance of the plane's wing for himself and then adjusted the controls to slowly exit the hangar.

DeVersa's eyes kept darting from the wings to Huxley and then to the instruments. Huxley didn't change position and judging by his wing position he didn't need to and within a minute the plane was clear of the hangar and safely on the apron. DeVersa left the cockpit and lowered the forward steps and waved his arm to Huxley to indicate he should come and join him. Huxley didn't need any second encouragement and sprinted over to the plane.

"O.K. We're going on a little test flight. Are you up for it?" DeVersa shouted above the noise of the engines.

"Wow, are you kidding?" Huxley said and climbed up the steps. Once DeVersa had raised the steps and closed the door he led Huxley into the co-pilot's seat and indicated to him to put on the seat restraints. The boy's eyes were as wide as saucers as he looked out of the small windows of the plane, his excitement could hardly be contained. DeVersa handed him a set of headphones to put on and DeVersa received a communication verification from him. DeVersa slowly taxied the plane from the apron to the taxiway that led to the main runway. DeVersa was constantly checking the instruments while Huxley just sat in amazement, saying nothing.

They arrived at the main runway and DeVersa did one final check of his instruments and a 360° visual check of the sky to ensure there were no other planes in the vicinity. Not that there would be any traffic, but the training was too instilled to ignore.

"Are you ready?" DeVersa asked as he looked over to his newbie co-pilot. Huxley merely nodded, a hint of nervousness had begun to creep into the boy's demeanor, but he was gallantly trying not to show it.

"No, son. I may not always be looking at you," DeVersa correct, "reply affirmative."

"Affirmative." Huxley instantly replied but still continued to nod his head. DeVersa pushed back the throttles and released the brakes; the jet smoothly sped forward and within a few seconds they were in the air, DeVersa was raising the undercarriage. Within minutes they were circling over the Naval Yard looking down at the U.S.S. Augusta but by now Huxley was only concerned about ensuring he didn't miss the opening of the sick-bag as he threw-up.

Chapter 37

Awkward Overtures

Bermuda

Amy awoke at approximately the same time as the crew of the Augusta was submerging into the depths of the Atlantic Ocean on their way to Admiral Stanford's funeral. Her first thoughts were of the unwanted overtures that Moose had been making during the previous day's get together, she felt that maybe Ivan and herself had been a little premature in signaling their intention of leading separate lives. In an effort to extricate herself from Moose's company Amy gave Ivan the responsibility of looking after Mir while she offered her assistance to Moxley for kitchen duties. At first, Moxley declined, profusely, stressing she was as much of a guest in the pub as the incoming crew. But Amy countered that she loved cooking and she had been suffering withdrawal symptoms since she had been in space, which wasn't too far from the truth. She told Moxley it would be a pleasure to help out, so reluctantly, he gratefully accepted. Amy didn't expect to see the Moose in the kitchen, she suspected he was sexist and didn't appear to be the type to be seen preparing meals for anyone but himself, let alone doing the washing-up. On that score, Amy was correct and for much of the rest of the day she was able to stay in the background until it was time to take Mir to bed.

Now, a new day had dawned, and Amy was certain Moose would be calling in on the pub to renew his attempts at courting her. Amy had to do something, she could tell Moose outright that any romantic ideas were not going to work but she had a feeling that could go one of two ways. He would either be deterred but not put off and would continue to harass her, or her impression of him was that he was the type of person who could just flip, and his actions may be unpredictable. All she had to do was keep out of Moose's way for a couple of days until the Augusta returned to take them to St. Santia. If Moose decided to also take the trip she would have a quiet word with Jason to prevent that happening.

By this time, Mir had woken up and was standing on the inside of the cot, smiling and gurgling at Amy. This prompted Amy into action, the plan of attack was simple. Amy would bathe and change Mir before calling in on Ivan to explain the situation. Amy wanted him to be by her side for the next two days, they could claim, that under the circumstances, they were trying to make a go of it for Mir's sake. That would surely be enough to prevent any further unwanted advances from Moose. Amy spent the next thirty minutes playing with Mir, bathing and dressing her, then she quickly showered and dressed before the two of them went to knock on Ivan's door. Amy knew that Ivan had been celebrating pretty hard the previous day and of course, all the time she had known him he had never imbibed any alcohol because of their situation. So, she wasn't sure what kind of a state he would be in when she knocked on the door. To her surprise, the door opened shortly after the first knock and standing there was a beaming Ivan.

“Dobroye utro, moy malen'kiy milyy.” Ivan said specifically to Mir, Amy knew that was Russian for ‘good morning my little darling’. She had heard it every morning for six months on the space-station. Mir responded by smiling and holding out her arms to her father. Amy handed over the child to Ivan.

“Come in, come in,” Ivan said to Amy, “to what do I owe this pleasure so early in the morning?”

“I wasn’t sure you would be in the land of the living after what you consumed yesterday.” Amy said with a laugh.

“I was drinking vodka. I’m Russian. No problem.” Ivan replied in between throwing Mir into the air and catching her, much to her delight. “But is there a problem?”

“Yes, there is, but not with Mir, don’t worry.” Amy replied and then went on to explain her uncomfortable predicament with Moose.

“Yes, I see,” replied Ivan, when Amy had finished, “that accounts for him sitting next to me for most of the day and pumping me with questions about you. I didn’t give it a thought at the time but it all makes sense now.”

“So, my thought is, that for the next two days we could pretend to be a couple again until we can leave the island on the submarine’s return. Just to stave him off. It would keep everything simple." Amy suggested.

"Or I could have a word with him." Ivan offered.

"No, I think he is the type to cause trouble." Amy responded.

"Oh, I think I could handle that big bear." Ivan retorted.

"Yes, you probably could but I'm concerned that after the year or so these guys have had in isolation he is the type to go over the edge. I wouldn't put it past him to use a gun." Amy argued. "It would just be a lot less complicated if we hung out together. It's just for two days Ivan!" Ivan thought for a while as he continued to play with Mir.

"Well, certainly it would be no hardship to be with you and Mir for a few more days." Ivan finally replied, who was by now on the floor playing with Mir, "and it would keep him at bay wouldn't it. Why not? Let's tour the island together."

"Great Ivan, thanks." Amy replied, extremely relieved. She certainly didn't want to return from the loneliness of space to suddenly be in a relationship with someone she didn't like, and she wasn't thinking of Ivan. She watched on with a smile as Ivan continued to play with Mir. "I think it's time we took her downstairs and found her some breakfast. Shall we go and find some food?" Ivan said to Mir, who replied with a giggle and a shaking of her arms. Ivan swept the toddler up from the floor and the three of them proceeded to go quietly downstairs to the kitchen.

In the kitchen Amy located some cereal and even some fresh fruit that had recently been picked. She prepared a carafe of coffee, surprised that the supply had not yet been exhausted and while she was preparing the rest of the breakfast items Ivan carried Mir into the restaurant area of the bar. Moxley had carried out a magnificent job of clearing up after the festivities and Mir's high-chair was still there. Ivan was seated with Mir as Amy brought through the breakfast things on a large serving tray. At the same time, Moose walked casually into the bar and smiled at Amy.

"Good morning Amy. How are you?" Moose said pleasantly.

"Oh, hi Moose, I'm fine. No hangover this morning?" Amy replied in the same vane.

"Hi Moose." Ivan said turning his attention away from Mir.

"No, I'm fine. I really didn't drink that much yesterday." Moose replied. Amy set the large tray down on an adjoining table and began to move the breakfast items over to the table Ivan and Mir were seated at.

"Whoops, forgot the OJ." Amy said and went back to the kitchen. Moose saw this as an opportunity to have a private word with Amy and he wasted no time as he entered the kitchen.

"Look Amy, I wondered if I could show you and Mir around the island. It's a beautiful day and you're only here for a couple of days at the most." Moose said sheepishly. But without any hesitation Amy replied and nipped any thoughts that Moose had right in the bud.

"Funnily enough, that's exactly what the three of us are going to do to-day." At first, Moose thought that he was one of the trio and he greeted her reply with a smile. "Ivan and I have decided to stay together for the sake of Mir, so we are going to use the next few days to get to know each other in the real world, if you'll excuse the pun." Amy didn't even engage eye contact, she continued about her business almost as if Moose wasn't there.

"Oh. That's great!" Was Moose's reply. "Well have a nice day then." Moose said pleasantly, although inside he was seething and the whole force of his anger was directed towards Graneski. He felt it was all that little punk's fault that Amy had decided not to have anything to do with him. Moose was scheming and when Graneski returned, that man was going to have an accident.

Chapter 38

The Trip to Nebraska

U.S.S. Augusta

DeVersa, did one low pass over the Augusta to catch everyone's attention before heading back to the airfield to land. He placed the pilot's checklist to a clip-board and began to follow the steps for landing. The clip-board was resting between DeVersa and Huxley.

"I'm going to call out and perform each of the steps on this checklist" DeVersa said catching Huxley's attention and pointing to the clip-board. "What I need you to do is make sure I don't miss a step. Can you do that?" DeVersa didn't really need Huxley's assistance but it was an attempt to get the lad's mind off his sickly demeanor. It seemed to work because DeVersa purposely omitted the step to bring down the undercarriage which Huxley picked up on immediately, with some alarm.

"Roger that." DeVersa replied calmly and continued with the remaining steps to complete a perfect landing.

After shut-down they left the plane with DeVersa assisting a groggy Huxley down the steps. DeVersa lifted the steps back up and indicated to Huxley to dispose of the bag containing his previously digested breakfast. DeVersa had one more thing to check, the re-fueling capacity at the site. So, when Huxley re-joined him they drove to the pumps that were a short distance from the hangar. DeVersa alighted the vehicle and walked over to the large man-hole covers above the underground tanks. DeVersa unscrewed one of the covers and using a flashlight shone it down into the depths of the tank. There certainly appeared to be enough fuel in the tank to provide at least a couple of tank-fills. He expected to make at least two or possibly three trips to Nebraska to replenish stocks and knowing the fuel situation was solved that was one less worry. The fuel-tanks had a manual pump, which although laborious was nevertheless effective. DeVersa and Huxley could manage the pumping but perhaps he could also enlist the assistance of Grover's team when necessary. Satisfied that there was no more he could do right now he replaced the covers and decided to head back to the submarine to see how everyone else was faring.

At the time DeVersa did his fly-pass of the submarine, Janet and Mary were busy packing and gathering instruments, together with what little documentation they had on ectogenesis. However, they were not too concerned at their lack of publications as they were certain enough papers would be available at the site in Nebraska.

Grover and his crew were returning to the Augusta in a convoy of three vehicles as they saw the jet fly over. They had commandeered a large cargo truck to bring back 60 crates of ready-to-eat meals to be transported to Nebraska, subject to any weight limitations that DeVersa might make. Initially, the truck wouldn't start but they managed to find some jump-start leads and fired it up from another vehicle. They then loaded up the crates of meals onto the truck, carefully ensuring a variety of entrees and that the date codes stenciled on the side of the crates were within three years of the current date.

On their arrival back at the Augusta, Grover and Lewes left the others to park the vehicles and proceeded to the War Room to meet with Janet and Mary. Grover made a call to Janet's room and when the two ladies arrived he and Lewes were seated at the conference table. They went through the perfunctory greetings and Grover got straight to the point.

"We have probably procured enough food for you to survive on for six months." Grover began to explain, "although, it would not be a particularly healthy diet without fresh fruit and vegetables. However, when we arrive in Nebraska the team could also scour the local supermarkets for tinned goods to supplement the rations, but for now, I think this is the best we will be able to do."

Both Janet and Mary had remained standing, arms-crossed and leaning against the wall. "What you have obtained is better than we could have expected, Grover, thank you." Janet replied.

"That's also assuming we will be able to transport that much on the plane." Grover added, "that decision, of course will rest with DeVersa."

"Understood." Janet replied. "There's not much more that can be done until DeVersa gets here so why don't you take your team to the galley and get some refreshments and once DeVersa returns we can re-convene here to finalize the planning?"

"Grover looked at Lewes, "sounds good," he said. Lewes merely nodded his head in agreement and they all left the room. Janet and Mary returned to their rooms to resume their packing and Grover and Lewes to hail the rest of the team to the galley.

It couldn't have been much more than thirty minutes later when DeVersa and Huxley appeared in the galley. DeVersa walked straight over to the coffee dispenser to grab a cup of coffee, hoping that was a commodity they could replenish while they were in dock.

"I noticed the truck outside with all the crates. Is that yours Grover?" DeVersa asked.

"Yes sir," replied Grover, "not sure how many of those crates we can store on that toy of yours."

"Ha!" DeVersa retorted, "probably most of them, we won't have a full passenger load. I'll work out the load and balance once we have all the required cargo worked out."

"The ladies suggested we convene as soon as you came aboard," Grover replied.

"Where? In the War Room?" DeVersa asked between sipping his cup of black coffee.

"Yep, I'll go and knock on their door." Grover replied, "meet you there." The rest of Grover's team rose and proceeded to the War Room. DeVersa gulped down the rest of his coffee and picked up a sticky-bun from a tray on the galley's serving area and began to follow the others. He was just about to leave the galley when he realized he was alone. He looked back to see a forlorn Huxley looking on like a lost puppy without his master. "Are you coming?" DeVersa asked with a mouthful of cake.

"Well, after what happened this morning I didn't think I would be coming." Huxley said dejectedly.

"What, you think you are the first person to throw-up on your first flight in a jet?" DeVersa asked sarcastically. "Get your butt down to the War Room sailor, on the double."

With the meeting underway it was mainly DeVersa calling the shots, asking all the questions and for once, Janet took a back seat and only spoke when asked a question. DeVersa was making notes on the whiteboard, writing down all the weights of the equipment and the stores for his calculations. They were joined by Jason who merely indicated to DeVersa to carry on while he stayed in the background just listening. DeVersa suggested they all leave the Augusta at 6:00 A.M. the following morning. Taking into consideration the journey to the plane, the loading of the cargo they should be in the air by 8:00 A.M. with arrival in Nebraska at approximately mid-day.

"Great, just in time for lunch." Lewes joked. Grover gave him a playful cuff on the back of his head while everyone else smiled, all except Jason who took this as an opportunity to step forward and say a few words.

“As you all know, I am not in favor of this little sojourn, however, I cannot control what people choose to do.” Jason said gravely, “I am only responsible for this vessel and those who chose to remain on it and I cannot jeopardize their safety. But of course, we will do everything we can to support you during this endeavor, if successful, it will benefit everyone. So, with that being said, we need to get back to Bermuda, DeVersa, what sort of timeline are we looking at for your return to Norfolk?”

“Well, theoretically, we could unload and return the same day.” DeVersa replied.

“With all due respects sir,” Grover interrupted, “I think it would be best if we had at least one day to reconnoiter the area to ensure the ladies’ safety before we depart.”

“Then we could expect you back two days from now and we will head back to Bermuda the following morning.” Jason said and DeVersa nodded his head in agreement.

“Well, good luck everyone and just in case, here are some emergency communication devices.” Jason said as he laid out on the conference table six small pager-like radios. “We will be monitoring for any emergency that arises. At the sight of the modules the faces of both Janet and Mary paled a little as they both remembered the last time they were forced to use those devices.

Chapter 39

Meanwhile, Back on the Farm

St. Santia

"A baby?" Maria asked in amazement, "from space?"

"Yes," Sheldrake smiled. "As yet, we don't have all the details, but I am sure they will be forthcoming."

"So, our little nursery has grown to five." John said.

"Well, we don't know that yet," Joan said poignantly, "we don't know that they will join us here."

"Why wouldn't they?" John retorted, "the baby would need socializing with other children, of course they will come here."

"John Hamax, you're talking as if the baby is a puppy!" Joan admonished him, and everyone laughed.

The conversation then flittered back and forth until Bob decided it was time to go and check on the chickens.

"Oh, Bob, perhaps the Connecticut could do with some eggs because I think we have plenty." Maria added.

"Sure, do you need a couple of fresh chickens as well?" Bob asked Sheldrake.

"I'm sure the cooks would appreciate that, thank you." Sheldrake replied as he rose to leave the gathering.

"No problem, should be there just before lunchtime" Bob replied. He too rose and was about to say his farewell but was interrupted by John.

"Mind if I join you?" John asked, "I think I need to socialize with other men." Everyone laughed once more as John and Bob walked towards the Mini-Moke, while Sheldrake began walking back to the Connecticut.

The girls were left with the children to discuss matters, mainly Marlene's welfare. But she was holding up very well and her demeanor certainly did not give rise to any concerns. Before they knew it, the time had passed quickly, and they could see Bob and John heading towards the submarine in their vehicle to deliver the goods they had promised.

"Oh, my goodness!" Joan cried, "I didn't realize the time. I had better get some lunch going."

"I'll come and help." Marie said.

"Hey, don't go to town." Marlene shouted after them as they walked in the house, "the crew will probably put on a big spread this afternoon."

As it turned out, after a light lunch, the crew did in fact put on quite the buffet and a good time was had by all. Awnings had been erected with tables and chairs which provided a wonderful view of both the beach and the houses. The residents were impressed, and it prompted Joan to make a suggestion.

"Raymond, you should leave this structure up, it would serve as a great meeting place, like a coffee-shop." Joan said.

"Well we could," Sheldrake mused, "we could even arrange for food and drinks to be regularly brought from one of the submarines."

"We could name it Sandbucks." One of the crew man offered, who coincidentally was in fact bringing trays of food over from the Connecticut.

"Sandbucks?" Joan asked, "how did you arrive at that?"

"Well, it's on the beach and the submarines are full of young bucks." The sailor replied. The group laughed but somehow the concept stuck, except the name was quickly abbreviated to SBs.

Sheldrake shared what little he had learnt from the new visitors in Bermuda and it was expected they would be returning with the Augusta to St. Santia. But enough of that, music was laid on and the three ladies were in demand to dance with various members of the crew. At the end of the evening the girls were exhausted and one or two of the crew were a little worse for wear, due to the copious amounts of alcohol that was available. Joan wasn't sure whether the Admiral would have approved of such a situation, but she was not able to condone the men as a very inebriated John had to be assisted back to the house while replying to Joan's admonishments with, "well I'm just trying to socialize."

Chapter 40

Flight Departure

Naval Yards, Norfolk, Virginia

The detachment of men travelling to Nebraska walked down the gangplank of the submarine at exactly 6:00 A.M. to tumultuous applause from the crew of the Augusta, who to a man had surprisingly risen from their slumbers to see the group off. Janet and Mary said their goodbyes to Dr. Moore and Jason respectively. Janet and the doctor merely shook hands although the gaze as they looked each other in the eyes indicated more was needed but she was still not quite ready. Jason and Mary held each other passionately and with a tear in her eye Mary pulled herself away and with one last, longing look at Jason she left the submarine with Janet.

Nothing much was said on the drive to the airfield, Mary and Janet were in the Jeep driven by DeVersa with his new side-kick, Huxley, while the rest of the group was travelling behind in the truck and another Jeep. On arrival at the plane, DeVersa began to give instructions as to where everyone should be seated as well as informing Grover where the luggage and cargo should be stored. For loading purposes most of the dried food was taken out of their crates and distributed in the passenger area of the plane.

While everything was being loaded DeVersa and Huxley went through the checklist in preparation for take-off. Once the truck was emptied and the cargo hold door closed, Grover's team drove the three vehicles to the hangar and parked them inside. They closed the hangar doors with a lot more speed than DeVersa and Huxley had done opening them the previous day and by the time they returned to the plane, DeVersa was ready for take-off. With everyone seated, Huxley left the cockpit to provide take-off and emergency instructions to the passengers. Although he was a little nervous giving out these instructions and ensuring the passengers did indeed have their safety-belts attached and their seats forward for take-off they obediently complied, albeit with a smile.

After taxiing to the appropriate runway indicated by the somewhat dilapidated, but still functioning, windsock, DeVersa made an uneventful take-off. DeVersa had chosen the Hastings Municipal Airport as his destination. The aviation manual described it as having two runways, both of which had adequate lengths to land the Citation, however, only one of them was long enough for take-off. The other attraction was that it was only thirty minutes from the Clay Centre.

Once they were in the air and the intended flying altitude had been reached DeVersa entered the directional co-ordinates before putting the plane on autopilot. He would have to periodically check landmarks to ensure they remained on track as GPS was no longer a dependable option. DeVersa provided Huxley with some charts that had their intended track clearly defined and asked him to verify some of the landmarks to ensure they were on course. While the poor matelot was left struggling with his first attempt at aerial navigation DeVersa walked back to the cabin to see how the passengers were coping. There wasn't really any need to, Grover was already fast asleep, Mary and Janet were reviewing some of the documentation they had on ectogenesis. Graneski and Lewes had brought some playing cards and were playing Crib while both Hernandez and Stenich were zoned out listening to music through their headphones.

DeVersa, the ever-consummate pilot, merely smiled and told everyone they were on schedule to land at noon.

"Just in time for lunch!" Lewes said, which brought a smile to the ladies. DeVersa then returned to the cockpit to supervise Huxley's attempt at navigation.

Needless to say, poor Huxley was turning the charts around and around in an attempt to distinguish a landmark that would match something remotely akin to anything on his charts. But DeVersa was expecting that and he calmly sat beside the confused young man and began to give him a quick basic ground course.

"First of all, hold the chart in the direct you are heading." DeVersa told the boy and turned the chart to coincide with their destination. "Now, the chart clearly shows many things, lakes, railway lines, towns, towers and land masses. So, all you have to do is find one of them and the rest will be easy. For example, we will shortly be passing between Roanoke and the George Washington and Jefferson National Forest. Then we should be flying almost parallel with Interstate 64 which heads east to west. We are flying low enough that you can distinguish the highways, they are great navigational aids. Especially when you know even numbered highways travel east to west and odd numbered ones are north to south."

"I did not know that!" Huxley said, somewhat amazed by that snippet of information, although considering he had never got his driving license he could be forgiven for not knowing that. Still, armed with this new wealth of knowledge Huxley avidly scoured the ground and tracked their progress for the rest of the flight. In fact, it was Huxley who correctly pointed out the Clay Center as it came into view. Just to the west of the town, on Highway 180, was their ultimate destination, the U.S. Meat Animal Research Center. DeVersa made a quick pass of the area and there didn't appear to be any obstructions on the highway, so he made the announcement for everyone to prepare for landing. He banked the plane and turned for a final approach but just as he was about to touch down, out of the corner of his eye, he saw a movement, just outside the very building that was the team's destination.

Chapter 41

On Board the U.S.S. Augusta

Naval Yards, Norfolk, Virginia

It was with a great deal of consternation that Jason said goodbye to Mary, but he knew there was no way he could stand in her way. Dennis was equally concerned about Janet but with her; he knew standing in her way would be an impossibility. All the two men could hope for was that Grover and his team would take good care of them and they would all make a safe return with their objectives fulfilled. Meanwhile, it was business as usual. After ensuring all systems were operating correctly Jason and Dennis proceeded to the galley for breakfast. Cook seemed to be coping extremely well by himself and the usual fare was available in the galley.

Once breakfast was over Jason went to organize a work-party to obtain some of the dried food rations to remain on board as an emergency measure. He also wanted to procure extra rations for the Connecticut as he was hoping Sheldrake would take a tour up the eastern seaboard of the U.S. to look for would-be survivors. Dennis returned to the surgery just in case one of the sailors had a medical issue that needed tending to.

Now that the funeral was over, and the rest of the crew were busy occupying themselves with the maintenance of the vessel, Tony had been pretty much left on his own, alone with his thoughts. He had concluded that there was no way he would continue to live a lie and stay with Marlene. It would be a wrench to not see baby Augusta as much as he would like but if all ties were severed now it would be much easier than if he continued to be close to her. Occasionally, as he laid in his bunk a crew-member would drop by and chat briefly with him. Tony would pretend he was reading and tell them how nice it was to get away from the stress of family life for a few days, not realizing just how much they would welcome such a problem. Consequently, the conversations didn't last too long, which didn't seem to bother Tony much as in his solitude he could see a future, a happy future in a loving relationship; and it wasn't with Marlene.

Chapter 42

Arrival in Clay

U.S. Meat Animal Research Center, Nebraska

Even before the plane had landed and had finished taxiing Grover was looking through the small windows at the snow-covered area for any signs of life. He had instructed the rest of his team to do the same so that both sides of the plane were being monitored. DeVersa stopped the plane as close to the Research Center as he possibly could but before he opened the exit door and lowered the steps he needed to discuss what he had seen with Grover. DeVersa wanted to tell Grover without alarming anyone else so, as a joke, he summoned Grover to the cockpit to receive rendezvous instructions.

A confused Grover entered the cockpit and while Huxley was stashing away his charts, still wearing his headphones, DeVersa explained to Grover what he saw.

"Are you sure it was a person?" Grover asked, not disputing that DeVersa had indeed seen something, he was just trying to confirm what it was. Given that this was a research facility some animals could have somehow survived the devastation.

"I can't be sure, but something definitely went into that building." DeVersa said pointing to the research center, "there's an open door on the far side. It was still open as we taxied by."

Grover, thought for a minute. "O.K., the girls stay on the plane with you, we will reconnoiter the place while you taxi the plane into a position so that you could take off immediately. Once we have determined what you saw and secured the area we will give you an all-clear on the radio. In the event you hear any gun-fire or receive an emergency call, take-off immediately and monitor the radio in case we need further assistance. Any questions?" Grover asked. DeVersa merely shook his head and went to prepare the door and stairs just as the girls were rising from their seats and putting on their backpacks in preparation for deplaning.

"If you ladies would be so kind as to wait on the plane until we have checked out the buildings." Grover said pleasantly, without any hint of concern.

"I don't think that will be necessary Grover." Janet replied, "we will just tag along, I'm sure we will be safe in your capable hands."

"I'm sorry miss, it was kind of an order not a request." Grover told Janet deadpan, looking directly into her eyes. For once in her life Janet didn't argue she returned to her seat in a huff but said nothing more.

Grover led his team of wannabe Seals down the few steps leading from the luxury jet and was pleased to see the men automatically positioning themselves in their V-formation without having to be told. No sooner were they on the snow-covered road, DeVersa had raised the steps back into their recess on the plane and the door was secured. The team were all wearing communication devices and DeVersa was monitoring their conversations as, to the surprise of everyone, except Grover, he began to taxi away from the building.

As the team approached the side of the building where DeVersa had seen the movement and the open-door Grover indicated with his left arm that they should continue in as low a crouch as possible. They approached a low wall and Grover indicated to Graneski and Lewes to cross to the other side where there was a parallel wall on the far side of a roll-top door. There were definite rustling sounds coming from inside the building but no voices. Grover utilized his periscope to scan the inside of the building, what he saw made him stand in amazement.

Chapter 43

Relaxing on Earth

Horseshoe Bay, Bermuda

As strange as it may sound, the two new adults on the island, who had been in space, in virtual isolation for some considerable time, decided they wanted to get away from everyone. Well, at least that is what they had told Moxley. The real reason was to distance themselves from Moose, who despite what they had told him, still erroneously believed he stood a chance with Amy, he never seemed to be too far away. The couple asked Moxley the best place to visit, he suggested Horseshoe Beach. He told them they could take one of the vehicles that was kept gassed-up. "It's a nice drive and the sand out there is one of the finest examples of a pink beach," he told them.

"Pink beach?" Ivan asked, "what is a pink beach."

"Well here in Bermuda, there are pink beaches. Basically, it is sand that is finely pulverized remains of calcium carbonate shells and skeletons of invertebrates such as corals, clams, and other shells. On the underside of Bermuda's coral reefs, there are dark red skeletal animals that grow profusely. When the red forms die, the skeletons plummet to the ocean floor, wave action erodes them then they become mixed with other debris on the seabed such as the white shells of clams, snails and sea urchins. The sea brings them to the shore creating a remarkable pink hue." Moxley explained.

"That sounds interesting, we should go there." Amy said quite excited. "Boy you really know your stuff Moxley."
"I memorized the brochures." Moxley replied.
"Anyway, it sounds great!" Ivan agreed.
"Here's a map," Moxley said as he passed them a pocket map that had been published by the Bermuda Tourism office, "I'll just pack you some food and drinks while you check out your route."
"No please don't go to any trouble, we can manage." Amy responded.
"No trouble, it's nice to have something to do for a change." Moxley said.
"How long will it take to drive there?" Ivan asked
"About thirty minutes." Moxley replied as he was on his way to the kitchen but then he stopped and turned to face them, "but stick to the main roads. We have cleared any remains of the devastation from the main drags, around the lighthouse and the golf course. The hurricanes and the sea took care of the beaches but if you go inland some of the sights aren't pretty." Amy cringed at the thought of bodies that had been lying around decomposing for this length of time. Moxley continued to shout from the kitchen as he prepared snacks for them.
"In the early days we thought the lighthouse would make a good lookout point to search for any other survivors. We arranged shifts to man the place but as time went by we realized that keeping the

beacon going would be just as practical. So, we set up some solar panels and the lighthouse keeps going 24 hours a day."

"So, if there is anyone out at sea they should see it." Amy said.

"Precisely." Moxley replied. "As callous as it may sound, we used a heavy-duty bull-dozer to clear the main roads and burnt the bodies as we went. But I know from my own experience while foraging, there are some areas that you just don't want to visit. I guess nature and time will eventually take care of everything but meanwhile, well you know?" Moxley returned carrying a couple of coolers filled with drinks, food and snacks for Mir.

"Thank you Moxley." Amy said sincerely.

"My pleasure, here are the keys to my Range-Rover, it's in the car-park and don't forget to drive on the left-hand side of the road." Moxley told them and they all laughed.

Approximately thirty minutes later Ivan, Amy and Mir were leaving on a family picnic just like any other family going out for a day-trip. As they left, Moose, who had been sitting outside, casually entered the bar and spoke to Moxley.

"So, where are our intrepid space-travelers off to then?"

"Just for a drive to Horseshoe Bay to take in some sights." Moxley replied, not giving it a second thought.

About an hour later, Moose could see the family of three on the beach as he turned his jet ski towards them and slowly rode the waves to the shore where they were seated.

Chapter 44

Reconnaissance in Clay

U.S. Meat Animal Research Center, Nebraska

Janet and Mary were not paying much attention to what DeVersa was up to as he raised the steps and closed the door, they just put it down to his reaction to over-zealous security instructions given by Grover.

"Boys playing bloody soldiers again." Janet quipped, but when the plane began to move she could no longer contain herself. Janet stormed into the cockpit determined to know what was going on.

"What the hell is happening here DeVersa?" Janet demanded to know, "why are you moving us away from the building?"

"Grover's orders ma'am." DeVersa replied calmly.

"But why?" Mary asked as she quickly caught up with Janet.

"O.K., I can tell you now." DeVersa said.

"Tell us what?" Janet asked.

"As I was making my incoming approach I saw a movement, something or someone went into that building." DeVersa said, pointing to the research center as they taxied by. "I informed Grover and as a precaution he has told me to be in a position for an emergency take-off, so I can get you two to safety. So, that's what I am doing." Janet was about to insist that he return to the center immediately when their conversation was interrupted by Grover's voice over the radio.

"DeVersa, DeVersa, this is Grover. You better swing back around her and let the ladies see this. Over." Grover's voice crackled over the radio.

"Grover, Grover, this is DeVersa, will do, over." DeVersa responded and then to the ladies, "well, I guess everything is copasetic," then he prepared to taxi back to the center.

DeVersa taxied back to where the others had alighted the plane just a few minutes earlier, only this time it was Janet and Mary champing at the bit to exit the plane. As soon as the door was opened, and the stairs were touching terra firma the girls were rushing down the steps and over to the building to see what Grover wanted them to see. Huxley, who had been quietly listening and watching the proceedings also began to exit the plane.

"No son, you just stay here with me a little while longer." DeVersa said and he held out his arm to bar the young man's path.

"Aw come on DeVersa, Grover said it was 'all clear' didn't he?" Huxley pleaded.

"Not exactly, anyway, it won't hurt to wait another five minutes now will it lad?" DeVersa replied calmly.

Reluctantly, Huxley sat back in his seat at just about the same time the ladies were entering the research center. For a few moments the two ladies stood in awe at what they saw. It was just then that the roll-top door that they had all just entered, came crashing down, barring their exit. All seven passengers that had arrived in Nebraska were now trapped.

Chapter 45

Foraging for Supplies

Naval Yards, Norfolk

The detail, sent by Jason to find some additional rations, were playing football on the dock as they waited for one of the crew members to go off and obtain a truck. It was Lester, a young Electronics Technician, who had agreed to locate a suitable vehicle. Lester, a short, diminutive character, originally from Detroit, who had worked on one of the auto-maker's assembly line before joining the navy. There wasn't much he didn't know about cars and he was quite happy to take the brisk, long walk to the main buildings and if necessary, find an appropriate vehicle, like a jeep, to seek what he was ultimately looking for. Lester was armed, as Grover had reported his findings to Jason regarding the obvious presence of people being in the area recently and had written down instructions on where the stores were housed. He had also told Jason that any party sent to the buildings should go with caution, which Jason did impart to the detail he sent and insisted on some of them being armed; and equipped with radios. But Lester had not encountered any obstacles and found a truck inside one of the warehouses that he managed to get started.

On Lester's return with the truck, the rest of the crew, five of them, piled into the back and slapped the cab to indicate to him that they were all ready. The raucous crew enjoyed the short but bumpy ride to the warehouse, the one found by Grover on the previous day, and as soon as Lester came to a stop they all jumped out of the truck ready to cherry-pick some goodies.

As they entered the building the crew was amazed at just how extensive the establishment was and the variety of goods it contained. As well as the boxes of dried rations there were uniforms, overalls, winter clothing and flashlights, something that would definitely come in handy. The detail was, more or less, retracing the footsteps of Grover's team made the previous day and they soon came across the abandoned camp-site. Although, like Grover, the objective was to just obtain food, this detail had the time to explore, there was no urgency to just *'loot and scoot'*, as was the case with Grover's team. So, the detail continued to meander through the maze of containers and packages, yelling to each other whenever an interesting item was discovered. For the most part, any new unearthing of an item was met with indifference until one of them shouted out, "chocolate, over here."

The remainder of the detail came running over and began to open the cartons marked 'CHOCOLATE – SLABS'. They began to act like bees around a honey-pot until one of them noticed a man, holding an automatic rifle and it was being pointed directly at them.

Chapter 46

Trapped in Clay

U.S. Meat Animal Research Center, Nebraska

Janet and Mary, like Grover's team, were indeed speechless when they first entered the Research Centre because there in front of them, alive and well, were all the types of livestock that they had hoped to create through ectogenesis. Cows, horses, sheep, pigs and goats, all housed in the building and all segregated in pens made of plexiglass. The animals, like the pens, were all immaculately clean and appeared to be in excellent health.

"How could this possibly be?" Janet whispered to Mary, just as the door came down to trap them inside. As if to answer Janet's question an officious voice came over on a loudspeaker.

"Put down your weapons. You are surrounded by armed personnel and you cannot escape."

Grover was embarrassed to be caught like this, the sight of the animals had made him let his guard down but his mind was now back on a war-footing and he was thinking quickly.

"Do as he say." Grover said to the rest of the team. He said it loudly and slowly and they began to comply with the request, laying down their weapons with deliberate movements. He couldn't see any microphones or any way that their captor could possibly hear them. They were trapped in a small area surrounded by plexiglass with the closed door behind them, but that also appeared to be their protection. Grover couldn't see anywhere that so-called armed personnel could possibly be pointing anything at them, convincing him that this was all a bluff. There was something else, the tone of the speaker's voice, heard on the loudspeaker, Grover felt it was that of a nervous man and the 'surrounded' threat was merely a ruse, but of course, he had to be one hundred percent certain before he made any counter-attack.

Grover was calculating an escape plan, he still had pistols and knives concealed on his person. Grover also knew that just one of his grenades was more than capable of taking down the door, but the possibility of flying debris had the potential for maiming or even killing one of the ladies or his team. He felt his best strategy was to bide his time, lay low and wait for an appropriate opportunity to escape to the jet, unless of course, that route was also now jeopardized. However, the answer to that question came quicker than he expected.

Chapter 47

Alone on a Beach

Horseshoe Bay, Bermuda

How wonderful to be on one of the most beautiful beaches in the world and not have a single tourist in sight, Amy thought. Here they were, Ivan, Mir and herself in complete isolation, not that they hadn't experienced solitude before, but this was different to being alone in space, this was so relaxing. The sand, the gentle waves rippling on the beach with not a cloud in the sky. It was also good for them too because she needed to discuss their future with Ivan. They always knew onboard the space-station that the two of them would never become a couple, their love-making had been purely a scientific experiment. Then, after the devastation, they didn't expect to live more than a few months after Mir's birth but their successful return to earth had changed things, the situation needed to be re-visited.

"This is great, isn't it?" Amy said as Mir grabbed a handful of sand and watched as it sifted through her fingers.

"Yes. Yes, it is." Ivan replied, "can you believe this is the first time I have ever been on a beach?"

"What?" Amy replied incredulously. "You've got to be kidding me!"

"No, not at all," Ivan replied smiling, "remember, I'm originally from Siberia, I went to university in Stalingrad and then straight on to the Yuri Gagarin Cosmonaut Training Center in Moscow."

"But you never had a vacation anywhere?" Amy was now facing Ivan with a look of total surprise.

"I may have been living in a more liberal Russia than during the Cold War but because of my training I was very restricted in where I could travel for my vacations. Don't misunderstand me, I was extremely well treated, and I always thought my days of travelling would be possible after a couple of missions. But...." Ivan's voice trailed off. For a moment there was silence, then Amy decided to breach the subject of their future.

"Well, Ivan, we appear to be in a situation neither of us expected to be in when we took on this undertaking." Amy said, now looking out to sea as if an answer would pour in on a wave.

"I don't think the situation has changed Amy." Ivan replied nonchalantly. Amy looked at him with a quizzical look on her face, but Ivan continued, "no, I don't expect you to spend the rest of your life with a man you don't love. Especially now that you have an opportunity to meet a potential soul-mate amongst the men from the submarines."

"But what about you?" Amy asked, "you will be alone, without female companionship."

"As will many others, but I have something they do not have, a daughter to love and nurture." Ivan said, but then a cloud appeared to cover his face, "you're not thinking of keeping her from me are you Amy?"

"Of course not Ivan, I would never dream of doing that to you." Amy replied immediately, "but I believe we will have to make the trip to St. Santia so that Mir can be with the other children."

"Naturally, she couldn't stay here. So, I will come too, and I could live close by." Ivan said excitedly. "I will be like an old father, vetting prospective beaus for the lovely Amy and my beautiful Mir and I will see them off with a shotgun if I do not approve." Amy and Ivan laughed as he tickled Mir and she responded with a giggle as more sand fell through her fingers.

The situation that Amy thought was going to be difficult was in fact not a problem and for a while nothing more was said, until she continued in a kind of joking manner.

"But what if I don't find anyone, I may become asexual and have no need for another partner." Ivan pondered this for a minute and continued in a philosophical way.

"You must." Ivan continued, "you must find the biggest strongest man amongst the horde of seamen and breed big strong boys, survival of the fittest and all that." Then he spread his arms and curled them, showing his muscles. It was just then that Moose came into view, astride his jet-ski and heading straight towards where they were sitting.

Chapter 48

Captured Like Pirates

Naval Yards, Norfolk

The men just stood rooted to the spot, the man holding the gun had a demonic look on his face, his hair was unkempt, his face was streaked with dirt, although his clothes were in good condition, courtesy of the supplies in the warehouse.

"You thieving bastards, what are you doing here hey? Trying to steal my stuff, are you?" The man asked with a distinct Latino lilt, but his voice was menacing, so much so that the crewman chose not to respond.

"Down on the floor, face down, you sticky-fingered, pirates." The man shouted, then veritably screamed, "NOW." The crewmen reacted instantly and laid down. For a couple of moments there was an impasse, the crewmen were helpless and the man with the gun was not quite sure what to do next.

"No sé qué hacer. no sé qué hacer." 'I don't know what to do,' the man was whispering in Spanish while his fingers moved nervously on his weapon as he patrolled backwards and forwards watching the helpless crew members. He was unsure of his next actions, until he saw a number of plastic ties hanging from one of the steel framed storage shelves. "I know, I'll tie them up, that's what I'll do, tie them up." He suddenly said in English.

To the crewmen, the man was, without doubt, deranged and each one of them was certain that the slightest movement on their part would set off a shooting tirade, so they remained motionless and soundless.

“You, you.” The man shouted and kicked the crewman closest to him, “get up, slowly now.” The selected crewman was Dale, an A-Ganger who maintained the submarine’s steering gear amongst other things. He also just happened to be the youngest amongst them, whether that was a coincidence or a planned move on their captor’s part, regardless, Dale gingerly did as he was told and slowly rose.

“Grab a handful of those plastic ties there.” The man said, indicating with his head to the ties he had just seen. Dale, again, dutifully did as he was told.

“Now, all of you, put your hands together behind your backs.” The man ordered. Dale also robotically, responded to the order. “No, not you. You dipstick.” The man said to a terrified Dale, while, despite the desperate situation the crewmen found themselves in, one or two of them couldn’t help but let out a snigger at Dale’s expense.

“You tie them up, starting with this one.” The man said as he kicked the nearest of the crewmen, one of the ones who had just laughed. Dale made a loop with one of the ties, bent down and placed the loop over the hands of the crew member. Dale pulled hard on the free end of the tie and the noise of the plastic ratchet seemed to satisfy the gunman as he closely supervised Dale’s every action. The man then indicated with his gun to repeat the same drill with the next man in line on the floor. Dale then proceeded with the others, all the time keeping his back to the armed man. For the last two prostrate men, instead of pulling on the free end of the tie on the crew member's wrists he pulled hard on a looped tie in his hands, satisfying the gunman that he had heard the ties being tightened. When Dale had finished he was ordered back to the concrete floor of the warehouse beside the others and he purposely laid between two of the crew members whose wrists were not completely secure.

"Now, dipstick, it is time to put your hands behind your back." The man said, and he walked over the prone crew members, until he came to Dale. He straddled over Dave and grabbed the ties from him. Dale thought this was the moment, the man would have to use both hands to tie him up, so the gun would be loose in the crook of the man's arms. He felt he could twist quickly enough to grab the gun and catch the man by surprise. The others, whose ties were not secured could then come to his aid. Well, that was his plan and he took a deep breath in preparation for shouting out 'NOW' when a quiet, calm voice stopped everyone in their tracks.

"Hello Dancey. What's new?"

Chapter 49

Aboard the Jet

U.S. Meat Animal Research Center, Nebraska

DeVersa and Huxley were listening intently to the radio and they heard the events as they unfolded. First the dropping of the door, then the voice that came over the loudspeaker and finally, Grover ordering everyone to lay down their arms. But what the captives couldn't see was a man that had run from the middle of the building to the end where they were, flicked an outside switch that operated the roll-down door, then retreated back to an entrance about half-way down the outside of the building. It wasn't until a few seconds after the man entered the building that the message was broadcast over the loudspeaker. This was all being witnessed by DeVersa and Huxley. Now, DeVersa knew the Cessna was relatively quiet but surely the man would have noticed the presence of a jet on the nearby road, even if he hadn't heard it. He was either too focused on the trespassers or figured all the occupants of the jet were trapped inside. Consequently, DeVersa's conclusion was the same as Grover's, this was a one-man operation.

"O.K. my man, time to earn your pay." DeVersa said as he located an automatic pistol that he had stashed in an inside pocket of his flying jacket. Huxley just looked on in astonishment and he was even more astounded when DeVersa reached behind him into his backpack and pulled out another gun and handed it to him. "Know how to use one of these?" DeVersa said nonchalantly, "you must have handled one during your basic training." Huxley, mouth agape, just nodded his head.

"Here's what we do. We will go down the steps and you will run to the back of the building where the others entered. Wait for me to get to that door over there." DeVersa pointed to the door that they saw the man entering. "Give me 30 seconds after I have gone in then locate the switch for the back door and utilize it. Make sure you shout out that it is you, otherwise Grover may cut you to pieces thinking it is one of their captors. Got it?" Huxley continued to nod while looking at the gun as if it was going to jump up and attack him.

"Now, tell me, what are we going to do?" DeVersa asked and Huxley reiterated the plan, ad verbatim.

"Questions?" DeVersa asked.

"What do I do after I have opened the door?" Huxley asked.

"Good question." DeVersa said. "Let Grover take charge."

They both rose from their chairs and moved to the steps.

"Ready?" DeVersa asked. Huxley nodded.

"1, 2, 3, Go." DeVersa said and they both went running towards the building. They, more or less, arrived at their designated points at about the same time. Although Huxley's destination was considerably further away than DeVersa's, the vigor of youth made up the difference. DeVersa paused for a few seconds to regain his breath then he slowly and quietly opened the door to the building.

Huxley waited the agreed half of a minute and on cue, found the switch and pressed it, not forgetting to step back behind the wall and cry out repetitively, “it’s Huxley, don’t shoot, it’s Huxley, don’t shoot.”

DeVersa had entered a stairwell with a double-door ahead of him and a single flight of stairs rising to the next level. DeVersa chose to ascend the steps and he reached the top just as Huxley successfully found the switch to the roll-top door. This had caught the attention of a man in a room that could only be described as a control booth, he also happened to be the only man in the room. The door to the room was slightly ajar, probably left open in the man’s haste to broadcast the message to the intruders. DeVersa went into a crouch position and pushed open the door.

“Freeze, put your hands in the air.” DeVersa said, very authoritatively. So much so that the man stopped what he was doing and raised his arms. Then in a more gentler voice, DeVersa continued, “we’re not here to hurt you but please don’t make a sudden movement for a minute or two O.K.?” The man nodded slightly, DeVersa rose, walked into the room then waited, hoping that Grover was on his way.

Sure enough, within a minute Grover had arrived. He had scrambled under the roll-top door as soon as there was sufficient room for him to roll under. Within another minute he had located the door DeVersa had entered and had burst through the door of the control room. DeVersa had dealt with Seal types before and especially having been caught with his trousers down he was pretty certain that Grover may take a little too aggressive approach with the once captor but now captive.

"Grover, relax, cover me." DeVersa said and without waiting for a response from Grover he began walking to face the man. As he approached the man he began to speak in a much gentler voice.

"My name is-," which was as far as he got as he saw all the animals that the control room was overlooking.

"My god, look what you have got here!" DeVersa rasped as he saw for the first time what the others had already seen.

"Yes, and it has been bloody hard work to achieve this under the circumstances," the man said in a distinctly British accent and despite the guns DeVersa and Grover were holding the man rose to attack him with a cattle-prod, using it as a cudgel. "And damned if I am going to sit back and let you slaughter these beautiful animals." But just as the man raised his improvised weapon he heard a voice behind him.

"You don't have to worry sir, we're here to help you continue with your work." Janet said as she arrived in the room.

Chapter 50

Confrontation

Horseshoe Bay, Bermuda

"How the hell did he know we were coming here?" Amy said rhetorically, as she saw Moose head towards them on his jet ski.

"I don't know, but maybe it's time we put this to rest right now." Ivan said angrily as he rose from the beach.

"No Ivan, now is not the time. Let me deal with him, please." Amy pleaded, as she now rose and faced Ivan. Amy knew Ivan was strong, athletic and had practiced martial arts back in Russia, but she didn't think violence was necessary and she certainly didn't relish a confrontation here in the middle of nowhere with nobody around. Ivan calmed somewhat but every muscle in his body was still tense as the Moose approached the shore on his jet ski. Amy waded into the water to greet Moose as he neared.

"Hi Moose." Amy shouted out amicably. "How did you know where we were?"

"Moxley happened to mention it and I thought you might like to see some of the island from a different perspective." Moose replied nonchalantly, as he turned off the vehicle and waded into the water to be beside Amy.

"Well that's very thoughtful of you Moose," Amy replied sincerely and before Moose could say any more she continued, "I bet Ivan

would love to join you." Without hesitation she turned to Ivan, "he wants to take you for a trip along the coast dear. I think that would be great, you should go."
"How exciting. I've seen it from space how cool to see it so close." Ivan said enthusiastically, knowing exactly what Amy was doing.
"I'll see you back at the room, anyway, I think Mir has had enough sun for one day." Amy added.

Ivan waded into the water towards the jet ski as Amy returned to be with Mir. A bemused Moose attempted a smile as his plan to be alone with Amy had completely backfired but for now he would go along with the tourist expedition and bide his time.

Chapter 51

Hostage Negotiations

Naval Yards, Norfolk

The man with the gun looked directly at the newcomer but his aim stayed trained on the defenseless crewmen, although the muscles around the man's eyes and face relaxed a little as he recognized who was addressing him, it was Bosun Giles. Lester had finished parking the truck and was slowly following the others into the building when he heard the confrontation with the gunman. He had immediately radioed the Augusta and Giles had responded with a couple of armed sailors.

"What's happening Dancey?" Giles said pleasantly as though he was greeting a friend he hadn't seen in some time, which in fact was true. Dancey had been aboard the Connecticut with Giles, furthermore, he was one of the few submariners who had stood up to the mutineers with Giles. The trussed-up crewmen wouldn't have known Dancey because they were all from the Augusta and Dancey had left the Connecticut on docking in Norfolk. Although they were intrigued to know why he was called Dancey.

"These men were stealing from me." The man called Dancey replied through gritted teeth.

"You pilfering little shits." Giles said officiously to the prostrate crewmen. "Why would you want to do a thing like that to a fellow submariner?" The men on the floor weren't quite sure what Giles was driving at but each of them knew this was Giles' way of placating a man that he obviously knew.

"That's a court martial offence." Giles continued, "do you want me to have these men charged Dancey?"

"I don't know boson." Dancey said with some reverence to Giles. "That seems a little harsh."

"Maybe, maybe." Giles replied looking as though he was trying to think things through. "I could send them back to the submarine and put them in the hole for a couple of days!"

"Sure, sure." Dancey replied, but surety was the last thing he was thinking.

"All right you lot. On your feet and get out of here." Giles commanded, and he waited for them to get up and watched them leave through the columns of stores. "In order, you slovenly sailors!" Giles shouted after them as he followed for a few paces to where Lester was waiting in the wings with a couple of other armed sailors. "Untie them and wait for me." Giles whispered to Lester. "I'll be fine here." Then he indicated with a sideways shake of his head for the others to join Lester.

Giles returned to the culvert of boxes where Dancey was still standing with his gun, aimed as though he was ready to shoot.

"O.K. Dancey," Giles said passively, "that's dealt with them. Now, how are you coping?" At first Dancey didn't reply. He just stood there, his fingers still twitching nervously on the rifle.

“You’ve got plenty of food and clothing here, nice little home from home, isn’t it?” Giles said casually as he read the labels on some of the boxes. “You must miss a hot shower though, hey? Look, we’ve discovered some survivors on an island in the Caribbean. Kids and all, how about that?” Giles continued but still nonchalantly looking at the boxes. “Yes, proper little village growing up there. A place that could use expertise like yours. They’re going to need serious help setting up solar, wind and water energy. We don’t really have anyone right now and when the gas finally runs out the poor children will be back to just fire.” Giles remembered that Dancey was an electrician aboard the Connecticut, a good one at that, and he was playing on the man’s skills, it appeared to be working as Dancey slowly began to lower his gun.

“Well, I could do that.” Dancey said.

“Of course you could, Dancey, of course you could.” Giles said smiling, turning to face the man head on. “Do you want to come back to the Augusta and talk about it. It’s not the Connecticut but it’s almost as good. We can get a hot meal inside you and you could clean yourself up. How does that sound?”

“Sounds pretty good bosun.” Dancey said with resignation and he dropped the gun to the ground.

“Jeez Dancey, you should know better than to throw your gun to the ground like that!” Giles shouted. After carrying out classic hostage negotiation tactics without actually being aware of it he resorted to shouting which could have jeopardized the situation. But Giles needn't have worried, Dancey merely smiled and replied,

"Why? It's not loaded."

Chapter 52

Animals Explained

U.S. Meat Animal Research Center, Nebraska

The man turned to face Janet, who was being followed into the room by Mary and instead of striking DeVersa, who was in the process of fending off the impending blow, despite having a gun in his hand, the stranger gazed at the two women, teetered and then fell to the ground. Both Janet and Mary immediately went to his aid.

"This man is spent." Janet said, "just look at him! His clothes are in tatters, I bet he has been running this place single-handedly."

"He's all skin and bones poor guy." Mary said. Janet noticed a cot in the corner of the room, covered in disheveled sheets and blankets.

"Help me get him to that bed over there." Janet ordered, which in fact meant 'you men, lift him to over there.' Which, is exactly what Grover and his team did.

"Has anyone got any water handy and a protein bar maybe?" Mary asked. Needless to say, Grover was prepared and handed both to Mary. The man had merely fainted and after a minute he began to come around, alarmed at first, when he saw all the people in the room, he tried to rise but both Janet and Mary gently settled him back down with soothing words and then offered him the food and water.

"Who, who are you?" He said croakily, "where are you all from?" Janet and Mary went on to tell them who they were and why they were there, while the rest of the men left the room to prepare some lunch and take stock of their surroundings.

"So that's why we came here." Janet said at the end of her explanation, "we were hoping to create some livestock using ectogenesis and then breed them for future generations of humans, but this is beyond our wildest dreams. However did you manage to survive the devastation and breed all these animals?" Janet asked incredulously.

"Devastation? Is that what you call it. All I know is that I was in here early one morning, to supervise the birth of a new calf, by the time I left the building everyone and everything outside was dead. I tried raising people on the phone, watching the telly for an explanation but nothing and I haven't seen another person since, until you walked in here." The man said nervously, as though these were the very people who had been the cause of what they called the devastation. But they soon placated him by explaining how they had survived and what they suspect was the origin of the devastation.

"I see," responded the man, still a little skeptical.

"So, now you know our names and how we survived, how did you and these animals survive?" Janet asked, "I'm intrigued."

Well, this building, although it wouldn't appear to be from the outside, is split into hermetically-sealed enclosures, including this control room. They all have their own air-purifying systems so when the devastation, as you call it, hit we were all safe."

"We?" Mary asked, looking around to see if there were any people in the vicinity.

"Well, me and the animals that is." The man said, he was sitting up now, but he looked pale and gaunt, his hair was greasy, and his personal hygiene left a lot to be desired. He was probably in his late thirties, but he looked a lot older. A tall man and had it not been for his lack of food he would probably have a very good physique. "The enclosures were built that way to protect the animals from possible airborne diseases. But who would have figured…." The man's voice trailed off as he thought of how the design had actually protected both the animals and himself from extinction.

"These animals are the result of the ectogenesis program that you came here for, well at least the original breeding pairs are. Their offspring were being monitored for possible defects, but to date, they have all been perfect, just perfect." The man said as he appeared to go off into a daze.

"You still haven't told us your name. You're obviously British, so what's your story?" Mary said with a friendly smile.

"Oh sorry, forgive me. Sir Harold Fletcher at you service. I'd shake hands, but you don't know where they have been for all these months." He tried to smile at his own little joke, but it was ignored by the two ladies whose brows were raised as they looked at each other for being in the presence of a knight of the realm.

"Oh, the Sir bit? That's nothing," the man said reacting to the women's questioning look that occurred between them, just happened to have worked on the Queen's Sandringham estate for a while so I found myself on the new year honors list. No big deal."
"Sure it is," Janet responded, "for doing what exactly? What is your field?" By now Janet was getting a little frustrated at not getting the answers she wanted to hear.
"Well, I set up a breeding program with some prize livestock they had amongst their cattle herd on the Queen's estate." Harold explained.
"So, you were responsible for breeding the cows?" Mary asked, believing Harold could be a great asset to the island community.
"No, that was the bull's job." Harold replied, giving a quick laugh at this own little joke but as he saw Janet getting more and more exasperated with his story, he continued. "I come from a farming family in Norfolk. England that is, not Norfolk in the U.S., so we knew the farm hands on the Queen's estate at Sandringham. I was being earmarked to inherit the family farm, so I was sent off to study Animal Behavior at the Anglia Ruskin University in Cambridge. After that I received an Animal Bioscience degree at Edinburgh University. That used to be formally called Livestock Husbandry, the program that is, not Edinburgh University. Unfortunately, by the time I returned to take over the farm, the land had been appropriated by the local council and it was no more. But I was offered the position at Sandringham and then after a few

years of that, I was invited to teach at the University of Guelph in Canada. But I missed the hands-on aspect of farming, so when this establishment explained their program and asked me to supervise the livestock in these new pens I jumped at the opportunity. That's it really." Harold said as if anyone could do it.

"So, you have been tending to all these animals alone and still managing to feed yourself?" Mary asked.

"Pretty much." The man replied.

"Where have you been finding food for the animals?" Janet asked.

"In the summer there are plenty of fields that provide enough food. The biggest problem has been finding enough petrol to get the combines working and keeping the generators going to maintain light and heating in here." Harold said opening his arms as he looked around him. "Nebraska isn't exactly the warmest state in the U.S. during the winter months."

"You can operate a combine harvester?" Janet asked.

"Yes of course. I told you, I grew up on a farm. Could drive just about anything by the time I was twelve years old." Harold said, again as if there was nothing to it.

"But the animals look so healthy considering they have been cooped up inside for all this while." Mary remarked.

"As I said, once the snow clears I can herd the animals out into the pastures so that they can graze on the fresh grass. I didn't think there was much risk of an airborne disease by then." Harold explained, "and of course, during the winter months I add supplements to their feed, proteins, vitamins that sort of thing. But unfortunately, I am beginning to run low on those and not sure where to replenish the supply."

"But what about you?" Mary asked, "where have you been getting your food?"

"Oh, about once a month I would take the morning to drive around for supplies and potential sources of petrol. I didn't want to be separated from my work for a longer period than that." Harold replied, but then his face darkened, "occasionally there would be an unfortunate death amongst the animals. I would carry out a post-mortem and if I felt it was safe to do so, reluctantly I would supplement my diet with some meat."

"Wow," Mary said, "you must be worn out."

"Plumb tuckered, as they say in these parts." Harold joked, and the girls laughed. "But there is one regret, the only thing I don't have here are chickens, just wish I could have saved the chickens." Harold lamented.

"Well, have we got fantastic news for you." Mary replied enthusiastically, "we have chickens aplenty."

"You are joking, aren't you?" Harold asked, eyes wide open in amazement at this piece of news.

"Nope," Janet replied, "in fact chickens are all we've got."

"So, we'll trade you." Mary said jokingly, "you can have some chickens and we'll take some of your livestock."

"Oh no, that will never do. These animals must never leave here." Harold said with all seriousness. "It's my job to make sure they survive. I was brought here for a reason. My job, don't you see?"

Chapter 53

Situation Defused

Naval Yards, Norfolk

Dancey and Giles left the warehouse and walked out into a beautiful, yet cool, sunny day. The crewmen, who were now untethered, were standing around with Lester and the two other armed men.

“Alright you lot, carry on with what you were supposed to do, no one has told you to stop.” Giles said to the idle men. “Lester, do you mind driving us to the Augusta?”

“Pleasure bosun.” Lester immediately replied, and he jumped into the cab and started the engine.

Nothing was said on the short journey back to the Augusta, on their arrival both Jason and Dennis were awaiting them at the top of the gangplank. Giles got out of the truck and helped Dancey down before assisting him up the gangplank. At this point Dancey thought he was in serious trouble and as soon as he set foot on the hull of the submarine he stood to attention in front of the two officers and saluted.

“That’s not necessary anymore sailor,” Dennis said kindly, “why don’t you just come with me to the sick bay and we’ll get you cleaned up.” Dancey was a little tentative to go with the doctor until he saw Giles nod his head, then he allowed Dennis to help him down the hatch. Jason watched the two men disappear down the hatch then he turned to Giles.

"We have been in radio contact with Lester, he was appraising us of the situation. You took a risk with an armed man whether you knew him or not. But, well done Giles." Jason said.

"Ah, it was nothing. Not much of a risk really, the gun wasn't even loaded." Giles said, blowing off the compliment. "The poor kid has been on his own all this while, got a little cabin fever, that's all. He'll be fine. Is there anything else you want done sir?"

"No, no Giles, nothing else. Go and relax, you have my permission." Jason said smiling.

"Sir." Giles replied with a quick salute and as he disappeared down the hatch Jason understood what the Admiral had seen in the man. Even though there was no longer a need for the position of bosun onboard a modern, nuclear, submarine, having someone with Giles' experience was invaluable. It was exactly why, that when Giles transferred to submarines he was still referred to as bosun even though his rank was Chief of Boat.

For a moment, this left Jason on his own, scanning the skies for DeVersa's return, although that was not scheduled until at least the following afternoon. He just couldn't help but worry about Mary's welfare and whether she was safe.

Chapter 54

Researching the Research Facility

U.S. Meat Animal Research Center, Nebraska

Janet and Mary looked at each other astounded. To travel all this way and find exactly what they were searching for; only to be confronted by someone who was not prepared to co-operate. But Janet didn't think this was the time to question Harold's motives.

"Harold," Janet said soothingly, "look, you now have nine pairs of willing hands to help you here. You no longer have to do this alone. Is there anything we can do?"

"No, not really." Harold said pondering the question. "All the pens are set up on an automatic feeding system, I just have to ensure all the hoppers are kept full. Which is precisely what I was doing when I saw your jet come in to land."

"Yes, DeVersa said he saw someone or something running into the building." Janet said.

"So, there's nothing we can do?" Mary asked, "because you definitely look as though you could do with a break."

"Well there is one thing. Did you bring any tea with you? I could go a cup of tea." Harold replied.

"I'm sure we can arrange that," Mary said, "how do you like it?"

"Strong, just a little milk, no sugar." Harold replied.

"We know how to make strong tea don't we Mary?" Janet said conspiringly to Mary with a wink of the eye that Harold didn't see.

"No problems." Mary said and left the room.

On her return, Mary was carrying three cups of steaming tea and she put two of them down on one of the desks and the other she gave to Harold. Harold took a sip of the brew and closed his eyes in ecstasy.

"That's a good cuppa," he said and continued to drink while they made small talk. It only took about five minutes for the sedative that Mary had dropped in Harold's tea to take effect.

"That's going to keep him quiet for about five or six hours I should think." Mary said. "God, the poor guy needs it."

"He sure does." Janet agreed but then practicality set in. "We need the men to take a look around to see if there is anything of use other than the animals in this building." Janet said. "You and I can take an inventory of the animals. I'm sure Harold keeps meticulous records, but I'd like to see the livestock for myself and do a head count.

The ladies went downstairs to find the men, leaving a sleeping Harold in the control room. Mary couldn't help but notice a slight grimace appearing on Janet's face every time she took a step down the stairs, but when Mary asked her about it Janet merely waved it off as a slight muscle strain.

They found the men sitting down in a kitchen area enjoying coffee complemented by fresh milk that the establishment had on offer. Janet put forward her plan and everyone agreed, except for DeVersa, who suggested that he stay behind and put together a meal with whatever he could find in the freezer. Nobody objected to that, so everyone had their tasks and they all left DeVersa in the kitchen to do his thing.

Huxley, who hadn't really been brought up to speed with the protocol of Grover's novice Seals, went with the ladies to investigate the pens of livestock. None of the three were by any means experts on farm animals but you didn't have to be to realize that the creatures in the pens were indeed fine beasts. There were various sections in the building, each one holding different species, cattle, horses, sheep, pigs and goats. The first section they inspected was the cattle, which was further divided into three pens each one containing a magnificent bull and three cows. There were two distinct breeds of cattle, the carefully printed labels on the pen differentiated them as Holstein and Angus, one they assumed was dairy the other beef. The next section contained sheep and was divided much the same way, three pens each containing a ram and three ewes. This set-up was repeated in the sections containing the horses, pigs and goats. Beyond those pens were more cows, young calves, mares with foals, more goats with kids, sheep, lambs, pigs and piglets. Janet made careful notes as Mary and Huxley reported the counts of the animal, gender and age, adult or recently born.

By the time Janet and Mary returned to the kitchen area Grover and his team were also returning. Grover reported that there was nothing that they hadn't already seconded back on the islands.

But right now, Janet and Mary were more interested in the aroma from DeVersa's culinary efforts that were overwhelming.

"Whatcha got cooking over there, Peter?" Mary asked him, putting a friendly arm around the shoulders of the chief chef of concoctions.

"Oh, just some kebabs. Pork, beef, lamb. Take your pick." DeVersa replied casually as he continued to toss the contents of the food in the various pans.

"Mary, we better go and check on Harold." Janet said.

"Sure thing." Mary replied.

When they returned to the control room Harold was still lying soundly asleep, so Mary remained behind while Janet went to explore the other facilities on the floor. She soon discovered the labs. where she assumed the ectogenesis experiments had taken place. Then a horrible thought suddenly occurred to her, if, as Harold had said this laboratory was a sealed room, how come he was the only survivor in this establishment? Was he so obsessed about protecting the animals that he would defend them at the expense of the lives of others? Then Janet chillingly realized, she had left Mary all alone in the control room with Harold.

Chapter 55

New Shipmate

Aboard the U.S.S. Augusta

Dancey had spent the night in the sick room under Dennis' supervision and after a shower, a hearty meal and a good night's sleep he had received a clean bill of health. As Giles was the only crew member Dancey had met before he was summoned to bring him up to speed and introduce him to the others.

"So, this troublemaker is fit to stay, I can't kick him off the boat?" Giles jokingly asked on his arrival at the sick-bay.

"Giles, he's had a good hot shower and all he needs is to be around some good company once more." Dennis replied.

"Not much chance of finding that on this tin-can." Giles jokingly replied, "come on Dancey, let's see what we can find." Dancey thanked Dennis and followed Giles out of the sick-bay with a little trepidation, he was not looking forward to meeting his once captives, now that he was to be onboard with them.

While Dancey was being checked out in the sick-bay the previous day, the crewmen he had briefly captured, who were none the worse for wear, had continued loading up emergency rations and a further stockpile of coffee before returning with it to the submarine. Later that evening when they met Giles in the galley they were furious at the treatment they had received from him and were determined to have nothing to do with their new shipmate until they had been informed that the gun Dancey had held contained no bullets. There was a brief silence then they all burst out laughing.

“Guys, he’s a good kid. Don’t be hard on him, he’s been living a hand-to-mouth existence since he jumped ship and hasn’t seen another person in all that time.” Giles said seriously. “So, try and forget what happened yesterday and cut the poor kid some slack eh?” There was a general nodding of heads from the group.

“So why do you call him Dancey?” Dale asked.

“Dancey? That’s the Latino in him, his real name is David Luis and he’s originally from Puerto Rico. He used to sidle down the gangways of the submarine doing his dance moves and couldn’t wait to get ashore and dance with the ladies. Hence, Dancey.” Giles explained.

“Guess he hasn’t been dancing too much lately.” Dale said.

“He will,” Giles replied, “he’ll have old Joan doing the tango at the next party, you mark my words.” The rest all laughed at the thought of Joan and Dancey cavorting around a make shift dance floor back on St. Santia.

As Giles and his ward entered the galley Dancey couldn’t help but notice that it was bereft of anyone except Cook.

“Where is everyone?” Dancey whispered to Giles.

“Let’s grab some nosh first and I’ll explain.” Giles said. “Morning Cook how are you coping?”

"No problems bosun, how are you this fine morning?" Cook replied pleasantly.

"Great, thanks. By the way, this is Dancey, our newest shipmate, although he will probably go aboard the Connecticut when we get back to St. Santia." Giles said, then turning to Dancey, "Dancey this is Cook, he's our cook. I know, it's confusing, isn't it?" "Hi Dancey." Cook said extending his hand. Dancey shook it.

"Hi," Dancey replied, even more confused now as this was the first time he had heard the Connecticut mentioned and that the Augusta was still in contact with it.

"Can I get you anything special Dancey?" Cook asked.

"Er, no thanks what you have here looks great but thanks for asking." Dancey replied, relaxing a little. Giles gave Cook a wink in thanks to the kind-hearted gesture.

Giles chose one of the more secluded tables in the galley and between mouthfuls he explained to Dancey what had transpired since their initial docking in Norfolk immediately after the devastation and what had brought them back to the Naval Yards.

"So, normally, as you see now, we don't operate like a typical navy, but when we are at sea, we revert to our naval training and disciplines." Giles explained, "so, you are going to have to make a decision, you have a choice of staying in Bermuda, St. Santia, the Augusta or the Connecticut. Or wherever you would like. But remember no decision is final, you can move around whenever you like, subject to transportation."

Dancey thought about this for a moment before replying. "I would like to visit Puerto Rico once more and see my home town." Dancey said sadly.

"Son, you must have seen the results of what happened when you travelled around before we picked you up. Trust me, it would be no different back home." Giles replied with not a little compassion. It brought tears to Dancey's eyes as he stared into his coffee and he didn't say anything for a few moments and neither did Giles.

"Didn't you mention that the families were going to need help setting up power and the such?" Dancey questioned.

"That I did." Giles replied, "that I did."

Chapter 56

Arrangements Agreed

U.S. Meat Animal Research Center, Nebraska

Janet burst into the control room fully prepared to scream for help and defend Mary, but instead, she was astounded to see Harold sitting up on his cot drinking from a bottle of water while Mary was still sitting exactly where she was when Janet had left just a few minutes earlier.

"Good Lord Janet, whatever is wrong?" Mary said quite alarmed and rose, ready to react to some impending danger.

"Oh Harold, you're awake!" Janet said trying to regain both her breath and her composure.

"Yes, I am. Despite the 'Mickey Finn' you laced my tea with. But as Mary explained I needed that and I tend to agree, I feel all the better for it." Harold replied cheerfully.

"I see," was all Janet could reply.

"Oh, wait a minute. Were you concerned about leaving this beautiful young lady alone in a room with a sex-starved crazy man?" Harold asked jokingly.

"Something like that." Janet replied, trying to mask her true concerns

"Well worry not," Harold replied, "certified asexual, that's why my employers love me. Throw myself into my work you see."

Although the man's current demeanor belied any aggressive tendencies Janet was still concerned.
"I was just looking at the laboratories, they are all sealed too aren't they?" Janet asked innocuously.
"Yes, tight as a drum." Harold replied, before taking another sip of water.
"So, what I don't understand is how come you are the only survivor?" Janet asked.
"I told you, the birth of the calf is the reason I was here, took place during the early hours of the morning. I was waiting for people to arrive to give them the good news, but nobody showed up. Normally, people would start drifting in around 7:00 AM." Harold replied matter-of-factly. "By the way, what is that smell?" The aromas of DeVersa's cooking had finally reached the control room.
"Our pilot also just happens to be a great chef, he's cooking up a storm down there." Mary said.
"I think it might just about be ready. Shall we go to dinner?" Janet said, somewhat calmer now that she had been satisfied with Harold's answer.

During a scrumptious dinner, Harold's first since the devastation, he learnt all about the two fledgling communities, on St. Santia and Bermuda, and the preparations that were being worked on to help with the survival of the next generation. At the end of the meal, during a lull in the conversation, Janet thought it was time to put forward her plan.

“Harold, you have been stuck here all by yourself for all this time, don’t you think it is due to move the operation to a place that has a nicer climate where you can get all the help you need?” Janet asked.

“Sounds tempting but I don’t see how that is possible.” Harold replied but Janet was prepared.

“While you were sleeping I did a head count, I bet you that Peter could find a suitable plane to transport the animals to the islands.” Janet said while DeVersa looked questioningly at her, this was the first he had heard of such a plan.

“Out of the question,” Harold replied emphatically, “absolutely not. If the plane went down we’d have nothing. All the effort rearing these beautiful animals wasted. No, I can’t allow it.”

“That’s why we could make three trips.” Janet countered. “A third of the breeding stock of each species of the animals to St. Santia, while the remainder stay here. On Peter’s successful return, the next batch to Bermuda and finally, the rest of the animals to St. Santia to a different farm. You can choose to travel with them or remain here. It’s a win, win situation for everyone Harold.”

“You would have help Harold,” Mary added, “you wouldn’t be trying to eke out an existence in a cold climate trying to forage for food.”

“I don’t know, such a risk.” Harold countered.

“Then think of the children Harold, the future generation of mankind.” Janet said. But nothing seemed to sway the obstinate

Englishman until an innocuous statement was uttered by Stenich, who like the others had been silent during this verbal battle.

"It would be great to get back to doing some farmyard chores again." Stenich said out loud, although it was more reminiscing than anything.

"Do you have farming experience?" Harold asked casually.

"Are you kidding me?" Stenich replied totally askance, "I'm from Minnesota, until I joined the navy that was the only experience I'd had."

"Well then." Harold said slapping the table with his right hand, "that's settled, when do we start?"

Chapter 57

Anxiously Waiting

Aboard the U.S.S. Augusta

Once Dennis had dispatched his only patient he did a quick inventory to see if there were any supplies he should think about obtaining before donning his duffel and joining Jason in the conning tower. As expected, Jason was once more searching the skies in anticipation of DeVersa's return in the jet.

"You know it is far too early for their return. I don't think you should expect them until well after lunch." Dennis said calmly.

"I know, I know," Jason replied.

"Doctor's orders, let's go inside and grab a bite to eat." Dennis said. "Come on." Jason, gave a resigned smile and followed his friend down the steps. When they entered the galley, they were pleased to see that the newbie, with Giles by his side, was laughing and joking with some of the crew. Salutations were made as the two officers selected some breakfast and found a vacant table.

"Good to see Dancey settling in." Dennis remarked.

"He certainly is, he looks 100% better than he did when he first came on board." Jason said.

"Yes, complete isolation from people can have a funny effect on people but I think he is going to be O.K." Dennis said. The conversation during the rest of the meal was just punctuated with generalities of no real consequence.

"Need to get back topside to see if there's any activity." Jason said as he began to rise from the table.

"No, you don't, stay where you are." Dennis demanded. Then he looked over to Giles.

"Giles, could you arrange a shift to man the conning tower. We're expecting the jet back anytime." Dennis said.

"On it." Giles immediately replied. "Right Dancey, time to earn your daily bread. You and I will take the first shift. Dale, Lester you relieve us at 11:00 hours. Got it?"

"Right bosun." They both said in unison, albeit with a great deal of feigned resignation.

During their shift in the conning tower, Dancey probed Giles with questions about the families on St. Santia and the men on Bermuda. A couple of times, Giles returned to the galley for coffee and muffins. Dancey appeared to be fine and enjoying the art of conversation again, more like the Dancey Giles remembered.

Dale and Lester arrived to relieve Giles and Dancey while the next shift would be scheduled for three hours later, although as it happened, it wasn't necessary as the jet was sighted at 12:50. Word was passed down to Jason who was visibly relieved, and the boat's crew prepared to go topside to welcome back the travelers. Eventually, a jeep could be seen heading through the gates and making a beeline for the Augusta, although, the crew were surprised and concerned to see only two members of the team returning, DeVersa and Huxley. But when they got out of the jeep they went to the back and emerged with a very large cooler. They were both smiling and DeVersa was almost buoyant with excitement as they crossed the gangplank, even though they were struggling with the weight of the cooler. They headed directly to Jason, who was accompanied by Dennis and Giles and plonked the cooler down on the hull of the submarine.

"Great news sir." DeVersa said positively gushing. "We don't have to leave the ladies behind at all, well not for long anyway. The center was housing live animals in a climate-controlled building that had protected them from the devastation. Cattle, horses, pigs, sheep and goats. All perfect specimens."

"We've brought some meat back with us," Huxley added, pointing to the cooler.

"But how did the animals survive the devastation if they were stuck in a building?" Dennis questioned.

"There was a guy handling the birth of a calf at the time the bugs struck so he also survived, and he's been managing the place ever since." DeVersa explained, "poor guy was at the end of his tether when we arrived, not sure how much longer he could have carried on single-handedly."

"So, why aren't the ladies and Grover's team with you now?" Jason asked, looking a little perplexed.

"Sorry sir, here's the plan." DeVersa took a breath and slowed down a little, he realized that he wasn't explaining himself very well. "Better yet, Huxley, you tell them." Huxley stepped forward.

"Sir, after negotiations with the gentleman manning the center, Sir Harold Fletcher, it has been agreed that we will fly a third of the animals to St. Santia, then a third of the animals will be flown to Bermuda, accompanied by Sir Harold. He will ensure the facilities are adequate and that the necessary, trained personnel are available to tend the animals. He will then return to the Clay center and fly with the remaining animals to St. Santia, with, of course, the ladies and Grover's team, who will be staying behind to help take care of the animals at the Clay center. Sir Harold will then set up house on St. Santia to manage the animals' welfare." Huxley took a deep breath, pleased with himself for providing the explanation without a stutter, but he still wasn't quite finished.

"It is expected that it would probably take about ten days for Peter to find suitable transportation and for Grover's team to modify said transportation to accommodate the animals. What Janet has asked us to ask you was that in the meantime, could you poll personnel at both locations, St. Santia and Bermuda, for people with any farming skills who are prepared to help take care of the livestock and to arrange work groups to prepare for the arrival of the animals." Huxley said and then backed away to stand behind DeVersa, knowing that Jason had never liked being told what to do by Janet.

"One other thing sir," DeVersa added sheepishly, "it would be appreciated if you could make sure the airports at Bermuda and St. Santia are clear of any obstructions for our landings."

Jason's reaction was quite the contrary to expectation, first of all, he was relieved that everyone, especially Mary, was still safe and that they would be returning to St. Santia in a matter of days rather than months. Furthermore, their objective had been met and livestock would be flourishing on the two islands.

"That's great news. So, we could aim to set sail at 20:00 hours this evening. Unless of course, you need us to remain here for a day or two while you find an appropriate plane Peter?"

"No sir, I know exactly what I need and where I can find it, thank you." Peter replied.

"I thought you might." Jason smiled.

"All we need are a few provisions for overnight and a couple of generators, just in case we have to recharge a battery or two. Oh, and if you don't mind, I think we have time to just get a shower and some chow then we will be out of your hair." DeVersa added.

"Of course, have at it." Jason said, then he went to the conning tower to address the crew. "All hands report to your stations, we will be leaving for Bermuda at 20:00, estimated time of arrival 08:00 day after tomorrow. By the way, if there is anyone on board with any farming experience please make yourself known to bosun Giles."

Jason proceeded to the control room to oversee the preparations for their departure and once satisfied everything was in hand he went to seek out DeVersa. He entered the galley to find it deserted, except for Huxley, who was avidly tucking into a large pork chop with all the trimmings. This surprised Jason as he thought there would have been plenty of time for DeVersa to shower in the meantime. Then he heard voices coming from the kitchen and realized that DeVersa was probably checking up on Cook, he hoped he was not chewing out the poor lad because he had done a terrific job during DeVersa's absence. Fortunately, DeVersa was helping Cook update the inventory with the cooler of meat they had just brought onboard, less one pork chop that Huxley was now devouring. When they saw Jason enter the kitchen they both looked up from the clipboard where they were annotating their inventory.

"Oh, hello sir." DeVersa said, "good job Cook, just finish up here, I'm proud of you, well done." With a pat on the back of the beaming young cook, DeVersa left the kitchen with Jason and went to join Huxley in the galley.

"So, Peter, I just want to home in on a specific timeline, so that I know when we have to be ready for your arrival."

"Sure." DeVersa replied, as they both began to walk into the galley's eating area.

"So, let's say to-day is day 1. Bearing in mind that we must travel first to Bermuda, stay there a couple of days and then set sail to St. Santia. When should we expect your arrival on St. Santia?" Jason asked. DeVersa gave it some thought and after using his fingers to assist in his calculations he arrived at his answer.

"Day 12 at approximately 14:00 hours St. Santia time." DeVersa replied confidently. "Could be a little earlier or a little later depending on the weather conditions." Jason didn't question the former pilot's reckonings.

"Excellent, then that should give us plenty of time to check the runways and prepare pens for the animals on one of the nearby farms." Jason replied. "Once we are in Bermuda we could radio St. Santia to get Sheldrake's men on the case. Where are you hoping to find a suitable aircraft?"

"Langley Air Force base, I'm sure they will have what I am looking for there, it's only a couple of hours away, subject to clear roads." Then tipping his head towards Huxley, "as soon as this glutton has finished feeding his face perhaps we could set out and arrive before it gets dark." Huxley was indeed masticating the last morsel from his plate and he smiled as the others laughed.

"Take care and drive carefully." Jason said as he stood and left the two men.

Thirty minutes later, Peter and Huxley were driving away from the Augusta serenaded by a couple of 'whoops' from the submarine's sirens. Jason was looking on in trepidation, the plan sounded all too simple, far too simple.

Chapter 58

Farm Hand Training

U.S. Meat Animal Research Center, Nebraska

The evening before DeVersa and Huxley left for their return to the Augusta a chain-gang was set up to off-load all the rations from the Citation to a temporary warehouse. The next morning, everyone, including Harold, rose early to see DeVersa and Huxley take-off to report back to the Augusta. Once the duo was airborne and heading out of sight it was time for Sir Harold to introduce his new farm-hands to the workings of the facility. Harold gave the group a tour of the barns and the feed-room where all the food was kept and introduced them to the schedule that had to be maintained to provide the animals with the correct amount of fodder and vitamins. There were also troughs of water that were kept full by gravity-fed systems. However, originally, the troughs had been attached to the mains water supply which had stopped working a few weeks after the devastation. So, Harold had procured a couple of water bowsers and through a series of attachments connected them to the water-feeders. As the bowser that was attached to the feeder got close to being empty, he would switch lines to the other one. Once one bowser was empty Harold would then drive it to a nearby lake to replenish the water. Sometimes, he was forced to break the ice on the lake and drop a line into the icy water to draw out the precious liquid. Harold would then return to

the facility with the bowser full of water, this laborious exercise had to be repeated twice a week.
“What you’ve accomplished here Harold is nothing short of amazing.” Janet said sincerely.
“It’s certainly kept me busy.” Harold acknowledged.

As they neared the cattle pens one of the cows began to moo at their approach. in expectation.
“Ah, it’s time for Daisy to be milked, isn’t it?” Harold said to the cow and patted her lovingly on its muzzle. “Right then Stenich, your first task, no automatic milking machines here, it’s all manual, there’s a pail.” Harold said, pointing to a clean bucket by the gate. Much to the Augusta’s crew surprise, Stenich calmly picked up the bucket, slowly opened the pen’s gate, closing the gate behind him and went towards Daisy to begin milking.
“What about the bull?” Mary said in alarm.
“No, we don’t milk the bull.” Harold said, laughing at his own joke.
“No, silly, I mean his presence in the pen.” Mary said, still somewhat concerned for Stenich’s safety.
“What JoJo? That pussycat!” Harold responded. “He’s used to seeing his girlfriend being milked aren’t you JoJo?” The bull turned to look at Harold as if he recognized his name being called, then turned his attention back to the feeder.
“Aren’t bulls ferocious and dangerous?” Mary asked, still concerned about Stenich being alone in the pen with such a large animal.

"Can be," Harold answered, "as they get older they can become more aggressive, but I've known this bull since he was a calve and as long as you are not threatening they tend to be docile. But, never let your guard down and as you can see Stenich is facing the bull, just in case."

"So, these black and white cows are Holsteins?" Janet asked, recalling her notes, "bred for dairy production?"

"That's correct," Harold replied, "over there are the Aberdeen Black Angus which are more muscular and bred for beef production. Proud to say that my old work place, Guelph University, was the site of the first Angus to be born outside Scotland."

"Couldn't you use the same breed for both dairy and beef?" Grover asked.

"Yes, you could." Harold replied, but quantity and quality would suffer. Because the Holstein is not as muscular as the Angus the quality of meat would be inferior and tough. As for the milk, the Angus usually only produces what it needs for its calf, so you would lose quantity." Grover nodded at the explanation.

About twenty minutes later the group had finished walking up and down the pens while Stenich had filled the pail with fresh milk, courtesy of Daisy.

"What do you normally do with the milk?" Stenich asked.

"Done already?" Harold said surprised, "I really thought it would have taken you longer than that."

"Told you, I'm from good farming stock." Stenich replied proudly.

"Well normally I keep a little of it and throw away the rest but now I have guests. I guess you should pour it into some clean bottles and take it to the kitchen."

"Sure thing." Stenich replied.

"Don't forget to clean-" Harold wasn't given the chance to finish his sentence.

"The bucket, yea I know." Stenich interrupted him but Harold was smiling, beginning to warm to his new help.

"How often do you have to milk the cows?" Mary asked.

"About two or three times a day." Harold replied casually.

"Where have you found the time to do all this by yourself, Harold?" You must be exhausted." Janet remarked.

"I hadn't really thought about it until now, but I have to admit, the more I think about splitting up the responsibilities the more I relish the idea." Harold said with a smile.

"Once I've bottled the milk would you like me to milk the other cows?" Stenich asked.

"Would you be so kind?" Harold replied gratefully.

"My pleasure." Stenich replied with enthusiasm.

"Harold, perhaps we should talk about your schedule and see what we can do to help you with your chores." Janet suggested, "why don't we return to the kitchen and discuss it."

Chapter 59

Finding a Plane

Langley Air Force Base Virginia

Under normal circumstances, DeVersa knew the trip from the Naval Yards to Langley would take approximately 45 minutes but of course these were no longer normal circumstances. Even so, they were making excellent time until they entered the Hampton Roads Bridge-Tunnel. There were a number of cars blocking their route, most of them they could butt out of the way, the others, they were forced to utilize the winch on the front of their vehicle to pull clear and create a path. Nevertheless, they were able to reach Langley at dusk and DeVersa headed for the biggest hangar on the base. He knew from past experience that the Coast Guard always had a plane fully prepared for takeoff at a moment's notice.

As they approached the giant doors of the hangar DeVersa was most interested in, he was pleased to see that, as expected, they were closed. DeVersa parked their truck beside a Judas door in one of the main doors and shut down the engine. DeVersa rummaged in the back of the truck for a flashlight and left the vehicle, followed, like an obedient puppy, by Huxley. The small door was unlocked so they entered into what was now, with the ebbing of the last streams of daylight, a dark abyss. DeVersa shone his flashlight onto the hulk of a huge plane and he smiled.

"Just what the doctor ordered." DeVersa said.
"What is it?" Huxley asked.
"That lad, is a Hercules CC-130, in my opinion, the finest cargo plane in the world." DeVersa replied with pride.
"Have you thought about where you are going to land that giant in Clay, Peter?" Huxley asked.
"Yee of little faith." DeVersa replied derisively, "you can land that baby on a dime, they used to land them on aircraft carriers. It will land on the same road we landed the Cessna."
"On the road? Peter, you're kidding me aren't your?" Huxley said disbelievingly.
"Nah, these things are designed to land on all sorts terrains. Sure, it might need a bit more tarmac to take-off but it's a nice straight road there in Clay, won't be a problem." DeVersa said confidently.
"O.K. There's no more we can do to-night. Why don't we bring our stuff onto the plane, check out battery power, have a snack and bed down for the night for an early start in the morning?" DeVersa smiled and patted Huxley on the back.
"Sure thing boss." Huxley replied and with his flashlight made a beeline back through the door back to the truck to begin bringing in their things.

Fifteen minutes later, DeVersa was in the cockpit checking out the controls and the plane's data, while Huxley, was making a couple of sandwiches in the vast expanse of the plane's cargo bay using the light being provided by the generator. DeVersa discovered the plane had extended fuel tanks and they were full. There was also enough battery power to be able to start the engines so that was about as much as he could achieve in the fading light, he would have to do a full walk around of the plane in the full light of day. For now, he was content to join Huxley, have a bite to eat and settle down to sleep on one of the cots that were stored in the frame of the cargo area.

Huxley had heard the history about DeVersa and how he had gone on a bender where he went from being a flying instructor, to the stockade, then a submarine's cook. What he didn't know about was his flying experiences and how many times he had flown a Hercules before.

"So, Peter, did you enjoy flying these cargo planes rather than a jet or a chopper?" Huxley asked casually between mouthfuls of a peanut and jelly sandwich. DeVersa's reply was equally as casual.

"I'll let you know tomorrow – I've never flown one before."

Chapter 60

Arrival at Bermuda

Bermuda

The Augusta had set sail promptly at 20:00 and after an uneventful journey they arrived back in Bermuda, as scheduled, at 08:00 some 36 hours later. A few of the Bermuda contingent were up and about to greet them and to assist with the docking. Just before everyone began to embark, Jason asked Dave, one of the Bermuda residents, to arrange for everyone to meet at the Happy Mariner at noon. Jason needed to discuss work parties and ask whether any of the submariners had any previous farming experience. Tony was standing beside Dave and agreed to give him a hand. Meanwhile, Jason had to figure out how he was going to house the new family on the return trip to St. Santia, assuming they still planned to travel with them. Although, it wouldn't be the first time the Augusta had had an infant on board, Jason smiled at the recollection of baby Augusta's birth onboard the submarine. Jason then went to the radio room to ask Sparks to radio the Connecticut to begin organizing the clearing of the airfield there and ask what farming experience any of the crew or residents have. They would also need to find two suitable venues for livestock. Our ETA is 08:00 hours four days hence. Sparks looked up at Jason, a look of disappointment on his face.

"I thought we were going to spend a few days here in Bermuda?" Sparks asked.

"We were, but we have a new challenge, we have to prepare for the animals." Jason explained but sharing empathy with Sparks, "don't worry, you'll still get a couple of days here and there'll be plenty more opportunities to goof off in Bermuda." Sparks shrugged his shoulders and began to send the message.

At noon all the Bermuda inhabitants were in attendance at the Happy Mariner. Jason had already spoken to Ivan and Amy, they had confirmed they would be making the trip to St. Santia to be with the other families. Consequently, Jason passed the news onto Giles to make arrangements for the cabins that Janet and Mary had been using to be prepared for the threesome from space. Amy also felt she needed to explain her relationship with Ivan and the uncomfortable situation that had arisen with Moose but stressed she didn't want any disciplinary action taken. After all, they would soon be heading to St. Santia and Moose would be remaining on Bermuda.

At the meeting, Jason explained what had been discovered in Nebraska and outlined the plans to bring the livestock from Clay to the two Atlantic locations. Jason also explained what had to be carried out to facilitate the moves.

"Now, the big question is, who amongst you are prepared to help out with the managing of the livestock here on Bermuda?" Jason asked. Jason was pleasantly surprised to see that just about everyone had their hands up. Moxley of course, hadn't raised his hand but that was understandable, someone had to run the bar.

"How many of you have farming experience?" This time the number of hands diminished considerably but some of the sailors still had their hands in the air. Amongst them were Moose, Dutch and surprisingly, Ivan. Jason asked about their expertise and indeed a couple of the men came from farming families and felt quite confident that between them they could handle the number of livestock that was being delivered to Bermuda, with the help of some trainee farm-hands of course.

"Dutch, do you think you could manage the farm hands and all the livestock here in Bermuda?" Jason asked.

"My name is DeBoer, it's Dutch for farmer. Yes, I could handle it." Dutch confidently replied.

"If that is the case," Moose began, "considering you will have two thirds of the livestock on St. Santia, and Ivan may be busy with medical concerns why don't I move there to help him out?"

Chapter 61

Flying to Clay

Langley Air Force Base Virginia

"That's a good one Peter!" Huxley said laughing.

"No, I'm serious. Never flown a Hercules before." DeVersa replied deadpan, tucking into his sandwich. "Tried it on a simulator a couple of times though." Huxley was just about to take another bite of his sandwich and he stopped, a look of panic came over his face.

"You're not joking, are you? You've never flown one of these before?" Huxley barely whispered.

"Relax, it's just another prop. plane, a big one mind you, but don't worry, we'll be fine." DeVersa said, perfectly relaxed as he took another bite of his sandwich.

Once DeVersa had finished his snack, he began to read through the plane's handbook that he had brought from the cockpit, carefully noting, amongst other data, take-off and landing speeds. Huxley couldn't eat another thing he was so tense with worry, so he nervously watched as DeVersa scanned through the pages. DeVersa was turning the pages as if he had a photographic memory but the reality was he was only looking for the more salient points. With an empty plane, weight and balance calculations were a non-starter so he skipped those references although he would certainly need them on the flight to the islands with the livestock. Once he reached the last page of the manual, he rose and went to the cockpit to return the handbook to its rightful place.

"Come on then. Let's set up these beds and get a good night's sleep for an early start in the morning, the first thing we will have to do is open those hangar doors." DeVersa suggested, but poor Huxley was still in a state of shock. Although, he went through the motions of setting up his cot, he certainly wouldn't get much sleep that night.

The next morning, DeVersa awoke to find Huxley had already prepared coffee and some cereal for breakfast. It still wasn't light outside but once they had eaten, DeVersa left the plane, closely followed by Huxley carrying the generator, to find the electrical control panel for the hangar doors. Unlike the hangar doors they had opened for the Cessna it was doubtful that the two of them could manually open the massive doors of this building. DeVersa found the appropriate electrical boxes by flashlight, then, it was easy for him to rig up power with the generator and once Huxley started the generator, DeVersa flicked the switches. There was a hum of motors and the big doors began to slowly open.

In the hangar there was also a small tanker used for refueling planes, DeVersa walked over to it and checked the contents of the tank. The tanker was full of aviation fuel so DeVersa decided he was going to take that with them too, it would solve some serious fueling logistics. Now, of course he would have to do some rough weight and balance calculations for take-off, but he wasn't too concerned about those.

Once the hangar doors were fully open, DeVersa had Huxley switch off the generator, then he reverse-engineered his wiring and asked Huxley to take the generator over to the tanker. "Hux, good buddy, you may need the generator on the battery in this tanker, we're taking it with us. Once we can start it we will drive it into the hold of the plane." DeVersa told the young man, "oh and don't get close to the plane, I'm taking her out O.K.?" DeVersa continued, Huxley merely nodded and continued with his task. DeVersa thought the kid was being decidedly quiet this morning.

DeVersa reached the cockpit, relaxed and began to proceed through the pilot's checklist. As DeVersa expected, everything was straightforward and before he knew it the plane was outside the hangar just as the sun was beginning to appear on the horizon. DeVersa pressed the switch to open the doors at the rear of the plane and the ramp proceeded to drop down. DeVersa made sure the plane was going nowhere and went to the rear of the plane to supervise the loading of the tanker. Huxley started the engine of the tanker, once the engine sounded steady he exited to store the generator in the passenger's side of the cab. Returning to the driver's side, he proceeded to negotiate the truck up the ramp to the cavernous cargo area of the plane. Once in the plane, the truck's engine was switched off, DeVersa and Huxley carefully secured the truck with straps. Satisfied that the truck was secure, DeVersa proceeded towards the cockpit while Huxley returned to the bottom of the ramp. DeVersa had almost reached the cockpit when he realized Huxley was not following him, so he stopped and turned to look back at him.

"Something wrong lad?" DeVersa asked with some concern.

"Sorry Pete, but you've never flown one of these before. I'm not sure I can come with you." Huxley said sheepishly.

"Is that what's bothering you?" DeVersa said and laughed. "Well look, here's the deal, we said we were leaving at first light, which is now. So, you can either come with me or drive yourself back to Norfolk and wait for a pick-up. I expect one of the submarines is scheduled to visit in, oh about six months. Your choice." Huxley looked a little dumbfounded at this ultimatum. "Huxley, you weren't concerned when you flew with me in the Cessna were you?" DeVersa asked.

"No, of course not." Huxley replied and was about to say something else when DeVersa continued, still laughing.

"Well, I hadn't flown one of those before either.

Chapter 62

Discussions at the Happy Mariner

Bermuda

Moose's remark had caught Jason off-guard and he could tell by the look on Amy's face, who was now looking directly at him in a pleading sort of way, she didn't want his presence on St. Santia to happen.

"I think I have a better plan, Moose," Jason replied, thinking quickly, "my understanding is that Sir Harold will be using St. Santia as his base so it might be a great idea if you worked with Dutch to be his conduit here. Ivan will need to be on St. Santia with his family, so it makes sense for you to continue to remain here." Jason had no idea where Harold was going to live but it was the best counter argument he could come up with. It was certainly enough to curtail any further discussion with Moose, who returned in a huff to the bar for another beer.

"Right then, work parties, initially, we'll need two," Jason continued, addressing the whole crowd once more, "one," as he held up his index finger, "to clear the runways at the airport and two," holding up another finger, "to find a farm and prepare for the arrival of the animals. Dave, why don't you organize the airport clean-up crew and Moose, you're in charge of the farm team. Any questions?" At this last statement Moose stood upright and his chest puffed out, Jason felt the man needed a project to take his mind off Amy and a sense of responsibility was exactly what was required.

"Yes, there's just one thing," Dave said, "the airport is about as far away as we could possibly be on this island. At least an hour there and back each day. I suggest we find somewhere to billet on site until we have ensured the runways are clear."

"Anybody have any objections?" Jason asked as he looked around the room. "What about a farm, do we have the same logistical problem?"

"No. There's a farm not twenty minutes away." Moose replied, "I think there are a few remains that will have to be cleared but I think the biggest problem will be providing sufficient amounts of water for the animals. There is no main water supply on Bermuda, they rely on harvesting water from the rooves of houses. Although, the farms have been there for centuries, they may already have adequate storage facilities."

"But what if they haven't?" Jason asked, "could we tap into some wells?"

"Bermuda has no underwater wells, no rivers, streams or lakes to draw from, that's why the residents used to rely on collecting rainwater and storing them in tanks." Dutch explained. "At worst, we may need to set up some piping to draw in sufficient water from other houses."

"Do we have the expertise to do that here?" Jason asked, suddenly getting a little concerned.

“With all due respects sir, that’s a daft question.” Moxley chirped in, “nearly all of us here are submariners, if there is none amongst us who can’t fit a pipe we don’t deserve to survive.” At that remark everyone burst out laughing as Moxley continued to dry some glasses like a typical barman.

With the meeting over, the men divided themselves into two groups to begin planning their ventures. Jason was just about to walk over to join Dennis and the space family, who had now moved outside to the patio, when his advance was blocked by Tony.

“Hi Tony, what’s up?” Jason asked.

“Nothing really,” Tony replied, although his demeanor said otherwise, as he looked downwards and wouldn’t look directly at Jason.

“It’s about the return trip to St. Santia,” Tony said sheepishly, “I won’t be joining you. I am going to remain here, on Bermuda.”

Chapter 63

Hercules Arrival at Clay

U.S. Meat Animal Research Center, Nebraska

DeVersa continued walking up the steps into the plane. Huxley hesitated for a moment then followed his mentor up the steps with a few grumbling words as he did so. They made their way into the cockpit where DeVersa raised the ramp and closed all doors to secure the plane. DeVersa began to read each item from the checklist that had been secured to the sun visor on the pilot's side by an elastic band. With each item, DeVersa familiarized himself with the piece of equipment or control it was referring to. Finally, DeVersa asked Huxley to go and double-check that everything was secure in the cargo area, he didn't want things moving around in flight. Huxley dutifully did as he was told as DeVersa did another pass of the checklist.

"Alrighty then." DeVersa said, on Huxley's return and he quickly thrust the checklist into a surprised Huxley's unsuspecting hands. "Put on your headset and start reading the list, just as you did when we took off in the Cessna." A bewildered Huxley forgot his nervousness, he donned the headset and began to read the first line of the checklist and continued with every response of 'check' from DeVersa. Before you knew it, the giant aircraft was crawling out of the hangar towards the airfield. As the first vestiges of light began to appear on the horizon, DeVersa passed Huxley a chart with their intended route already marked out.

"Same again, once we takeoff I have to make a slight bearing to 270 degrees, the trip is straight west, should be uneventful. Copy?" DeVersa asked calmly.

"Copy." Huxley replied and sat back in the seat as the huge plane began to surge forward.

Much to Huxley's relief, DeVersa was correct. Except for some turbulence here and there, the flight was indeed uneventful, and they touched down safely on the road beside the Research center. Just like DeVersa said he would.

Graneski was the first one to greet them but the others were not far behind him to see the huge plane. Grover, of course, had parachuted from a Hercules during exercises so he was familiar with the aircraft. Eventually, Harold and the ladies arrived and DeVersa provided them with a quick tour making suggestions as to how they should sectionalize the pens using the structural ribs inside the cargo bay. DeVersa provided them with the timeline that had been agreed with Jason.

"So, that means we have nine full days to prepare pens in the plane. Does that give us enough time?" Janet said to nobody in particular.

"Absolutely," Harold replied emphatically. "We have, stored in that barn over there, plenty of pre-fabricated fencing. All we need to do is build the pens in the plane. It will require lots of sawing and hammering but I'm sure we can do it. Pity we can't use the power tools though."

"Why can't we use the power tools?" Huxley asked.

"We don't have any spare generators." Harold replied, "they're all being used to look after the animals."

"We have a generator." Huxley said matter-of-factly.

"Well there you are then." Fletcher's eyes beamed, "We just have to design and measure, then we can get started."

For the remainder of the day, Harold worked with the ladies and Grover to design the pens and decide upon the size of the area required to accommodate foodstuff and sufficient water for the trip. Harold decided to add a mild sedative to the animal's food to help relax them during the trip to St. Santia which was expected to take approximately five hours. During the next few days, Harold determined which animals would be making the trip while Grover's team worked on building the pens and fixing them up in the plane, under DeVersa's supervision. It had been decided that Harold would indeed accompany the animals while the ladies and Stenich would remain behind to care for the remaining livestock at the center. Harold was satisfied that Stenich, under his tutelage, had learnt enough to handle everything for the few days he would be away.

Eventually, departure day arrived, the pens had been installed, spare food and water had been loaded onto the plane, so, it was just a matter of herding the animals up the ramp into their selected sections. For this, the team had jerry-rigged a pathway that led to the ramp with ropes and spare fence pieces. They would only be loading a few animals at a time, so it would be relatively easy for them to shepherd the animals along the path. They loaded the animals one genre at a time with Harold leading each male of the species along the pathway with the rest of the family following behind, urged on by Stenich. Once the last of the livestock was loaded and the pens secure they loaded half of the rations they had brought with them on the Citation, the other half would be delivered to Bermuda next trip. Then, it was just a matter of raising the ramp of the Hercules and taking off. For that of course, they needed DeVersa, who had been seconded by Harold to drive into the town of Hastings to fetch some extra syringes from the pharmacy located there. While they were waiting for DeVersa's return, Harold inspected the security of the pens one last time and checked on the animals' welfare, satisfied, he joined the others on the roadway as they waited for DeVersa's return.

It must have been an hour later with still no sign of DeVersa, that Huxley suggested he should drive into town to see if DeVersa had encountered a problem. Grover, agreed to accompany him and as the journey should only take them an hour at the most, to get there and back, everyone remained on standby, however, Harold's optimism about the merits of the project was beginning to wane.

Chapter 64

Augusta's Arrival at St. Santia

St. Santia

In anticipation of the Augusta's arrival, Sheldrake had moored the Connecticut away from Jason's preferred docking on the jetty. As the Augusta burst through the waves about a mile shy off the jetty, a welcoming whoop emitted from the klaxon of the Connecticut. This was the signal for the crew of the Connecticut to scramble to their various forms of transport that were moored to the submarine to head for the beach to become a welcoming committee. It was also the signal for the families on the island to walk down the hill to welcome the new members of their community.

Many of the Connecticut's crew were on the jetty to assist with the mooring of the Augusta and once Jason, Dennis and Giles had walked down the gangplank they turned and waited for the family of Amy, Ivan and Mir to leave the vessel. Word hadn't yet reached St. Santia regarding the status of Amy and Ivan so when they walked along the jetty, smiling and waving in response to the applause they were receiving, it wasn't apparent to anyone on the beach that they were not an actual couple. Needless to say, Amy, who was carrying Mir, made a beeline for the awaiting ladies and the children. Mir's eyes lit up at the sight of the other toddlers and while the families were getting acquainted with each other, it was the turn of the crew members to exit the submarine. All this time,

Marlene kept glancing over at the jetty in anticipation of Tony's return.

"Daddy will be here soon Augusta, don't worry." Marlene cooed to her daughter. But, as the number of seaman leaving the submarine reduced to a trickle with still no sign of Tony, a bad feeling began to develop in the pit of her stomach. That bad feeling was accentuated when a smiling Jason approached Marlene's group and bypassed the others to talk specifically to her.

"Do you have a minute Marlene?" Jason asked cordially.

"Sure. "Marlene replied, but she had sensed what he was about to tell her. As they moved out of air shot of the group, Jason's face turned from a picture of happiness to a mask of seriousness.

"Look Marlene, I don't quite know how to tell you this, so I will just come straight out and say it." Jason said, looking directly into Marlene's eyes. "Tony decided to remain on Bermuda, he didn't give me a reason why and I didn't ask. Frankly, it's none of my business. I'm so sorry."

"Oh, don't be." Marlene replied trying to put on a brave smile. "Had he have returned here it may have made things even more difficult. At least this way it is final, out of sight out of mind as they say."

"You don't seem too surprised." Jason said a little perplexed.

"No. It was coming, I expect he met someone during the trip." Marlene said, confusing Jason even more, as with the exception of Amy there were certainly no women he could possibly have met.

"It's complicated." Marlene replied in response to Jason's confused expression.

"Will you be O.K.? Do you want me to tell Maria?" Jason asked with some concern.

"No, no, no. I'll be fine." Said Marlene, as a tear began to roll down her cheek belying her true feelings.

"Would you like me to escort you home?" Jason asked tenderly. Marlene thought for a minute as she bit her lower lip.

"You know," Marlene finally answered, "that might be a good idea. Thanks. When you get back maybe you can also apologize to our new guests for my premature departure."

"Of course I will." Jason said quietly, then they both began walking towards Marlene's house.

Maria had watched the verbal exchange between Jason and Marlene; and as they began to head for Marlene's house she was about to run over to her when she felt a hand on her arm gently restraining her.

"I don't think Tony has returned." Joanne whispered in her ear. "Let her be for a bit." Subconsciously, Maria began to search around for Tony and indeed she could see no sign of him. Then she noticed Augusta's baby-buggy that Marlene had left behind. By now baby-swapping was in full swing and Amy now had hold of Bob and Maria's baby, Joanne was holding Mir and the other little loves were crawling around the many feet forming the group.

"You haven't decided on a name for him yet?" Amy asked, as she was smiling at the baby boy.

"No, not yet." Bob replied as Maria was a little distracted by Marlene's departure with Jason, "we've been too busy, what with one thing and another."

"Oh, look, Marlene has had to return home for some reason, but she has left her push-chair behind." Maria said, and she was about to grab it when Ivan took charge.

"Let me please." Ivan said as he effortlessly picked up the push-chair. "I have been cooped up in a space-station and a submarine all this while. I need to find my legs again." Before Maria could say anything, Ivan was gone and striding towards the departing couple.

Jason and Marlene had almost reached the house when Sheldrake waved to Jason from the jetty.

"I guess he has an update for me." Jason remarked.

"You go Jason, I'll be fine now." Marlene said and indeed she appeared to have recovered from the initial shock.

"Are you sure?" Jason asked, a little concerned. "Raymond can wait you know?"

"Really, I'll be fine, you go and thank you." Marlene said. Jason waved and began to head for the jetty to meet with Sheldrake. Just as Marlene reached to open the door she heard the voice of a breathless Ivan call out behind her.

"Marlene, you forgot your buggy." Ivan said, as he placed the carriage down on the concrete patio in front of the door.

"Oh! My goodness, I forgot all about that." Marlene said putting her hand to her mouth in surprise. Then noticing how Ivan was perspiring, "you look as though you need a cold drink of something."

"Ha! I'm not yet back to fitness. Now I am back on earth I hope to begin working out again." Ivan said, between deep breaths.

"Come on in." Marlene said, "let's see what we can find." Marlene proceeded to open the door she was still holding and beckoned for Ivan to enter. Once Marlene was in the kitchen she went straight to the fridge, still carrying an inquisitive Augusta who was trying to steal glances at their new guest.

"Would you like water, juice, cola or some other soda?" Marlene asked as she moved objects around in the fridge to see what she had in there.

"You have a cola?" Ivan's eyes opened with delight, "that was a rare luxury growing up in Russia."

"Cola it is." Marlene replied. "I think I will have one too." Marlene began to open the cans and pour the contents into glasses before adding some cubes of ice.

"Colas were hard to come by where I lived. My father worked on a logging camp in a remote part of Siberia. Everything was hard to come by."

"Funny coincidence, I grew up on a logging camp in Canada." Marlene replied.

By the time Maria arrived with Amy and Mir, Marlene and Ivan were each enjoying a cup of tea and cookies, chatting and laughing like long lost friends.

Chapter 65

Preparations Underway - North

Bermuda

The day the Augusta departed, Dave and his crew, which included Tony, drove in a convoy of trucks and scooters to the airport to begin clearing the runways while Moose and his men went off to prepare the farm. Because of the distance from the airport to the farm, both teams would also be on the lookout for suitable vehicles to transport the livestock once they were unloaded from the plane.

On arrival at the airport, Dave's crew noticed a few planes strewn on the three main runways. It must have been a particularly busy time when the devastation struck there. Some of the planes were stacked in line in preparation for take-off and there were a couple more along the tarmac. The planes had stopped askew so that they completely straddled the runway. For some reason, one of the aircraft had burst into flames, and all that remained was a charred, metal, carcass of frame and wheels. Unfortunately, the decaying charred carcasses of people were still clearly visible in the burned-out remnants.

After a couple of passes along the runways the group parked on the grass in the triangle of the intersection of all three runways.

"O.K." Dave began. "We need to clear all these planes from the runways, so we will have to find some tow-trucks to do it."

"Push-back trucks." Tony said.

"What?" Dave asked

"Push-back trucks." Tony repeated. "I used to work at Logan airport during my vacations when I was at college. We should be able to find some outside the terminals."

"Can you drive one?" Dave asked.

"Nothing to it." Tony replied, "But I don't know about that lot," as he turned to point at the mangled mess on the main runway."

"Man, I think we will need a bull-dozer to shift that stuff." Louis said.

"There may be just what we need over there?" Tony said as he pointed to a half-built building that appeared to be a new terminal that had been under construction. "Let's take a drive over there to see what we can find." Dave suggested.

The assorted convoy of vehicles headed towards the terminals, the existing one and the new one. The good news was that between the two buildings they were able to find exactly what they were looking for. The bad news was they would have to clear the badly decaying bodies that littered the area and the vehicles. Fortunately, this was anticipated so they began to don protective gear and cleared the bodies. This task took the remainder of the day to complete so once they had set up generators to re-charge the batteries of the selected vehicles they would need the following day it was decided to return to the triangle where they originally stopped to set up camp.

Camp was literally that, they had brought with them tents, cooking gear and enough food to last them a week. The tents they were using were of the pop-up variety, obtained from one of the few camping stores on Bermuda. So, in no time at all, tents were erected, fires were lit, and the pleasant aroma of food being grilled was emanating from the camping stoves. After dinner, a quick discussion was held regarding the next day's schedule, a few stories were shared and then everyone bedded down for the night.

The next morning, they returned to the vehicles that would be needed for moving the planes. Tony was familiarizing himself with one of the push-back truck's controls before he started up the vehicle and headed for the first of the planes that needed to be shifted. Meanwhile, Dave, Louis and the rest of the team tried to figure out how to manipulate the plethora of switches and levers on the large bull-dozer that was parked in the construction site. They didn't need to know much, the huge, curved business end of the vehicle was in the perfect position to clear the mangled debris from the runway, it was just a matter of figuring out how to get the vehicle started and moving.

By the time Tony had attached the tow-bar on his truck to the first of the planes he was attempting to move he heard the roar of the bull-dozer's engine break the silence and a plume of smoke could be seen billowing from the vehicle's exhaust. It was Louis who had been designated to drive the bull-dozer, after all, Dave had suggested it was his idea in the first place. Louis, however, wasn't quite so confident, a young African American born on the wrong side of the tracks in Memphis who joined the navy under duress from a local judge. Louis had been given a choice, join the navy and learn a trade or go to prison and waste his life away. Louis chose to become a store person, which didn't really qualify him to be a heavy vehicle driver, but then, neither did any of the others have the required qualifications. So, Louis sat his six-foot frame into the driver's seat and after suggestions from the rest of the team he managed to turn on the engine, then, got the thing into forward gear to begin trundling down the runway towards the obstruction.

By the time they reached the burnt-out plane, Louis was sweating profusely in the steel-protected, enclosed cabin. Except for Dave and Tony, the rest of the team rode on the bull-dozer like soldiers on the side of a tank, appreciating the breeze as they went along. But instead of being armed with rifles and grenades they were carrying brooms and shovels procured from the construction area. Louis came to a stop some fifty yards short of the plane while the other men jumped off and began to assess the best angle of attack. Dave had driven along separately on one of the scooters that another crew man had brought from the Happy Mariner. Once Louis began working on the obstruction Dave would go and check on Tony to see if he needed any assistance.

Louis remained in the bull-dozer, looking at the remains of the plane, his thoughts went to all the people who had been killed in what was left of the aircraft. Were they just arriving or just leaving? Had they been holiday makers or Bermudians leaving or returning from visiting family? Louis would never know, all he hoped was that the devastation had killed them before the fire had consumed them. The brows of his youthful face scrunched into furrows as he thought briefly about his own family. Louis' father, a second-generation sanitary worker, did not earn a great deal of money. Despite the fact that Louis' grandfather had participated in the 1968 Memphis Sanitation Strike, part of the Civil rights movement, to demand extra pay and improved working conditions. Louis' mother cleaned houses, when she wasn't too pregnant with his four sisters and two brothers. It certainly hadn't been their fault that Louis had turned to crime, in fact he had feared his mother more than the judge. Louis had just been trying to bolster the household income, he hadn't committed the robbery for himself. The judge had recognized that fact and provided him with the opportunity to join the service. In doing so, he would be providing the family with extra income, he had been sending back part of his pay to his parents and of course, there would be one less mouth to feed.

The sound of many voices shook Louis out of his reverie. Each one was suggesting a different approach to the movement of the obstruction.

"Do you think you will be O.K. Lou?" Dave asked as he rode his scooter up beside him. "I just want to go and check up on Tony."
"You go ahead Dave, I'll be fine, I'll radio you if we have a problem." Louis replied in his friendly Tennessee drawl. Louis waited until Dave was clear then amidst all the gesticulating, pointing and shouting he revved the engine and went full-speed to a point fifty yards from the front of the plane. Without stopping and still at full-speed he continued towards the wreck of a plane while the rest of the team began to scatter in all directions as they realized what Louis was doing.

The bull-dozer hit the plane with a resounding cacophony of sound and pieces of the aircraft began to scatter in all directions almost like one would imagine the 'Big Bang' would have been, but on a much smaller scale. But despite the pieces that were being strewn around, the main bulk of the craft remained intact and was being pushed backwards onto the now long, unkempt, grass at the side of the runway. The tail of the plane only began to yaw a little once the front of the plane had left the runway. Louis reversed the bull-dozer back onto the runway and turned the vehicle to survey the bits that were left, which weren't that many. The rest of the team were looking on in awe, they had expected this to be at least a two-day enterprise.
"Y'all going to just stand there or are you going to start sweeping?" Louis shouted. In response, Louis received quite an assortment of

verbal epithets and hand-gestures but sweep they did, while Louis continued clearing the larger pieces that still littered the runway.

It was just after lunch by the time the runway was cleared so Louis reported in to Dave. Coincidently, Dave and Tony had finished towing the planes, so they agreed to meet at their base. By the time they'd had lunch no one felt like driving straight back to the Happy Mariner via the farm, they still had to return to the terminal to retrieve all the other vehicles that they had arrived in. So, it was agreed they would get the vehicles later that afternoon, return, have dinner and in the morning, they would de-camp and head out to visit Moose and his crew.

They arrived at the farm mid-morning and the first people they saw were Moose and Dutch, no surprise there, surveying the farm house.

"Hi guys." Dave said from the open window of the truck he was driving.

"You lot done already?" Dutch asked.

"Yea, wasn't that bad as it turned out." Dave replied, "but we haven't come across any suitable trucks to transport the animals."

"No worries," Moose replied, "got 'em in spades here."

"So, what help do you need here?" Dave said while he looked around for the others who were supposed to be helping Moose.

"We're done too." Dutch replied.

"A few carcasses to clear that's all. There was a warehouse full of straw, I checked it out. There was no mildew or rot, so we moved it into the barn. Other than that, everything has been straightforward." Moose replied, then continued and turned to view the farm house, "although there is one thing." Everyone looked at the farm house as though it was haunted. It certainly was an old building, but it had obviously been well-maintained.

"We're thinking of moving in there," Moose nodded towards the house, "it would make sense. It's already divided into separate sections, so we could both live there. Moose said pointing first to Dutch then himself. "Then if Sir Henry or whatever his name is, decide to stay, there's another section he could live in temporarily."

"Wow, sounds like you have it all worked out Moose." Dave said.

"Yea, but it needs cleaning out a bit." Dutch said with a concerned look on his face.

"What do you mean, like a spring cleaning? We could all help you with that." Tony said enthusiastically.

"No, not exactly," Moose said. "Bodies, lots of bodies. I think they must have been using the farm as a bed and breakfast and the place was packed." There was silence for a while as everyone looked at the house until Moose spoke again. "I'm torn between burning it down and re-building or just living somewhere close by, but this would be ideal."

"I have no problem removing the bodies Moose," Tony said, thinking back to the shock of that initial sighting of Dexter and his sons on their boat in the Caribbean, "we had to do that in the early days on St. Santia. I'm used to it."

"No, that's not it, I'm not squeamish, I could do it." Moose quickly countered, "it's just, well, living there after all those people had died there, kind of sacrilege."

"You're getting sentimental in your old age Moose." Dave replied. "We don't have the expertise to re-build a new house in such a short time and even if we did, those resources would be better suited on St. Santia. Look at the size of that roof, how much water will that be storing when it rains?" Moose pondered this and eventually nodded his head in agreement.

"Come on, let's get started." Dave said, then began to put on a protective suit to begin clearing the house. The others had no hesitation in joining in and although it was as bad as Moose had suggested, the bodies were cleared from the house then taken in a truck to the nearest beach where they were burned, and the ashes left to the elements.

As they were winding down, Dave radioed Moxley to inform him that both teams would be heading back to the Happy Mariner that evening. So it was that the two tired teams arrived back at the pub to be greeted by a full roast pork dinner, courtesy of meat brought on the Augusta from the freezers of St. Santia and the epicurean skills of Smee. At the beginning of the meal Dave celebrated the success of their projects with a toast. In fact, by the end of the night, many toasts had been made and as everyone began to disperse back to their respective homes, Tony accompanied Dave back to his condo, where he went to spend the night.

Chapter 66

Preparations Underway - South

St. Santia

Sheldrake did indeed have an update for Jason. A team had been sent to clear the runway and because of its relative proximity to where they were, the team had returned each evening and reported to Sheldrake.

"I'm pleased to tell you that the runway is now fully functional and ready for the animals' arrival." Sheldrake informed Jason. "As for the farms, we have found two fairly close by. One was a dairy farm and the other raised cattle for beef. The men have done sterling work clearing what is left of the carcasses and burning them. The dairy farm is ready, and the other establishment should be cleared tomorrow. Their next task will be to clean out the barns, unfortunately we have not been able to find any straw, so we will be using wood-shavings to line the floors. I understand that would be adequate until we can procure suitable amounts of straw."

"Sounds like you have everything in hand then Sheldrake. Well done." Jason said. "What about transporting the animals from the airport?"

"Yes, plenty of vehicles to facilitate that." Sheldrake replied, proud of himself that he had thought of that one too, because they weren't part of the original instructions. "The farms had appropriate trucks and they have been serviced, fueled and ready for action."

"Well, all we have to do is wait." Jason replied.

"Would you like to inspect our efforts?" Sheldrake asked.

"I could, but I wouldn't know what I was looking at." Jason replied, "I'm a city boy from Tampa, never been on a farm in my life." They both laughed.

For the next few days, the main priorities were preparing the farms and getting Amy, Ivan and Mir settled. A suitable house was found within walking distance and while the place was being cleaned-up Amy, Ivan and Mir stayed with Marlene. During the day, the womenfolk would walk to the seconded property to prepare for its new occupants while Ivan would join Bob, John and the other men carrying out whatever needed to be done to prepare for the coming of the livestock.

Both objectives were finished well ahead of time and a house warming party was held for Amy, Ivan and Mir. Although, after the party, much to the surprise of everyone, except Amy and Marlene, Ivan returned to Marlene's house. This was a talking point for the next few days, but it was soon superseded by the pending arrival of the livestock.

On the expected day of arrival, the trucks were driven to the airport to be in position for the plane's landing. Jason remained on board the Augusta awaiting a radio message from DeVersa detailing his ETA. On receipt of the call, Jason would alert everyone, on both submarines and the island, with a blast on the klaxon. However, by late afternoon, with no sign of the plane, Jason was beginning to grow increasingly concerned, he began pacing up and down the hull of the Augusta, searching the sky for any sign of a plane. Not for the first time, Jason was beginning to think, the plan was too simple, far too simple.

Chapter 67

In Search of Their Pilot

Hastings, Nebraska

As Huxley drove the Research Centre's SUV into town, Grover was on full alert and sticking to the directions given by Harold, it didn't take long before they had found the SUV that DeVersa had taken. It was parked down what was once one of the busiest streets in Hastings. Grover indicated to Huxley to remain in the vehicle while he checked out the surroundings. Grover quietly got out of the SUV and walked in a crouch to DeVersa's SUV. He stole a glance inside to see if DeVersa was in fact there, but the vehicle was empty, except for a box of syringes that had prompted the trip. Grover, still in combat mode, moved towards the open door of the building the SUV was parked beside. Grover stole a quick look inside, slowly coming to his full height and relaxing his arms so that his weapon was pointing downwards. With a sideways tilt of his head, Grover indicated to Huxley that he should come over. Grover waited for Huxley to arrive, then they both entered through the door. It was clearly obvious, from what they could see, that they were flying nowhere that day, DeVersa was blind drunk.

DeVersa, barely conscious, was sitting on a bar-stool, holding onto an almost empty glass containing the remnants of what looked like whiskey. DeVersa's head was lying on the long wooden bar, that was part of the drinking establishment, beside him were a couple of empty bottles. At the sight of the two men entering the bar he attempted to lift the hand that contained the glass and his head. DeVersa mumbled a toast to the arrival of his friends but all it resulted in was him falling off the stool with the remaining whiskey spilling from the glass onto the floor. Between the two of them, Grover and Huxley lifted their drunken pilot from the floor and half-carried, half-dragged the man out through the door and into the SUV DeVersa had driven into town. Grover radioed the team that they should unload the animals as they would not be going anywhere that day, but he gave no further details.

Harold was livid, it was a real '*I told you so*' moment for him and basically, he was not prepared to continue any further with such a wild, risky adventure. Harold continued to moan and complain during the entire evacuation of the livestock from the plane. The others took the tirade in silence, their disappointment was palpable, but what was even worse was not knowing why the trip was off. By the time the last of the animals were safely ensconced back in their pens the small convoy of two SUVs reached the center.

While Harold went into the control room to ensure his charges were comfortable the team remained outside to get the story on DeVersa. Huxley parked his SUV slightly ahead of where the team was standing which gave Grover room to park beside them. Grover exited his side of the vehicle and went around to the passenger side to reveal DeVersa in all his glory. As Grover opened the door, DeVersa almost fell out, in fact, if it hadn't have been for Grover holding him in the passenger seat, he would have fallen out. DeVersa was now singing, or at least mumbling almost incoherently, the song, 'Anchors Aweigh' accompanied with arm movements on the appropriate notes.

The ladies' reactions were of complete disgust, but a couple of the submariners couldn't suppress a grin. Huxley, who now joined them, was somewhat disillusioned, he had known of DeVersa's history, his fall from grace as a pilot because of his binge drinking, nevertheless, it came as a severe blow to witness it first-hand. Grover meanwhile, began to drag the man out of his seat with a view of getting him into a bed to sleep off his drunken stupor. Huxley lent a hand while Janet and Mary decided to visit Harold in an effort to placate him and bring the project back on track.

By the time evening came around, Harold was back on board and DeVersa had returned to the land of the living, albeit barely. Everyone, except DeVersa, was in the kitchen, Grover and Mary were concocting the evening meal when the disgraced pilot walked gingerly into the room.

"I've let you all down." DeVersa said, his voice was gravelly.

"No fucking kidding." Graneski let slip, then realized Mary and Janet were standing in the room with them. "Whoops, sorry, that just slipped out." But if the ladies had heard the profanity, they didn't let on, they were still focused on DeVersa.

“I’m so sorry.” DeVersa said. “I don’t know what to say.” He sat down on the nearest chair as if he didn’t feel confident he could remain standing much longer. He put his head in his hands and began to sob. Nobody spoke for a few moments until Janet broke the silence.

“The simple fact is Peter, that unless you can fly us back to St Santia we are stranded here. You realize that don’t you?” Janet gently asked the embarrassed man, who merely nodded his head.

“If we postponed the trip another day do you think you will be ready?” Janet asked, Peter again nodded his head.

“Harold has been somewhat concerned because of this delay but we have assured him this will NOT happen again until all the animals have been flown to the islands.” Janet continued in that officious tone she excelled at, “so far, he has kindly agreed to continue with the venture providing Huxley is assigned to you day and night to ensure this episode is not repeated. Is that understood Peter?” DeVersa nodded his head in agreement once more.

“I will report to Mr. Hargreaves on our return and accept my punishment.” DeVersa said forlornly.

“Peter, that won’t be necessary.” Mary said gently. “We have all discussed this and it has been agreed, nobody outside this group need to be aware of what you did to-day. As far as they are concerned we had some logistic glitches at this end, that’s all.”

“We understand everyone deals with life in different ways.” Janet added in a much softer tone than her previous tirade, “you are aware of your shortcomings and now so are we, we will help you. After all, another couple of days isn't a big deal in the great scheme of things, is it? So, look, don't worry about it, relax, we will head out tomorrow. O.K.?" DeVersa gave one more silent uncontrollable sob before there was an interruption.

"Grub's up!" shouted Grover. As Huxley came over to fill his plate with the evening's fare, Grover had a few private words for him.

"Do not let him out of your sight. Do ya' hear?"

Chapter 68

On the Beach

St. Santia

It was the following day on St. Santia and Jason had gotten very little sleep the previous night. Although, he was still optimistic that the plane's delay was the result of a misunderstanding of the timeline and its arrival remained imminent. Jason left the submarine and walked over to a shaded gazebo that was part of SBs. SBs now had chairs and a food table that was regularly being replenished with snacks, cups and a large carafe of coffee. It was a wonderful meeting place for the residents and the crews of the submarines to take a break from their chores, ask for some extra assistance or just chat. Just about everyone passed through the café at least once a day.

Sheldrake was sitting at one of the tables talking to Amy and Mir as Jason went to the food stand and poured himself a coffee. Jason considered taking a pastry, but he had noticed his clothes appeared to be a little tighter than they should, so he passed. Jason walked over to Sheldrake's table just as Amy stood and began preparing to leave.

"Something I said?" Jason asked jokingly.

"No, of course not." Amy smiled as she whisked up Mir from the beach. "You just missed Maria, I said I would be right behind her, that's all."

"No problem." Jason replied as he sat down beside Sheldrake.

"Still no sign of the plane then?" Sheldrake asked.

"No, not yet, but I'm sure everything is fine. I must have got my days wrong, that's all." Jason replied smiling, belying his true feelings. Sheldrake wasn't fooled either, he knew the man's meticulousness for details.

"But I've had another thought." Jason continued quickly, trying to change the subject. "Something that struck me when the ladies were talking to me about this trip. It makes sense to me that if there had been any survivors after the devastation wouldn't they seriously consider moving south where there are more natural food resources?"

"It would make sense, yes." Sheldrake mused.

"And we have committed to return to Norfolk on a regular basis in the event that any of the men who had left wish to return to the fold as it were." Jason explained.

"You mean, like Dancey?" Sheldrake replied.

"Yes, like Dancey. But what if there are survivors out there that don't even know we exist?" Jason asked.

"What are you suggesting?" Sheldrake asked.

"I am suggesting," Jason replied slowly, "that once this little project is over and the animals are settled, on both islands, that you ask for volunteers to sail around the Gulf to see if you can find any stragglers out there."

Chapter 69

Hercules Departure from Clay

U.S. Meat Animal Research Center, Nebraska

Departure day had arrived, once more, only this time DeVersa had not been allowed to leave the vicinity. In fact, during the loading of the animals, he was firmly ensconced in the cockpit of the plane with Huxley, diligently working with him on the route to St. Santia. Once all the animals were loaded and the pens secured, the giant doors of the plane were closed. Harold boarded the plane along with Lewes and Graneski, it had been agreed that for this trip, Grover, Hernandez and Stenich would remain with the ladies. DeVersa was preparing to start the engines and he indicated to the small crowd on the road to retreat to the building to avoid any wake turbulence. When DeVersa felt the group was a safe enough distance away, he started each engine. With Huxley's assistance DeVersa went through his pilot's checklist and satisfied that all was in order he began to ease the throttles and slowly roll the plane down the road.

Before entering the plane DeVersa had checked the wind direction and felt the best option for take-off was to go to the end of the road, carry out a 360° turn and depart past the research center. As the plane passed by the research center it was already airborne, Huxley waved to the group, who were now standing by the door and they reciprocated. In just a few moments DeVersa had reached his desired altitude and turned the plane to the correct bearing for St. Santia. DeVersa told Huxley to broadcast a message to the others on the plane. The three human passengers smiled as a nervous Huxley informed them that their flight time to St. Santia was expected to be five hours and the local temperature at their destination was 84° Fahrenheit or 28° Celsius. Not that Huxley knew the temperature on St. Santia, but it had been pretty much that warm every day since they had arrived there. Once Huxley's message was over, Harold rose to check on the welfare of the animals, while Graneski had already dealt the cards as he and Lewes resumed their never-ending game of Crib.

Back at the research center the group returned inside to resume their duties. Grover was going to prepare the food and together with Hernandez would assist Stenich carrying out any of the tasks as per Harold's written schedule. Meanwhile, Janet and Mary would monitor the controls and assist where required. This meant that the group separated as the ladies went up the stairs to the control room and the others went about their duties on the ground floor. Mary noticed that Janet was not displaying her normal boundless amount of energy as she climbed the stairs and it was obvious she was attempting to put on a brave face.

"Are you sure you're alright Janet?" Mary asked her.

"Of course." Janet replied, "a little tired that's all." Mary was about to accept the explanation when suddenly Janet tripped on the top step. This time, not only did her face contort into a mask of pain but she also let out a brief cry of agony.

Chapter 70

Hercules Arrival at St. Santia

St. Santia Airport

At 13:45 in the afternoon, Sparks received the long-awaited radio message from the incoming Hercules.

"U.S.S. Augusta, U.S.S. Augusta this is the livestock plane. Over." Huxley said with a little more confidence now.

"Livestock plane, this is Augusta. What is your ETA? Over." Sparks replied.

"Estimated arrival in 15 minutes. Over." Huxley said.

"Will pass on the message. Good to hear from you." Sparks replied and immediately paged Jason. On hearing the news, a very relieved Jason gave two good blasts on the klaxon which spurred the entire community into action. The families grabbed their children and boarded their Mini-mokes to drive to the airport to witness the unloading of the animals. The trucks to transport the animals to the farm had been readied and left at the airport so the men who had been designated to drive the trucks took off in an assortment of SUVs, mopeds and motor-bikes. Jason drove himself and Sheldrake in a convertible while the rest of the men made their way by any means possible.

The arrival of the convoy of vehicles coincided with the landing of the plane and everyone cheered and applauded DeVersa's softest of touchdowns. The plane taxied towards the group of people, a couple of the children had their tiny hands over their ears and were crying at the loud noise being made by the Hercules' propellers and motors. Once the engines had stopped, DeVersa pressed the switch to lower the huge ramp at the rear of the plane to reveal, what appeared to everyone watching, a cavernous room with the baying of animals echoing inside. Barriers had been erected to form a lane for the animals to be herded into the transport trucks. The barriers were plentiful at the airport and the guys had done a terrific job bringing them to the arrival point. Once the ramp had fully descended, final adjustments were made to the barriers near the plane, to ensure there were no gaps for the animals to escape through.

The first person down the ramp was Sir Harold, who was greeted with cheers and wild applause. Harold waved, a little embarrassed, not only by the warm reception he was receiving but by the fact he was still wearing clothes fit for a Nebraska winter and not a hot, sunny afternoon in St. Santia. Behind Harold was Lewes and Graneski, who had already stripped down to more appropriate attire. They were closely followed by DeVersa and Huxley, who motioned to Harold to go over to meet Jason and the other officers. Within five minutes he had been introduced to the St. Santia families and the new arrivals. After having been on his own for so long he was beginning to find it all a little overwhelming. He used the animals as an excuse to extricate himself from the hand-shaking rituals to check the barriers and inspect the trucks.

Satisfied, with the arrangements, Harold decided that the herd of Black Angus would be the first to be transported in the flotilla of trucks that had been brought to the airfield. Harold was a little concerned with the number of people who had shown up to witness the arrival of the animals. The critters had never seen this many people, so Harold asked Lewes to pass the message to be as quiet as possible as the animals were herded to the trucks. Harold returned up the ramp with Lewes and Graneski, a few minutes later, Harold was leading the big Black Angus bull, down the ramp to the response of a few 'oohs' from the watching contingent. Walking gingerly behind the bull were the other cows and calves. The animals were still a little groggy from the sedative Harold had administered to them, but they managed to follow blindly along the path and into their designated truck. As the last of the herd was in the truck, the wooden gates were put into place, the doors closed, and the truck was on its way to take the livestock to their new home. Another truck reversed into place, the barriers were adjusted, and the process was repeated for the next genre.

Everything was going well until it came to the unloading of the final group of animals, the Holsteins. Mir, who had not yet adjusted to the warm clime of the island was beginning to get a little hot and bothered. Mir gave out a little cry, just as one of the cows was passing. Before anyone could react, the concerned cow walked over to Mir and planted a huge, wet, lick on the top of her head. The cow continued walking and the effect on Mir was immediate. Mir stopped crying, and everyone began to laugh at the spectacle.

Harold was more than pleased with the efforts carried out in preparation of the animals' arrival and no longer had any qualms about bringing the remaining animals.

"What you have done here in such a short time is bloody marvelous." Harold said to Jason.

"We aim to please." Jason replied. "Once you have finished up here we have a cabin reserved for you on the Augusta for the night. You can clean up and we can find you some more, shall we say, suitable clothes. Unless you would prefer to stay in a house instead?"

"No, to stay on a submarine for a night would be quite exciting." Harold replied, "after all, it will only be for one night as we will be heading back to Clay for the next shipment."

"Yes, but first, tonight, we have a little shindig arranged to welcome you to St. Santia. Jason said, "the chefs and the ladies are putting on quite a spread for you. The meat won't be fresh though, we're still using frozen supplies."

"Oh, a little knees up, hey?" Replied Harold, enthralled with the idea.

"Knees up?" Jason asked with a confused look on his face.

"Yes, the shindig, you're having a knees up," Harold replied, "haven't you ever heard of 'Knees Up Mother Brown?" Jason now looked even more confused than ever and it was exacerbated by the arrival of Sheldrake who had overheard Harold. Both Sheldrake's parents had been born in England, so he was familiar with the expression and immediately burst into a chorus of 'Knees Up Mother Brown' willingly accompanied by Harold.

Jason left the barn shaking his head while Harold and Sheldrake were performing a strange ritual amongst the wood shavings.

Chapter 71

Awaiting the Return of the Hercules

U.S. Meat Animal Research Center, Nebraska

"Janet, you are clearly not alright." Mary said in a stern voice. "For starters, let's get you lying down." Mary then assisted Janet into the control room and helped her onto the cot that Harold had been using. "Now, tell me, what's wrong?"

"I was having a problem with my water works but now I believe it has spread to my kidneys." Janet replied, through gritted teeth.

"How long has this been going on?" Mary asked.

"Oh, just about since we were airlifted back to the Augusta." Janet said.

"You mean, ever since the raping and you haven't told Dennis about this?" Mary asked incredulously.

"I thought it would go away, well, for once, I was wrong." Janet replied sardonically.

"Oh Janet. You silly girl. This could be serious, you have almost certainly got a kidney infection. We must return on the next flight." Mary said.

"No, stick with the plan." Janet insisted. "Even if we went to Bermuda, there's no doctor there anyway. We would have to wait for a submarine to be dispatched from St. Santia, I might as well wait until Peter returns from Bermuda to fly the last shipment of animals to St. Santia."

"No Janet," Mary replied with equal insistence, "change of plan. Peter will fly the next batch to St. Santia with us onboard so that we can get you seen to. Meanwhile, young lady, you stay put. You will need some pain-killers and plenty of water."

"There's too much to do Mary, I can't just lie here." Janet said as she began to rise from the cot.

"You stay there," Mary told Janet in no uncertain terms. "If Harold has managed to cope with all this while being by himself I am sure we can manage for a couple of days with more people and fewer animals." But the obstinate Janet was still not convinced.

"I will just sit at the controls." Janet retaliated by once more trying to rise and again, Mary gently brought Janet's shoulders back to the cot. It was then that Grover entered the room to receive further instructions but what he saw forced a look of concern to cross his face. Mary gave him a summary of Janet's condition and the proposed change of plan.

"Stefan, as usual, Mary is overreacting, I will be fine." Janet said, using Grover's given name to try and win him over. But he wasn't buying it and yet again Janet attempted to rise but this time it was Grover who restrained her.

"You want that I tie her to the bed?" Grover said to Mary but keeping a forceful hand on Janet's shoulder.

"No Stefan, I don't think that will be necessary. Will it Janet?" Mary said. Finally, with a nod of her head Janet acquiesced, laid back down on the cot and relaxed.

“Good, now let me go and prepare you something that will help you with the pain.” Mary said.

Grover accompanied Mary downstairs to the kitchen. As soon as they entered the kitchen Mary closed the door, sat down and burst into tears. Grover said nothing, he merely sat down beside her and put a consoling arm around her shoulders. Stenich made a brief entrance into the kitchen and left as quickly as he came. After a few moments Mary stopped crying, looked directly into Grover’s eyes and said, “Janet’s condition, it’s bad, I think it is really bad.”

Chapter 72

Hercules Flight Back to Clay

St. Santia Airport

Harold experienced his first 'shindig' on the island and did indeed enjoy a thoroughly good 'knees up'. Fortunately, during the meeting of just about everyone on the island he kept his alcoholic drinking to a minimum and was ready to take-off the next day with the rest of the team. Harold was also secure in the knowledge that there was sufficient expertise on the island to take care of the animals until his return. A number of the seamen had been brought up on farms and some, who had no experience, were prepared to learn and help out. In fact, one of the men had already moved into the farm house at one of the selected sites. Lewes, the Communications Officer, whose duties had diminished since their arrival on St. Santia had been raised on a farm in Wichita, Kansas. Lewes' elder brother was slated to inherit the farm and working for his older brother was not a situation he relished, so he chose to join the navy. Naturally, he jumped at the opportunity to supervise the farm, savoring a new purpose in life.

During the festivities, Harold spent most of the evening in discussion with Sheldrake, sharing stories of vacations in England, particularly the West country where Sheldrake's parents were both born. Harold had told Sheldrake that it was such a beautiful part of the world that he had always dreamed of retiring there.

Coincidently, Sheldrake mentioned that his parents had visions of also retiring there to see out the rest of their lives.

Meanwhile, Huxley had stuck to DeVersa like a limpet all evening long, ensuring Peter only drank from the non-alcoholic punch bowls. Huxley would love to have had a good stiff drink, but he took his responsibility seriously and choose to match whatever DeVersa was drinking. Another time, DeVersa would be annoyed by having some kid watching his every move but he liked Huxley. He also accepted that this was a situation brought about by his own stupidity, so instead of treating it as a punishment they used the time to get to know each other.

Amy socialized with just about everyone, getting to know them all a little better, she even participated in a few dances with the men. It was also the evening that it became obvious to everyone that Marlene and Ivan were now an item. Bob was a little saddened that his friend and ex-lover, Tony, had decided to leave Marlene and remain on Bermuda. But Bob wasn't going to dwell on the fact, unlike Tony, he took his responsibilities seriously and was determined to create an environment for his son and the other members of the next generation.

The Hamaxs also enjoyed themselves, Joan mainly taking care of the children with Maria, while John, as was his wont, imbibed in a few drinks with the men and swapped ribald stories. Although, Dancey took the opportunity to take turns with Joan and Maria to enjoy a tango or two. Jason and Dennis watched over the proceedings, each nursing a glass of wine that lasted the entire evening. Every so often people would arrive at their table to chit-chat with the officers, but they were too preoccupied with thoughts of the two women in Clay to really be good company.

So it was, that the next morning, bright and early the Hercules took off and headed back to Clay for the next shipment of animals to be taken to Bermuda. It was a smooth flight and after a successful landing at Clay the group entered the Research building. They were looking forward to sharing stories of the settling in of the animals on St. Santia and the great party they had all attended. But the mood of the incoming group suddenly changed once they became aware of Janet's illness and the change of plan. The group immediately accepted the new itinerary, even Harold, but DeVersa had a concern.

"We don't have enough fuel to return to St. Santia!"

Chapter 73

Re-positioning Flight

U.S. Meat Animal Research Center, Nebraska

"What?" Harold shouted out to DeVersa. "are you telling me that if we flew to Bermuda you would be jeopardizing the lives of those animals by not having sufficient fuel?"

"Absolutely not." DeVersa replied calmly. "My calculations were based on the original schedule and utilizing the fuel in the tanker we had brought from Langley. Going to Bermuda we know there is a large airport there with aviation fuel, the plan was to top-up there before proceeding on the second trip to St. Santia. Because St. Santia has no such facilities, it has only a small airport, we would not have enough fuel to make the return trip."

"So, we're screwed then." Mary whispered.

"I never said that." DeVersa said still keeping his cool repose. All eyes were now on the pilot. "All we have to do is transfer the fuel from the tanker into the plane, which is what we had planned to do anyway. Then, drive the empty tanker to a local airfield, re-fill the tanker and add that to the plane. That's all! That extra tanker-full would be sufficient to make the flight to St. Santia and back. We replenish the tanks with another tanker-full on our return and we should be good to go." For a second you could have heard a pin drop. "It's not a big deal guys. In fact, Lincoln Air Base is just over an hour away, we could fuel up now and leave as soon as the fuel has been transferred. Tomorrow morning, we'll return for a second fill-up while you are loading the animals. Where's the problem?"

"Do you have every airfield memorized in your head Peter?" Mary asked skeptically.

"Of course not," DeVersa replied smiling, "I'd noticed it was there when I was researching for the trip. Always good to have a backup plan."

While the fuel was being transferred, DeVersa and Huxley enjoyed a coffee and a sandwich, then, accompanied by Grover, they headed off in the direction of Lincoln. DeVersa had asked Grover to join them in the event that some manual pumping was to be required, they may need his muscle. Grover jumped at the opportunity, he was only too glad to get away, he'd already had his fill of milking and muck clearing.

Lewes and Graneski went off to seek out the other members of their team, Hernandez and Stenich, to see if they could offer any assistance while Harold wanted to speak to Mary to see if she had experienced any issues during his absence and of course to obtain further details about Janet's condition.

"I think it's bad. Harold." Mary said as tears began to well up in her eyes.

"Come now," Harold said, trying to be as gentle as he could. "You don't know that for certain."

"Look, there's something you don't know about Janet and me, something happened to us." Mary said, looking down at her hands as she twiddled with a tissue. Mary went on to explain the situation when they were kidnapped by a group of sailors from the Connecticut and viciously raped.

“Janet came off worse, she was gang-raped by four men almost constantly for two days. At least with me it was only the one guy.” Mary paused for a while and a shiver went down her spine at the thought of those events before continuing. “I think she has been harboring a kidney infection and not told anyone, secretly taking antibiotics and painkillers that have now come to the end of their usefulness. So, yes, I think it is that bad.”

“I’m sorry Mary, I didn’t know, how dreadful!” Harold quietly said.

“But, everything is O.K. here, Stenich has been brilliant, I really haven’t had to do much.” Mary said, trying to put on a brave smile and changing the subject, “so why don’t you go and check on things while I prepare dinner.” Harold was about to say something else but felt it was best to comply with Mary’s wishes.

At the time of the year the group was visiting the Research Centre darkness falls a little earlier in Nebraska than on St. Santia, so, initially, it was not a concern that DeVersa and the boys had not returned from their trip to Lincoln as day turned to night. By the time dinner was ready and everyone, except Janet, was in the kitchen awaiting the trio’s return, snow had started to fall outside. Inside, anxiety levels were beginning to increase.

Chapter 74

In Search of Fuel

Lincoln Airfield

It took just under two hours for DeVersa to drive the tanker to Lincoln Air Force base. On the way they encountered a few obstacles, especially on the ramp onto I-80, but by using the tanker as a battering ram they were able to clear a path without too much difficulty.

"Are you confident there will be fuel at this airfield Peter?" Grover asked, not because he doubted DeVersa's reasoning but more to kick-off a conversation. Grover had tremendous respect for DeVersa as both a pilot and a cook, despite his relapse a few days ago.

"Better be." DeVersa replied, "it's the Air Refueling Wing for the Nebraska Air National Guard. "Another few pilot-training lessons we could have Huxley here flying one of those refueling jets and we wouldn't have to worry about driving tankers around, hey?" DeVersa pushed Huxley on the shoulder as they all laughed at that possibility.

At the airport, which is shared by both civilian and military planes, DeVersa made a bee-line for the east side of the runways where the National Guard installations were.

"Well, would you look at that?" DeVersa exclaimed.

"Look at what Pete?" Huxley asked, who like Grover, was searching around for whatever it was that DeVersa could see.
"Right in front of us." DeVersa smiled and pointed to a fleet of full-size tankers. "Grover, my friend, it doesn't look like we will be needing your services after all."

Grover stopped the tanker he was driving, which was dwarfed by the full-sized trucks lined up on the apron. He exited and walked over to the first truck in the line. Using the ladder at the rear of the truck's cab he climbed the utility ladder and walked along the tanker until he came to an inspection cover. DeVersa unscrewed the cover and looked inside the tanker, meanwhile, Huxley and Grover left the vehicle and watched DeVersa's exploits.
"Eureka!" DeVersa called out, much to his pleasure, not only was the tanker full, it also contained the correct aviation fuel. "Huxley, see if there are keys in the ignition and give it a whirl would you please?" Huxley climbed into the cab and obliged, but he was met with a gentle ticking noise as he turned the key.
"Flat battery," Huxley shouted out through the open door, "not surprisingly, being stuck out here in the open for all this while. I'll set-up the generator to re-charge the battery."

While Huxley was setting up the battery cables DeVersa closed the inspection cover and climbed down from the tanker.
"So, Pete, why so many tankers parked here?" Grover asked.

"Well, there would always be a small fleet available but you're right, I wouldn't have reckoned on this much fuel." DeVersa thought, "perhaps they were about to have an exercise, that's the only thing I can think of."
"Suits us though." Grover added.
"Sure does, we will only need one trip after all." DeVersa said. The two men then went behind the trucks to visit the installation. In the huge hangar were several military jets, Sabres, Phantoms and Thunderstreaks but they all appeared tiny against the Boeing KC-135 Stratotanker, the main refueling plane. DeVersa was in his element looking at the array of flying machines parked in the hangar and gave Grover a bit of history on each one of them.
"You obviously miss this Pete." Grover said sympathetically.
"Sure do," DeVersa replied a little distantly. "But after what I did it was felt best for everyone that I stayed away from aircraft. They believed it would cure my problem." There was a pause before DeVersa continued, "well, that didn't work did it?"

DeVersa and Grover were both laughing as they returned to the tanker just as Huxley fired up the engine.
"Can you move that pile of junk out of my way?" Huxley shouted to DeVersa, referring to the small tanker they had used to drive there, which was now blocking the path of their new, seconded vehicle.

Once the mini-tanker was relocated and DeVersa was ensconced in the driver's seat of the new tanker, Huxley in the middle of the bench-seat and Grover on the passenger's side, they were ready to roll.

"What I intend doing is going back on the highway the way we came." DeVersa said.

"Well that make sense." Huxley said sarcastically.

"No, you prune, I mean exactly the way we came which means driving back on the wrong side of the road because we have already cleared a path.

"Oh, good thinking Batman." Grover said.

"This has taken no time at all, should be back in plenty of time for dinner." DeVersa said as the big tanker began to trundle towards the highway.

The decision to retrace their route appeared to be a sound one as they drove the wrong way up NW 12 St. to gain entry back onto I-80 but it soon became obvious that they could push away all thoughts of returning to Clay in time for supper. Snow was beginning to fall, and a serious problem loomed in the powerful beams of the trucks headlamps.

Chapter 75

Concerns

U.S. Meat Animal Research Center, Nebraska

Mary went to look in on Janet and to provide her with an update on the schedule. Janet was still insisting that they should not change the plan on her behalf, but Mary couldn't help but notice that Janet had taken a decidedly turn for the worse.

"They're not back yet?" Janet asked from the constraints of her cot.

"No, not yet and it has started to snow, I hope they're alright." Mary responded.

"DeVersa and Grover? I'm sure they will be. Probably encountered a couple of snags, that's all." Janet replied confidently.

"I'm sure you're right, Mary replied, "then we can get you safely to the Augusta and get Dennis to fix you up."

"Well, maybe not Dennis, I think I might be a little more comfortable with Amy checking me out." Janet said.

"Amy? But didn't she say she was a gynecologist? If it is your kidneys that are the problem wouldn't it be better if you were examined by Dennis?" Mary replied somewhat surprised at Janet's thought process.

"Yes, but Dennis and I are, well you know, getting a little closer, I just wouldn't be comfortable, that's all." Janet countered.

"But he was the one who took care of you before." Mary argued.

"Yes, but I didn't exactly have a choice then, did I?" Janet responded, sounding more like her old self.

"True. But what about Ivan? Not sure what he specialized in." Mary suggested.

"No!" Janet replied quickly and emphatically. Then continuing in a gentler vein, "I would like Amy to examine me then they could all confer. There, that's settled."

Shortly afterwards, Harold came in, had a quick conversation with Janet on her welfare then went back to look at the controls and printouts regarding the remaining animals in the center.

"Well, everything looks in order I'll leave you to it." Harold said and went to leave the control room.

"Any sign of our intrepid trio Harold?" Mary asked.

"'Fraid not," Harold said from the doorway, "and it looks as if the snow is beginning to get heavier."

Chapter 76

Trip Back to Clay

Wilds of Nebraska

Ahead of them was a 90°turn that needed to be negotiated to reach the highway. It had been easy enough in the mini-tanker but the turning circle on the truck and trailer was going to prove quite the challenge. If it had just been the road it wouldn't have been an issue, it was the other vehicles in the way that was the problem. DeVersa could not use the rig as a battering-ram as he had with the mini-tanker because of all the forward and reversing manipulations he would have had to complete. In addition, with thousands of gallons of fuel behind him, the risk of fire would be ever present if any sparks were to be created as they bludgeoned other vehicles aside.

DeVersa slowed the truck and finally stopped to think the problem through. After careful thought he finally decided to uncouple the rig, leaving the tanker at a safe distance and he would use the truck to bulldoze any obstacles out of the way. DeVersa explained to the others what he was going to do, then making sure the rig was lined up in a straight line he switched off the air supply to lock the trailer brakes then gently backed up the cab to help release the fifth wheel locking lever. In the back of the cab were some chocks, he told Grover and Huxley to place them at the back of the tanker to prevent the trailer from moving. DeVersa turned off the ignition and climbed out of the cab, snow was beginning to gently fall so the quicker they got this done the better.

DeVersa lowered the landing gear of the trailer with an extra few turns in low gear to lift some of the weight off the tractor. Then, DeVersa disconnected the air lines from the trailer and secured them. Then came the tricky bit, DeVersa told the others to stand clear, he raised the release handle lock and pulled the release handle to the 'open' position. There was always a risk that the trailer could move at this juncture in the proceedings and DeVersa knew it was important to keep clear to avoid injury. Satisfied that the trailer was not going anywhere, DeVersa returned to the cab and gently drove it forward until the fifth wheel came free from the trailer, he then paused, to prevent the trailer from completely falling to the ground in the event of the landing gear, which was now supporting the full weight of the tanker, should collapse. DeVersa secured the truck and returned to the trailer to ensure the ground was indeed supporting the trailer and the landing gear was holding up. Satisfied, DeVersa climbed back into the cab and waved Grover and Huxley to join him.

For the next two hours they completely cleared cars, trucks and debris for a half kilometer stretch of the ramp until DeVersa was confident they were now able to negotiate the tight bends with the big rig. DeVersa drove back to the parked tanker and he gently reversed the cab in line with the trailer. By reversing the uncoupling procedure DeVersa had carried out earlier, the rig was soon back together again. Once the chocks were removed they were all back in the cab and proceeding on their way to Clay, grateful they were no longer exposed to the elements. Although, DeVersa, who now had the windshield wipers on full to combat the increasing amount of snow that was falling, was concerned about the effect the conditions would have on their return trip to the Research Centre.

Chapter 77

Group Reunion

U.S. Meat Animal Research Center, Nebraska

Mary decided they couldn't wait to serve dinner any longer, she dished up for the five of them at the center and plated some food for the others, to be eaten once they arrived. By the time dinner was over and the dishes had been cleared away, the snow had stopped falling. It had been one of those snowfalls that looked worse than it really was and had only lasted for about twenty minutes. It was now very late and Graneski was just about to take one of the SUVs to go in search of the errant men when the sound of a truck's horn could be heard in the distance. Graneski and Lewes rushed outside, despite the negative temperature of a Nebraska evening and them, dressed in just T-shirts and jeans, but they didn't care. They were relieved to see lights heading towards them, getting brighter and brighter and the sound of what appeared to be a large truck getting louder and louder.

DeVersa stopped the truck beside the center to allow his two passengers to leave, then he continued driving the truck and parked it next to the Hercules. They waited for DeVersa to walk to the door and they all shook hands before entering the kitchen area. Mary had already heated-up their dinners and had laid the plates on the table, but they were not allowed to sit down until she had given each of them a welcoming hug.

Between mouthfuls of food, Grover explained the difficulties they had encountered and DeVersa assured them that their fueling issues were now completely solved with the tanker they had parked outside.

"Will you be too tired to leave tomorrow Peter?" Mary asked with some concern, "you've had a very trying time of it to-day."

"Nah, I'll be fine." DeVersa replied confidently, "I can have a little lie in while you are loading the animals and I'll be good to go."

"Who is going to open the plane's doors and stuff?" Huxley was quick to ask.

"Why you are," DeVersa replied almost as quickly. Then there was a brief look between Grover and Huxley as if to say, 'so, who will be minding you, Peter?' But Mary came up with an answer to that question, whether she was sharing the same concern as the other two was hard to say.

"I'll look in on Peter once you start loading the plane and I will make sure he gets some breakfast inside him before he leaves." Mary offered.

"Which brings us to the next point," Harold interceded, "obviously, Mary and Janet will be making this trip with Peter and Huxley, but who will remain behind? I would prefer to make the trip, there will only be a third of the animals left here and I believe my presence would be best suited on the plane. Which means at least Stenich must remain here." Stenich nodded his acquiescent.

"I don't mind staying," Lewes said.

"I can stay," Hernandez volunteered.

"You know me, wherever." Grover said.

"Probably with us on the plane along with Graneski," Harold replied, "just in case we need some muscle."

"Suits me." Graneski replied.

With the personnel's roles agreed they bade their good nights and retired to bed. Early the next morning, after a quick breakfast of cereal and coffee, all the men, except DeVersa, were outside preparing to load the plane. It was a beautiful Nebraska morning, blue sky and not a cloud in the sky but it belied the cold, sub-zero temperature as the men crunched through the two inches of snow that remained from the previous night's brief storm. Huxley supervised the topping-up of fuel from the tanker and by the time most of the animals were loaded, DeVersa had made an appearance. The first thing he realized was that the snow would have to be cleared off the wings of the plane before they attempted a take-off. Outside were an assortment of brooms and snow-shovels so DeVersa put on his coat and carried some of the tools over to the plane and explained to Grover what had to be done. While DeVersa returned to the building to complete his breakfast Graneski and Lewes climbed up to the plane and began to clear the snow off its wings.

A couple of hours later with just some snow remaining on the fuselage of the plane everything was ready for take-off. Grover and Graneski returned to the main building to help with Janet's boarding. They had fashioned a stretcher out of one of the cots in the sleeping quarters and they were carrying Janet to the plane with Mary alongside. Janet was well wrapped up for the journey and she even managed a smile as they walked up the ramp of the plane.

"You're beginning to make a habit of this Stefan." Janet said, referring to the last time Grover had carried her to a helicopter after her unfortunate incident.

"Don't you worry about it ma'am." Grover replied.

With Janet safely secured just behind the cockpit and everyone, except Harold, strapped in, it was time to take-off. Harold was still outside conversing with Stenich providing him with some last-minute instructions while Lewes and Hernandez listened in. Then, Harold turned away from the men and with a quick wave bounded up the ramp of the plane to join the others who were eagerly awaiting take-off. No sooner had Harold sat down, the ramp was up and DeVersa had the plane motoring to the end of the road.

DeVersa was cognizant of the snow on the plane but he figured most of the precipitation would blow away during the run-up to take-off. Even then, the cargo weight, with a full tank of fuel, was well within the plane's capabilities. Nevertheless, DeVersa was going to utilize as much of the road as possible to reach the appropriate take-off speed.

"Pete, you didn't come this far down the road to take-off last time. You still concerned about the snow?" Huxley asked with a little trepidation.

"No, but, just in case, I want to give this baby as much opportunity to lift-off as possible. Doesn't hurt to err on the side of caution does it?" DeVersa replied.

"Just that I thought we needed to get to St. Santia as soon as possible." Huxley said.

"There's an old saying lad, 'it's better to lose a minute in life, then your life in a minute'." DeVersa retorted. Huxley didn't continue the discussion, fortunately, DeVersa's calculations were spot-on and the passengers in the massive Hercules enjoyed a text-book departure.

After a couple of hours flying time DeVersa asked Huxley to attempt to raise the Augusta on the radio. There was no reply, but Huxley began to call every five minutes and about thirty minutes later the somewhat surprised voice of Sparks responded.

"Hercules, Hercules this is Augusta reading you 3 by 3."

"Augusta, we're hearing you loud and clear. Now hear this," DeVersa began, "inform the captain, change of plan. We are arriving with another batch of livestock to St. Santia, ETA in approximately 2.5 hours. We also have a medical emergency and will need immediate assistance. Copy?"

"Livestock arriving here in 2.5 hours and a medical team to be available." Sparks summarized.

“Acknowledge and out.” DeVersa replied. He felt there was no point in giving details at this stage and Sparks, bless his heart thought DeVersa, didn’t ask. They just needed to get the ball rolling for their arrival, DeVersa would elaborate when they were closer to arrival but less than ten minutes later they received another call from the Augusta.

Chapter 78

Medical Emergency

St. Santia

At the time of the radio call from DeVersa, Jason and Sheldrake were in SBs discussing the Connecticut's upcoming trip to Florida.

"The only concern I have," Jason said, "is that you don't have a doctor on board."

"That's true, Dr. Filmore left ship in Norfolk, but, we do have Henshaw, he is an excellent medic, trained for field conditions I understand." Sheldrake explained.

"I guess you will only ever be 24 hours away," Jason mused, "so that shouldn't be a problem." It was just then that Jason received a call on his radio.

"Jason here." Jason said curtly.

"Sir, plan change. The Hercules will be arriving in a couple of hours with livestock and they need a medical team on hand." Sparks relayed the information. A funny coincidence that they should just be talking about medical issues and they receive a medical emergency.

"Sparks, contact Dennis and warn Lewis to be ready to receive the animals. Then broadcast 'all hands to the beach'. I will arrange a livestock team to go to the farm." Jason replied.

“Sheldrake, you locate that Henshaw fellow to get medical transport of some kind to meet the plane, then, get all your available crew ashore.” Jason told the captain.

“Sir.” Sheldrake replied and began to radio the Connecticut.”

There were a few men milling about on the beach playing a pick-up game of football and Jason was about to run to them to obtain assistance as Giles was walking towards SBs for a coffee.

“Giles,” Jason said abruptly, “do you by any chance have your whistle on you?”

“Yes.” Giles replied.

“All hands on deck.” Jason said and began to run to the Augusta, Giles didn’t need to be told twice and Jason hadn’t gone two steps when the shrill sound of Giles’ whistle caught the attention of just about everyone in the vicinity. Suddenly, crews of both the Augusta and the Connecticut were running towards the jetty.

Just as Jason arrived at the jetty, he saw someone riding away on a motor-bike and assumed that would be Henshaw on his way to find a suitable vehicle for transporting a patient.

“We have a medical emergency and I need someone to go and find Amy and tell her to get down here immediately.” Jason said.

“On it sir.” Dancey replied and began running to find an available vehicle.

“We also need to get hold of Ivan.” Jason added.

“I’ll go.” Walters said, “I can just run up to the house.”

"The rest of you, cattle duties, some more animals are moving in." Jason told them. "We need to position the cattle trucks and assist Lewis in any preparations. You have two hours. Giles?"

Now the wheels were in motion and Giles was in charge Jason could return to the Augusta to receive additional information regarding the medical emergency.

Chapter 79

Incoming Patient

St. Santia

By the time Jason had reached the radio room on the Augusta, Dennis was already receiving an update from Mary. Mary had joined DeVersa and Huxley in the cockpit to explain Janet's condition to Dennis. Dennis had asked her a number of questions and realized there was nothing further he could do until Janet was examined and underwent tests.

"Dennis, all I know is that there is a medical emergency, so I have arranged transport and gotten word to Amy and Ivan to be here. What's going on?" Jason asked Dennis.

"It's Janet," Dennis answered, "my first impression from what Mary has told me is that she has a kidney infection and it's serious." Dennis was obviously upset by the news and his hands were shaking a little.

"Antibiotics can fix that can't it?" Jason asked with all the aplomb of a layman.

"Yes and no. We can get rid of the infection, but it depends on how far it's gone and what damage has been done to the kidneys. It appears she has been living silently with this for a while. Well ever since…." Dennis' voice trailed off then he continued, quietly, "she doesn't want me to do the examination, she would like Amy to do it."

"I'm so sorry." Jason replied, "I didn't know that when I had Amy contacted."
"No, that's good Jason thank you." Jason replied, then he appeared to snap out of his comatose state, "I need to prepare the sick-room, perhaps it would be best if Amy met Janet off the plane and she could be with her on the drive here."
"Certainly." Jason said and left Dennis to prepare.

Jason returned to the jetty and reviewed the beach that a few minutes ago was busy with the crews of the submarines and was now devoid of anyone. Approaching, he could see Amy in one of the Mini-mokes, it was being driven by Bob. Ivan had also been contacted and could be seen scurrying down the hill, Bob stopped to pick him up. Jason walked to the end of the jetty to await the arrival of the Mini-moke. Jason explained the situation to the two doctors and Amy agreed it would better if she was there when the plane arrived. Bob was more than willing to drive Amy to the airport, Mir had been left with the Hamaxs, so she was in good hands. Ivan climbed out of the back of the Mini-moke and went on board the Augusta to see if he could assist Dennis with anything.

Jason decided to travel with Bob and Amy to meet the incoming plane as there was no more he could do by staying on the Augusta. When they arrived at the airport Lewis was there ensuring the barriers were still well positioned from the original delivery of animals. Now all they had to do was wait for the arrival of the

Hercules and eventually, the plane came into view but there was still no sign of Henshaw and any transportation.

Chapter 80

Sirens Approaching

St. Santia

At the very first get-together after the Connecticut had arrived on St. Santia, Henshaw had been introduced to Tony and as soon as he had found out that the submariner was a medic Tony told him of the small British army installation he had discovered while they were foraging for supplies. It was nestled up in a secluded part of the hills. Tony told Henshaw about all the vehicles parked there and the medical supplies. So, during some downtime, Henshaw had taken a ride to locate the outpost and investigate the premises. Tony had indeed been correct in that there was very little in the way of supplies that would bolster their inventory and he agreed, it appeared to be there to assist in hurricane evacuation preparations. But there was one thing that Henshaw had remembered that he thought may one day be useful. Hidden in one of the buildings, amongst all the transport vehicles, was an ambulance, that is where Henshaw had decided to go.

On arrival at the outpost, Henshaw headed straight to the building containing the vehicles and parked his motor-bike by the ambulance. Henshaw leapt into the cab of the ambulance, the key was already in the ignition but when he turned it, there was no response. Henshaw really didn't have time to find a generator to recharge the battery, so he was about to think of a plan B when he realized the vehicle had a standard shift. The army base was at the top of a steep hill, if only he could get the ambulance to the gate he would be able to bump-start the engine by letting it roll and releasing the clutch with it in gear. Henshaw wiggled the gear lever to ensure it was in neutral, he released the hand-brake and turned the steering-wheel a little towards the door. Henshaw then exited the vehicle and placed his sturdy back against the rear of the ambulance. Henshaw then placed both feet against the wall and pushed with all his might. The vehicle began to move and using that initial momentum he managed to push it as far as the entrance to the building, where it refused to move another inch. Henshaw took a couple of minutes to regain his breath and then thought of another bright idea. Henshaw only had to get the vehicle over the slightly raised bump in the doorway that bore the tracks of the building's doors. Henshaw felt once that was achieved he could keep the ambulance's momentum going to the gate and voilà, down the hill. Henshaw went back into the building to retrieve his motor-bike, then using a discarded piece of rope he threaded it through the front bumper of the ambulance. Henshaw then tied the two ends of the rope together to form a loop which he secured over the handlebars of his motor-bike. Henshaw started the motor-bike, put it in gear, revved the engine and slowly released the clutch. Almost imperceptibly the motor-bike began to inch forward, the front wheels of the ambulance made it over the bump in the doorway at which point, Henshaw gave the motor-bike full throttle and the ambulance's rear wheels fair bounced over the obstruction. With the ambulance's momentum picking up, Henshaw slowed the motor-bike and released the rope from the handlebars, turned the motor-bike away from the oncoming ambulance, switched off the ignition and leapt off. Quickly, Henshaw found his feet and jumped up to the cab of the ambulance to adjust the steering while attempting to sit down. The momentum of the ambulance was slowing now but it was just a matter of a few feet before gravity would take over as it hit the incline of the hill. As it just about came to a halt, Henshaw shouted out some verbal encouragement to the inanimate object and miraculously the vehicle began to pick up speed as it reached the beginning of the slope. Henshaw was cheering at the top of his lungs as the ambulance began to hurtle down the hill. Henshaw turned on the ignition, depressed the clutch, placed the lever in first gear, released the clutch and pressed the throttle. The roar of the engine was music to his ears as Henshaw changed gears and eased on the brakes to slow the vehicle down.

After a few yards with the engine running, Henshaw stopped the vehicle to remove the rope before continuing down the hill. Henshaw's arrival at the airfield coincided with the Hercules touching down and just to make sure everyone was aware of his presence, he turned on the ambulance's siren.

Chapter 81

Prognosis

St. Santia

Henshaw drove the ambulance to the mouth of the barriers, where the plane would be stopping to unload the animals. Henshaw parked the ambulance and walked to the rear, opened the doors and pulled out the mobile stretcher. By now, Amy had joined him, they exchanged brief greetings then turned to wait for the jaws of the Hercules to open. As soon as the ramp was down Henshaw was wheeling the stretcher up the ramp towards Janet, this wasn't the first time Henshaw had been involved with air-lifted patients.

Mary was pleasantly surprised to see a stretcher being wheeled towards them and everyone made way as Henshaw and Amy bent down to look at Janet. Janet managed a smile and a quick 'Hi' as she saw Amy and raised her hand as way of a greeting. Amy returned the smile and immediately went to feel her pulse. Once Amy gave Henshaw the nod to go ahead and lift the patient, Henshaw seconded the help of Grover to lift Janet onto the stretcher. Henshaw gently, but quickly placed straps around Janet to secure her and began to wheel the stretcher down the ramp to the ambulance. Henshaw deftly pushed the stretcher onto the ambulance and Amy climbed into the back with Janet, who was being accompanied by Mary. Amy continued with her examination, taking blood pressure, temperature and gently probing Janet's abdomen.

As the ambulance neared the Augusta, Henshaw gave a couple of quick blasts on the siren to alert the Augusta's crew that they were approaching. Jason and Sheldrake formed part of the welcoming committee while Dennis and Ivan remained in the sanctuary of the sick-room making last minute checks on availability of swabs, instruments and drugs. Moving the mobile stretcher along the jetty and up the gangplank was a relatively simple process but negotiating the patient through the supply hatch was a bit more of a challenge, however, with the assistance of some willing crew members Janet was safely transported to the sick-room.

"Hey trouble, how are you doing?" Dennis asked with a smile as he grasped Janet's hand.

"Still causing trouble apparently." Janet replied with a whisper.

"Don't worry, we'll soon fix you up." Dennis said, with an optimism he really didn't feel.

"Henshaw would you scrub up and take a blood sample please?" Amy asked.

"Sure." Henshaw replied and without hesitation he moved to the sink to begin washing his hands.

"O.K., ladies and gentlemen," Amy was now addressing both the two doctors and Mary, "thank you for setting up, we'll take it from here." Dennis was expecting this, although he was still reluctant to leave, but Ivan wasn't aware of Janet's wishes and was about to protest his dismissal when Dennis took him by the arm and led him to the door, closely followed by Mary.

"We'll be in the War Room when you're done." Dennis said to Amy, "Henshaw will show you where it is." But Amy was already back to her examination.

In the War Room Dennis, Mary, Jason, Sheldrake and Ivan were all eagerly awaiting Amy's initial diagnosis and when she walked in, still removing her surgical gloves, her expression said everything.

"My estimate is a month at the most, maybe a few weeks." Amy said, then plonked herself down in a seat next to Dennis and held his hand.

Chapter 82

Life Saving Attempts

Aboard the Augusta

For a moment, the shock of Amy's revelation silenced the occupants in the room. Just a mere few days ago Janet, a driving force of the new community, appeared to be in fine fettle and now she was on the cusp of losing her life.

"You were right, Mary," Amy began, "it's her kidneys, they are badly infected and in poor shape. It's only a matter of time before they completely shut down." Mary responded by holding her head in her hands and bursting into tears, Jason moved to console her.

"What about a dialysis machine?" Sheldrake asked, "I'm sure we could find one."

"She's too far gone for dialysis I'm afraid, the infection is too great." Amy countered.

"What about a kidney transplant?" Dennis asked.

"First we would have to clear the infection before that could occur. Then we would have to find a compatible donor, our donor pool is not so large so the chances of finding an appropriate fit are remote. Even if we did find a new kidney for her; do we have the appropriate expertise for carrying out a transplant? Then there is the question of post-operative drugs, the biggest risk in these types of procedures is to prevent rejection, we'd need to procure the

appropriate medicines which....” Amy’s voice tapered off, she wasn’t being a defeatist she was just explaining the reality.
“Well, let’s look at this logically, step by step. Could you clear up the infection?” Ivan asked.
“It’s possible, but we still couldn’t save the kidneys.” Amy responded.
“Fine, so let’s say we took blood tests of everyone who was prepared to donate, could we perform the operations if we found a donor?” Ivan asked. “I for one have some surgical experience. Dennis what about you?”
“I could do it.” Dennis said, “It is not a particularly difficult procedure compared to other surgical operations, the risks, as Amy suggested, mostly occur during the post-care. But we do not have the facilities to do two simultaneous operations.”
“But we do have two medical rooms on the two submarines.” Sheldrake suggested.
“Yes, but what about the drugs, Janet would need them for the rest of her life.” Amy interjected, “where are we possibly going to find those?”
“I am sure we could find the appropriate drugs at various hospitals amongst the islands in the area. Even if their dates have expired we would have to take that risk and once we have exhausted those, we begin to manufacture them ourselves.” Ivan said with confidence.

Again, there was silence in the room, Ivan had made it sound all too simple but the skepticism amongst the others was almost palpable. At that moment, Henshaw entered the room to inform the occupants that Janet has been moved to a bed and she appears to be comfortable, he was just about to take his leave when he was called back.

"Henshaw!" Ivan shouted with a smile, "I need you to take a blood sample from me."

At first, the medic appeared a little confused until Amy explained the possible solution to Janet's condition, then everyone else in the room made the same request.

Word got out that a donor was required and to a man and women, everyone volunteered for the test. It was also arranged that Henshaw would fly to Clay with the livestock crew for the final transportation of the animals to Bermuda. There he would obtain blood samples from donor volunteers in the Bermuda detachment before the final flight back to St. Santia. Of course, Henshaw's absence would delay Sheldrake's departure for Florida but there was ample time for that.

That evening the usual get-together was held, albeit, subdued in the light of Janet's condition. Henshaw and Amy worked diligently on the samples as quickly as they were being provided. By the time Henshaw was to leave for Clay, the majority of the tests had been immediately eliminated because of incorrect blood-types. John Hamaxs' was a match but was promptly eliminated because of his age, they didn't want to hurt his feelings, and those of his wife, by saying they wouldn't use theirs even if they were a fit, so they took their blood anyway. Amy continued to work on the successful matches and of those she had tested to date, a few more samples passed the tissue typing stage but of those, they all failed the cross-matching phase. It would appear that all Janet's hopes rested on an appropriate donor being found amongst the Bermuda detachment. So, it was with high hopes that Henshaw flew off to Bermuda, via Clay, his presence there was to turn out to be a life-saver, but it wasn't the finding of a kidney donor.

Chapter 83

An Accident on Bermuda

Bermuda

Both trips, back to Clay and onto Bermuda, went ahead without a hitch. In addition to the usual suspects, Henshaw was in attendance and as Mary's presence was no longer necessary, she stayed behind on St. Santia. There was a brief pause before the contingent left Clay as Harold did one last nostalgic round of checks to ensure everything had been shut down in an orderly fashion, even though no one was ever expected to set foot in the installation again.

On the plane's arrival in Bermuda the passengers were welcomed by almost the entire Bermuda detachment, only Moxley and Smee had remained at their posts to prepare the evening's meal. Harold was briefly introduced to the crowd and in return, they cheered. In contrast, Henshaw's introduction was greeted with mocking jeers, the ensemble knew what he was there for, the radio waves had been buzzing with the news.

Under Harold's supervision the disembarking of the animals went smoothly, and he was more than impressed with the facilities. Moose and the rest of the crew had gone to town on the preparations for housing the animals. Each breed had their own shelters, pens and grazing fields supplemented by a good water supply. Moose also explained his expansion plans and a back-up plan for obtaining water from other areas during periods of drought. Harold was confident that the animals were in good hands and he went to the evening's festivities in a euphoric mood. Not only because the welfare of the animals was assured, but also because he had always wanted to travel to Bermuda. Although a holiday there had always been a little out of his price range. Now, here he was enjoying everything the island could offer, for free.

Once the animals were settled, the dining and drinking got underway soon afterwards, however, it was mandatory that for those who were prepared to become a donor, no drinking could occur prior to a blood sample being given. The first one to give a sample was Moxley who insisted no one would be getting a drink until they had a band-aid on their arm; to prove they had given a sample. Moxley didn't care if they were prepared to donate a kidney or not.

"So, to get plastered, we must have a plaster, is that it Moxley?" Lewes asked.

"I was once thinking of dressing as a band-aid for Halloween," Graneski added," but I decided against it."

"Why's that?" Lewes asked.

"It would be hard to pull-off!" Graneski jokingly shouted out. Everyone laughed, except for Moose whose hate for the man had suddenly been rekindled. Moxley pushed his arms away in an ignoring gesture to the remarks.

Every one of the Bermuda detachment did indeed provide a blood sample. Henshaw exchanged greetings with some of his old Connecticut shipmates as they came through the line. Henshaw also thanked Tony for informing him of the British base and explained to him about the ambulance he had found to transport Janet. Once all the samples were taken, Henshaw added more ice to his medical cooler and found some space in a refrigerator to store it. Then, it was time to relax a little, even so, Henshaw would refrain from drinking too much.

Henshaw was not the only one who was watching their alcoholic intake. Huxley was still under orders to watch DeVersa. Moose, with his new-found responsibilities had a personal cut-off at two beers and Dutch, who most always followed Moose's lead, did likewise. Moxley, of course, always abstained at times like this, he had been a witness to the exploits of drunken sailors far too often, someone had to retain order and civility amongst them. Fortunately, the night passed without incident and everyone went to bed having agreed a good time had been had by all.

The next morning, the St. Santia group prepared for their flight back to the island. Henshaw collected his cooler and replenished its contents with a little more ice. The group bade their goodbyes to the few that had risen to see them off. Graneski had also made it out of bed and volunteered to drive the St. Santia detachment to the airport. On the way to the airport, Harold wanted to stop off for one last look at the animals. Time was not an issue, if they could get back to the plane before all the ice in the medical cooler melted, Henshaw explained.

On their arrival at the farm, having radioed ahead, Moose and Dutch were there to greet them. Harold promised he wouldn't be long, so Henshaw elected to remain in the vehicle while the others went to look at the animals. The group started off in the Black Angus pen, as that was the nearest, before moving on to the other cattle and livestock. Graneski, however, was quite obsessed with the bull and remained to just study the magnificence of the animal.

Graneski had been standing with his feet on the bottom rung of the gate for a few minutes, the next thing he knew, he had been hurled onto the floor of the pen with the bull running towards him. Quickly, Graneski managed to make it back to his feet and reached for the gate but one of the horns of the bull caught him in the leg before he could grab the top rail. Graneski let out a shriek of pain and fell against the gate as the bull retreated to the far end of the pen. The bull was just about ready to make another charge when Graneski suddenly felt strong arms grabbing his body and lifting him out of the pen.

"Boy, that was close." Graneski said, but then he looked down at his leg, all he could see was a torrent of blood spurting out of the femoral artery.

Chapter 84

A Life Saver on Bermuda

Bermuda

Grover had split from the main group and returned to talk to Henshaw, he was a city guy and had seen enough of the animals, he just wanted to get back to St. Santia and chill out for a few days. Grover had been standing by the open window of the vehicle talking to Henshaw when he had heard Graneski's cry. With a speed that belied his size, Grover was in the barn and reaching over the gate to grab Graneski. As soon as Grover saw the tear in Graneski's leg, or at least the profusion of blood pouring from it he knew the seriousness of the injury. Grover carried the injured man outside and laid him down on the old-fashioned, cobbled-stone, ground leading to the barn.

"Henshaw, get your arse over here!" Grover shouted as he began ripping off his T-Shirt, he wasn't aware that the medic had also responded to the cry and was standing right behind him. Grover rolled his T-shirt up into a ball and stuffed it into the hole created by the bull.

"Full pressure on that Grover, I have to get my kit." Henshaw said as he ran back to the truck, "and keep his leg in the air."

"I feel cold Grover, I'm going to die, aren't I?" Graneski whispered as his whole body began to shiver.

"Nah, Henshaw's on it. You'll be fine." Grover replied with a smile, not expecting the poor guy to pull through. Henshaw returned with his bag of tricks and pulled a bandage from it and began to free it from its wrappings.

"O.K. Graneski, I'm just going to put this bandage on, you may see a bit of blood for a few seconds but don't worry. O.K.?" Henshaw explained.

"I'm going to die, aren't I?" Graneski repeated.

"What? From this little scratch?" Henshaw replied and began to administer a HemCon bandage that was intended for just such an emergency. The bandage was designed to seal the wound until proper treatment could be administered.

"But I do have bad news, you will have to come with us and visit the sights of St. Santia to get you fixed up. So, you will be subject to our company for a few more days." Henshaw explained. "Grover, can you get some blankets, coats or something to keep him warm, shock is beginning to set in." As Grover returned with some blankets the rest of the group were returning and they immediately came over to see what had happened.

"How did you manage to fall in the pen?" Harold asked.

"I was standing on the gate and it was like my legs lifted up and I fell in, I guess the bull took exception to me being there." Graneski managed to reply through clenched lips. Pain was also beginning to set-in, Henshaw had anticipated this and gave Graneski a shot of morphine to make him as comfortable as possible. Grover was still propping Graneski's leg in the air to reduce the blood flow to his leg. Henshaw returned to the vehicle to review his files then took charge.

"Dutch, could you radio Dave and tell him to contact the Augusta and get them to prepare for a Femoral Artery Repair, we should be there in," Henshaw paused then looked at DeVersa before continuing, "ETA would be?"

"Three hours flying time." DeVersa immediately answered.

"Tell them four hours or less." Henshaw added.

"On it." Dutch replied.

"Moose, once we get Henshaw on to the truck can you drive us to a hospital before taking us to the airport?"

"Absolutely." Moose merely replied.

It took a further ten minutes to position Graneski comfortably on the vehicle before Moose drove them to a hospital. Henshaw kept checking on the condition of Graneski while jotting down a list of items on a scratchpad. As Moose pulled into the road leading to the hospital, Henshaw told him to head for the 'Emergency' department.

"Hey Lewes, can you come and give me a hand please?" Henshaw asked Lewes and they both ran to the doors of the hospital building. Henshaw found a supply room and began gathering tubes, needles and all kinds of medical related paraphernalia. Checking the list to ensure he had collected everything he needed, Henshaw and Lewes ran back to the vehicle and as soon as they were seated, Moose continued driving to the airport.

No sooner had Moose come to a stop by the plane, Grover carried Graneski up the ramp and laid him down on the same cot that had been used for Janet. Wasting no time, DeVersa was in the cockpit starting up the plane and closing the ramp. Goodbye waves were exchanged as the ramp was being closed and Henshaw began to unwrap the assortment of goodies he had procured from the hospital.

"This is just your way out of getting out of being thrashed at Crib." Lewes said to try and cheer up his card-playing buddy, in fact it did produce a faint smile on the pale face of the patient.

"Oh, don't worry Lewes." Henshaw said, "you'll still be sitting beside each other on the trip."

"I will?" Lewes replied with a surprised look on his face.

"Sure," Henshaw replied nonchalantly, "I checked the list of blood samples we took before we left St. Santia, you're the same blood type. So, instead of thrashing poor Graneski, you'll be giving him a dashing. A dashing of your blood, that is. Relax Lewes, just let me stick this needle in you." It could have been a combination of the look on Lewes face or the fact that the mission was now over, either way, Grover began to guffaw at his team-member's misfortune.

"Don't know what you're laughing at Grover." Henshaw said casually, "you have the same blood-type too. Halfway through the flight, you're up."

Chapter 85

Emergency Operation

St. Santia

John Hamax was waiting at the airport in the very ambulance Henshaw had taken from the compound. Amy was also there to prep. Graneski for the operation that would be carried out by Dennis with Ivan assisting. Grover and Henshaw carried the patient to the ambulance and would accompany Amy to the Augusta. From the ramp to the ambulance, Henshaw provided Amy with a quick synopsis of what had happened, the treatment he had administered, blood pressure, temperature and pulse. By the time the ambulance arrived at the jetty, Graneski was out of it, courtesy of the injection Amy had dispensed. As crew-members were loading Graneski onto the Augusta, Amy turned to the two men.

"I can't believe he is still alive, your quick-thinking Grover and your expertise Henshaw, well done. If we were still awarding medals you would be up for them." Amy said and shook both of their hands. It may not have been obvious to anyone watching but the hand-shake with Grover appeared to linger a little longer than it should before she turned and scampered onto the Augusta.

Once more, the War Room was the meeting place to hear about the condition of a patient. Grover and Henshaw were present enjoying sandwiches and coffee with the rest of their group who had been transported by a convoy of Mini-mokes. Jason and

Sheldrake had joined them, they were just discussing the accident when Amy entered the room and sat down beside Grover.

“Graneski is going to be fine, they’re just finishing up in there.” Amy said smiling as she removed a medical hat from her head, forcing her long blonde hair to cascade down to her shoulders. “I’m still a little confused as to how it happened though.”

“All we know is that Graneski said his legs seemed to come away and he fell in, that’s it.” Henshaw replied.

“But there was no one else there,” Grover said, “we were the only ones not on the tour, we were -.”

“That’s not quite true,” Harold interrupted, and everyone turned to look at him. “Moose had said he had to return to the barn to check on something.”

“That’s right, he did.” Huxley added.

“But why would Moose want to hurt Graneski?” Henshaw asked, “in fact, why would anyone want to hurt Graneski?”

“I think I know why,” Amy said, talking to no one in particular. “and I think it would be best for Graneski if he remained here on St. Santia instead of returning to Bermuda.”

Chapter 86

Preparations for the Connecticut's Departure

St. Santia

All eyes were now on Amy.

"I know this may sound conceited but when I first arrived in Bermuda and it became known that Ivan and I were not an item, Moose began to take a lot of interest in me. So much so that I asked Ivan to pretend we were going to try and make a go of it together to put Moose off. It only partially worked, but I remember Graneski had made a couple of jokes, innocent at the time, but they were at Moose's expense and I think he may have taken exception to them. Of course, I can't prove a thing, just as we can't prove Moose somehow lifted Graneski into the pen with the bull."

A silence filled the room for a while until Jason pitched in.

"I'll have a word with Giles to see if there has been any previous history of violence with Moose, but I think you are right Amy, we can't prove a thing and all we can do is keep aware of the situation." At that point, Dennis and Ivan entered.

"Henshaw, wonderful work, I don't know how you did it." Dennis said.

"You saved his life." Ivan concurred, and everyone began to slap Henshaw on the back. "He will be up and about in a few days." Dennis continued, "meanwhile, he is sharing a room with Janet as I am afraid space in our sick room is limited." At the mention of

Janet's name, the travelling members of those who were present immediately inquired about her welfare. Dennis looked down and was about to answer but Amy jumped in.

"No change presently." Amy said, "as for donors, unfortunately, there are no compatible matches here on St. Santia, hopefully we will have better luck with the samples you have brought back from Bermuda." Amy looked at Henshaw. "I will start working on those right away."

"On a lighter note," Jason thought the group need lifting a little, "Sheldrake here is taking the Connecticut to Florida, he is already to leave but he was waiting on Henshaw's return. When do you think you will be up for it?" Jason looked at Henshaw, he seemed to be the focus of attention right then.

"Do you think I could finish my sandwich?" Henshaw replied. It had the effect Jason intended and everyone was smiling, it was agreed that the Connecticut would depart in the morning.

The following morning, a great deal of activity could be witnessed on St. Santia. Final preparations were being made for the Connecticut's departure and at 10:00 A.M. the submarine slipped under the sea on its journey to Florida. DeVersa, checked in on Cook to ensure he was coping and everything was in hand. Afterwards, DeVersa and Huxley drove to a travel shop and obtained street maps of the nearest islands in the Caribbean. For the next few days, DeVersa would be obtaining flying machines to visit as many hospitals as possible to seek out a shopping list of drugs that would be required in the event of a kidney transplant operation being performed. It also gave DeVersa an opportunity to begin teaching Huxley the basics of flying. Amy began the task of checking the blood samples from Bermuda and job duties were distributed amongst the Augusta's crew to assist in the maintenance of the livestock and chickens.

During DeVersa's travels a collection of pharmaceuticals were gathered, with the assistance of his ever-present side-kick, now co-pilot, Huxley, but their efforts all proved to be moot. After a couple of days analysis, Amy determined that no compatible donors existed on Bermuda. A few days later Graneski was declared fit enough to leave the sick bay and return to a residence on the island, however, he was not allowed to carry out any strenuous activities. Graneski had also been informed of Amy's suspicions and concerns about his safety if he was to return to Bermuda. It was suggested that it would be better if he remained on St. Santia. Graneski remarked that the real reason was that Grover couldn't do without him and would be quite happy to remain on St. Santia.

At about the same time as Graneski's release from sick bay, Janet took a distinct turn for the worse, much to Mary and Dennis' sorrow. Janet was becoming feverish and delirious, Amy did what she could but there was little that could be done.

In between bouts of consciousness Janet was well-aware of her condition and her thoughts would sometimes return to her childhood, when she was playing with her parents. One night, in one of her particularly bad spells of delirium, she saw her father, she felt him touch her brow and she heard his voice.

"It's alright sweetheart. Daddy's here. You're going to be alright."

Chapter 87

Along the Coast of Florida

Aboard the U.S.S. Connecticut

Sheldrake was trolling along the coast of Florida, sounding the submarine's klaxon every fifteen minutes. There were look-outs positioned forward and aft of the submarine, Sheldrake, along with Giles, were in the conning tower scanning the coast through their binoculars. The submarine had surfaced mid-morning, the day after leaving St. Santia, it was now late-afternoon. Sheldrake was now discussing with Giles the merits of staying off-shore or docking at Fort Lauderdale when a shout came from the forward lookout.

"Flare at 12 o'clock."

"Hard to port," was the order Sheldrake immediately gave to the control room, and as the submarine began to turn towards the shore all lookouts started searching for the source of the flare. Sheldrake gave a double blast on the klaxon to try and assure whoever fired the flare that it had been seen.

"Another flare, dead ahead, on the beach, two people waving." Once more came a shout from the forward lookout and all eyes turned to the area of the beach being indicated by the lookout's pointing hand. After a few seconds searching, the people on the beach were spotted by all the lookouts.

"I see them." Sheldrake acknowledged, "Be ready to launch a dinghy." Sheldrake shouted before addressing the control room. "How close can you get to shore?" Sheldrake asked.

According to the charts they were off Las Olas Beach in Fort Lauderdale. "I suggest we stop now sir, we are just about at our limit, the water-level drops-off quite quickly." The control operator reported.

"Stop engines and launch the dinghy." Sheldrake ordered, before switching to a hand-held radio.

"Bosun Walters?" Sheldrake aid into the radio.

"Sir." Walters immediately replied.

"Will you take Dancey with you to find out about these people. Are there others with them? Are they interested in joining our little community? But be wary O.K.?" Sheldrake said.

"You got it." Walters replied.

All eyes were on the dinghy as it raced over the ocean to the couple that had been waving to them on the beach. Dancey stayed in the dinghy as Walters alighted and introduced himself to what looked like a man and a woman. A dialogue was taking place and after a few moments Walters walked away from the couple and Dancey began to assist them into the dinghy. Sheldrake couldn't understand what Walters was doing so he called him on the radio.

"They have agreed to come with us, but I think you'd better handle this sir."

Sheldrake tried to ask Walters what he meant, and he tried to raise him on the radio, but Walters was now walking back to the dinghy and further attempts to raise a response were being ignored. Sheldrake was fuming with anger at the behavior of his bosun and was going to have serious words with him. As a result, Sheldrake was making tracks down the hull of the submarine towards where the boat was approaching to dock. The first person off the dinghy, helped by Giles, who had accompanied Sheldrake, was a tall man, probably fifty years of age with unkept dark hair wearing a pair of thick rimmed glasses.

"Hi, this is my wife Barbara," the man said to Sheldrake, he took the hand of the lady he was with as Walters was assisting her from inside the dinghy. "And my name is Patrick Delaney.

"Captain Sheldrake at your service. Welcome aboard." Sheldrake replied politely, belying how he was really feeling because of Walters' attitude.

"I understand you may have some idea of the whereabouts of my daughter, Janet, is that true?" Patrick asked, "last we heard she was on the Augusta."

Chapter 88

Gulf of Mexico the Time of the Devastation

Cancun, Mexico

The Delaneys had just completed a cruise through the Panama Canal and had disembarked in Cancun to visit a construction site of a different sort. Patrick was the owner of a large construction company and was also interested in some of the underwater development that was being built in the Cancun area. Patrick was bored with the general condo developments he had been involved in over the last few years which, is why he had retired, but now he was seeking a new challenge. He had been following the progress of the underwater houses that had been built in Dubai, but he wanted to go beyond that and have a home that was completely self-sufficient much like the U.S. Navy's SEALAB. Patrick had been working with Mexican authorities in the Cancun area and between them they had developed a housing prototype with its own air, hydro and fresh water generating systems. Both Patrick an Barbara were experienced scuba-divers, so they were eager to try living underwater for a couple of nights. The prototype had been secured in only twenty-foot of water and the Delaney's scuba gear had always been close at hand, so they did not consider the experiment any riskier than a normal dive would have been. The area of the underwater housing was barricaded off by several buoys and had been designated a restricted area to boating by the Mexican government who saw the tourist potential of such a venture.

The Delaneys had always had a loving relationship and Barbara's trust in her husband was absolute, nevertheless, although their first night underwater was filled with excitement, there existed a hint of trepidation. Once darkness fell and they had turned out the lights, the watery gloom was almost surreal as fish scurried past their quiet habitat. Although all the utilities were working perfectly, they both had a restless night and were quite looking forward to travelling to the surface and meeting with their support group. Patrick had been writing a copious number of notes regarding enhancements and tweaks that could be made. Barbara had been contributing updates from a decorative perspective and of course Patrick was suggesting structural improvements. So, after their first night, they awaited the arrival of their support group, whose approach they would see from a camera attached to a screen in their living area. The screen provided them with a 360° perspective of the surface and they could control the angle and zoom from inside the prototype. As the boat carrying the support group approached the restricted area the Delaneys donned their scuba-gear and left their grotto on the sea-bottom to meet with them. The support group was led by the foremen who had overseen the building of the prototype and he listened intently to Patrick's suggestions. In turn, the group provided a few more supplies packed into a water-tight, weighted, container that the Delaneys took back to their underwater home, where they would stay for one more night.

After one more day and night in the prototype, and a lot more notes, the Delaneys packed their sparse number of personal items into the water-tight container and once more awaited the arrival of the support group. Up until that point, the Delaneys had every confidence in their support group but as a few minutes delay turned into an hour they were beginning to get a little anxious. They looked at the screen one more time but there was not a vessel to be seen in the Gulf, in any direction. As time was moving on and they still had to get back to their hotel, pack and make it to the airport they decided to utilize the little skiff that was attached to a buoy within the restricted area. The Delaney's waited for an additional thirty minutes before an impatient Patrick decided to head for shore to express his disappointment with the support group. Barbara, however, was more concerned about returning the rental car in a timely fashion. But as they neared the shore and began to see bodies floating in the sea, they began to realize that the rental car was about to be the least of their worries.

Much like the other handful of survivors throughout the world at the time of the devastation, the Delaneys were suddenly faced with an incredible feeling of helplessness. All this death and the Delaneys had no explanation for it, worse still, they had no sense of the existence of any survivors. The Delaneys decided to head for the dock where their support group was based. As Patrick expertly approached the dock they began to see the bodies of their support group strewn around the buildings and the boat. Their initial reaction was to flee the area to try and find assistance, but it was becoming increasingly more obvious to them that this was not a local phenomenon. On docking, Patrick told Barbara to remain in the skiff as he was going to try and reach help, but she informed him in no uncertain terms that he would not be leaving her behind by herself.

Similar to the exploits of other survivors after the devastation, Patrick attempted to raise local police, Coast Guard and a myriad of other emergency numbers, to no avail. After discussing a few options amongst themselves, it was decided that they would stick to their original plan, go to their rental car, drive to their hotel, collect some things and then on to the airport. Their rental car was parked at the back of the building that was being used as the base for their support group. Patrick and Barbara, made the short walk to their car in only a few minutes, trying to ignore the bodies of men, women and the carcasses of dead birds, cats and dogs. They were still totally befuddled by what had caused this carnage, all they knew was that they had to get out of there.

Patrick managed to make the trip to the hotel, albeit with great difficulty, Barbara sat in the passenger seat, tears streaming down her face as she looked down at her hands in her lap, trying to ignore the death that surrounded them as they drove through the streets. Many cars, containing dead drivers, constantly barred their way and many diversions had to be taken but eventually, Patrick reached their hotel and managed to drive their car directly to the entrance. If they were expecting to find any improvement regarding their situation at the hotel, they were sadly disappointed. Without stopping at the hotel's concierge, they walked up the stairs to their room, which remained exactly as they had left it. For a few moments they experienced solitude and a departure from all the horror they had just witnessed. They just hugged, then sat on the bed to have a rethink of their predicament.

After a while, they decided upon driving home to Naples, Florida. They considered taking a boat across the gulf but decided that in the event of a breakdown, would there be anyone to assist them? They collected a few drinks and snacks from the mini-bar in their room, retrieved their passports and money from the safe; and returned to their car to begin the lengthy trip to Naples. Hoping that at some point during their journey they would meet others or reach a point beyond this wide swath of death. Looking at the maps, Patrick estimated that the trip would take between 50 and 60 hours of driving time so it was going to be a long journey.

It took the Delaneys a month to reach their home in Naples, on the way, they often had to exchange vehicles to overcome traffic jams and obstructions. During their journey they scavenged for food in supermarkets and at gas stations yet never encountered another living person. They deduced that the cause of all the death was an airborne disease and being underwater is why they had managed to survive. After a few weeks in the Naples area they seconded a recreational vehicle and travelled to Miami in search of other survivors. In fact, during their explorations they sighted two sailboats heading out to sea, but they were too far away for the occupants of the boats to see them on shore. But this gave the Delaneys hope, they now knew there were other survivors, they just had to be patient and persevere.

Having seen the sailboats, the Delaneys decided to remain on the coast and they settled in the Fort Lauderdale area. But they needed to be prepared if ever they saw signs of marine activity again. Their plan was to build bonfires all along the beach made of anything that was highly combustible, there was certainly enough items to choose from. They would store matches and lighter fluid in sealed plastic bags to protect them from the elements and affix them to a stick firmly embedded in the sand on the land side of the pyre. They would always carry additional lighters and flares with them wherever they went, and spares were stored in any vehicle they seconded. After any bad storm, which were prevalent in Florida, they would re-check their bonfires and their fire-starters and if necessary, replenish. Apart from gathering food and fuel for their vehicles, this was pretty much their lives until they heard the Connecticut's klaxon. Within seconds of the sound, Patrick had lit a flare, Barbara quickly followed suit and they began running towards one of the bonfires to get it lit but once they heard the acknowledging call from the submarine they didn't feel it was necessary.

Now their preparations had finally borne fruit and they were onboard the Connecticut with some other survivors, better yet, their daughter, their only child may still be alive.

"Come aboard Mr. Delaney, Mrs. Delaney. Do you have any possessions or items that you would like us to retrieve for you? Otherwise, we will set a course for St. Santia." Sheldrake asked, still avoiding an answer to Patrick's question.

"No, no, we have nothing." Patrick replied, and Barbara shook her head in confirmation.

Then, let's go below and I will bring you up to speed." Sheldrake responded, "Giles, escort Mr. and Mrs. Delaney to the War Room and see if they need any refreshments."

"But what about Janet, is she alive?" Patrick asked.

"All in good time Mr. Delaney, all in good time." Sheldrake said calmly, then he waited for the Delaneys to follow Giles down the conning tower to the War Room.

"All personnel, all personnel, prepare to dive. Set a new course for St. Santia. Full speed ahead." Sheldrake called on the ship's radio. Just then Walters, arrived to hurry down below.

"Bosun!" Sheldrake shouted in an authoritative voice and Walters stopped as if he knew what was coming.

"You did the right thing Walters, of course I didn't know that at the time but well done. Now, could you tell Hench to meet us in the War Room please?" Sheldrake told the worried man.
"Certainly Sir." A relieved Walters replied, he knew that Sheldrake was going to be upset because of his failure to respond on the radio, until he had found out the reason why and fortunately he understood. Walters scurried down the steps in search of Henshaw while Sheldrake made one last look around the hull to ensure no one was left topside and all hatches were secure before following Walters down below.

In the War Room Patrick and Barbara were already seated and Giles was trying to make them feel comfortable which was difficult because the Delaneys were already of the opinion that something was amiss. Henshaw entered the room closely followed by Dancey who had garnered some coffee, sandwiches and pastries from the galley and placed them on the table in front of the Delaneys. The aroma from the coffee was intoxicating to them but their immediate concern was about their daughter and they couldn't think of eating or drinking until they were made aware of her welfare. Sheldrake nodded to Giles and he shut the door. Sheldrake began to address the Delaneys with a very solemn voice.
"Regarding your daughter, I'm afraid it is a case of good news, bad news."
"What do you mean?" Barbara asked.

"Your daughter is in fact alive, on our sister sub, the Augusta, moored at St. Santia, which is where we expect to be in less than twenty-four hours. However, you must prepare yourselves, Janet is critically ill with a severe kidney infection and she is not expected to survive beyond a few more weeks.

Chapter 89

Returning to St. Santia

Somewhere in the Caribbean

Sheldrake explained to the Delaneys what had happened to Janet and the condition she was now in, he turned the conversation over to Henshaw to explain what steps had been taken to date. Henshaw told the Delaneys about the unsuccessful search for a kidney donor but of course, with their arrival the situation had now changed. Provided one of them was prepared to become a donor.

"Well of course we will." Both Patrick and Barbara replied in unison.

"Needless to say, we will need to carry out the necessary blood work but being their parents, that should be just a formality." Henshaw explained.

"I will get on to the Augusta and inform them of the good news." Sheldrake said then left the room.

"Why don't you relax for a while, enjoy some refreshments," Henshaw said pointing to the coffee, sandwiches and pastries, "you can join me in the sick room a little later, so I can take the necessary blood samples." The Delaneys briefly smiled and Henshaw poured them each a cup of coffee before leaving the room with Giles close behind him.

"God, to come this far only to find out she might not be alive by the time we get there." Patrick said when they were alone. Barbara didn't answer, her mind was in too much of a turmoil. Patrick reached for a sandwich and scoffed it down, Barbara merely pecked at the offering, too confused to consume anything.

Once Patrick had finished his coffee he stood up and spoke to Barbara.

"Come on then, let's get this done." Patrick said, referring to the blood test, he went to the door, opened it and looked down the corridor, "now where would the sick-room be?" Fortunately, he didn't have to look far, it was a few doors down on the opposite side with a sign that said, 'Sick Room' emblazoned on the door.

"There it is." Patrick said and walked the few steps to the room before tapping lightly on the door.

"Come in!" Henshaw said within the room. Henshaw had been preparing the necessary phials, needles and labels to extract the appropriate tubes of blood to carry out the tests. Patrick entered and waited for Barbara to come in behind him.

"I'll wait out here until you're done." Barbara said.

"There are seats in here, come on in." Patrick said. But Janet shook her head and stayed in the corridor. A couple of minutes later, Patrick was all done and standing in the doorway of the sick-room with the tell-tale piece of cotton-wall in the crook of his arm, held on by a band-aid.

"Your turn, come along." Patrick said. Barbara walked gingerly into the sick-room and sat down where Henshaw indicated as he gathered fresh equipment for her test. As Barbara sat down, Patrick went to sit down in the waiting area of the sick room.

"Patrick, I'm feeling a little squeamish right now, I'd rather you left, if you don't mind." Barbara said. Patrick was about to say something but then thought better of it.

"I'll meet you back in that room we were just in." Barbara added. Patrick left in a huff but didn't say anything.

"Now Mrs. Delaney, just relax your arm for me please." Henshaw said once they were alone.

"Before we do this, tell me, do you carry out the blood work yourself or will that be someone else on the Augusta?" Barbara asked. Henshaw thought it a strange question and was taken aback for a second before regaining his composure.

"I carry out the initial work, obviously if the blood-type is incompatible there is no point continuing with any subsequent work." Henshaw replied, he was about to explain some of the subsequent testing before Barbara interrupted him.

"So, you are the one who is going to find out very quickly that Patrick is not Janet's biological father."

Chapter 90

Preparing for Dual Operations

St. Santia

Once more the entire population of St. Santia was on the beach to greet newcomers to the island, this time, onboard the Connecticut. It was beginning to feel that new arrivals were becoming a regular occurrence on St. Santia based on the comings and goings of the last few weeks. The Delaneys' appearance as they exited from the Connecticut was met with loud applause and they waved in response but of course, their first duty was to immediately board the Augusta to visit with Janet.

Janet was, more or less out of it, and although Patrick spoke a few words to her, he didn't think she heard any of them. At first, Barbara wanted to remain with her daughter, but Amy persuaded her that there was nothing she could do, and it would be best to go ashore and let them prepare Janet for the trying times that lay ahead. Reluctantly, the Delaneys left and walked ashore to meet with the residents of St. Santia. As usual, plenty of refreshments were available in SBs and everyone was jostling to be introduced to Janet's parents.

"Who is this little chap?" Barbara asked as Maria walked over with her son in her arms. Bob was beside her and he spoke first.

"Actually, we haven't got a name for him yet, things have happened so fast around here that we just haven't come up with one." Bob explained. "We call him 'thing' right now."
"Well, we'd better come up with one soon, Amy, our new GP, has just told us that I'm expecting another thing." Maria said, surprising just about everyone within ear-shot, except Bob, naturally he had been informed. Verbal congratulations began being heaped upon the couple and it certainly seemed to lighten everyone's mood, including the Delaneys.
"Why don't we call him Dexter? He was the first person we saw after the devastation." Bob suggested.
"Hmm," Maria replied and after a little thought "that's as good a name and reason as any, why not?"
"So, Dexter it is." Bob said.

A little later, Amy came from the Augusta to join the group and took the Delaneys to one side. Henshaw had already informed Amy of the compatibility situation and she had prepared a suitable explanation as to why Barbara would be the most suitable donor.
"Normally, in donor operations we would be carrying out rigorous cross-matching tests and preparing both patients for the operational trauma that we would be performing." Amy explained, "however, circumstances are such that we do not have the luxury of time and as you are the parents it is felt that immediacy outweighs the risk."
"We understand." Patrick said.

"All the blood tests to date have been positive and we would like to perform the operations tomorrow morning, beginning with the kidney extraction at 8:00 A.M. and the transplant for Janet immediately afterwards."

"Do I have to sign anything?" Patrick asked.

"Mr. Delany, we live in a different world, who are you going to sue if it all goes wrong?" Amy said with an ironic smile.

"Of course, what was I thinking." Patrick replied. "So, let's get on with it."

"Hold your horses, there's just one thing." Amy said, "tests to date have shown that your wife would be the most compatible donor, which is common in these situations." Amy said, bluffing her way through the conversation. Patrick was a little aghast at first, believing he would be the logical choice and he looked first at Amy then his wife and then back to Amy.

"We would like to begin the pre-ops now, if that is not too much of an inconvenience." Amy quickly added, trying not to let Patrick dwell on the issue.

"Sooner the better," Barbara replied, relieved for the first time since she had been informed of the transplant and she began to walk towards the Connecticut with Amy. Patrick was about to escort her over to the submarine when Barbara stopped him.

"There's nothing you can do Pat, is there doctor?" Barbara said, then looking at Amy who smiled and shook her head. "Why don't you just stay here and get acquainted with everyone and come across later." Reluctantly, Patrick remained and found himself gravitating towards talking to the Hamaxs, although older, they were closer to his age-group than any of the others.

Meanwhile, Barbara strode purposely towards the Connecticut with Amy.

"Thank you for doing this," Barbara said to Amy as soon as they were out of earshot of the rest of the residents, "I mean, keeping this a secret."

"Not at all Mrs. Delaney, it happens more than you realize." Amy replied.

"Call me Barbara." Barbara said. She was about to expand on the circumstances that led to her infidelity but decided Amy wasn't really interested and frankly, the fewer people who were aware of the details, the better.

Chapter 91

Transplant Preparations

Aboard the Connecticut and Augusta

Barbara was taken on board the Connecticut and reintroduced to Henshaw who provided her with the usual sexless garb that patients are subject to wearing prior to an operation. Although the majority of Henshaw's experience had been with male patients, during his training he did deal with many female patients. Indeed, his first assignment was on a female ward in a Naval hospital, so he was comfortable when a semi-naked Barbara emerged wearing her new attire. Henshaw led her to a bed in the sick-bay and after a few minutes they were joined by Dennis, Ivan and Amy. Introductions were made, procedures described, and the risks were clearly explained. Barbara was just glad it was all happening so quickly, she had never had an operation in her life and certainly didn't want to spend days thinking about it. Once the meeting was over everyone, except for Amy, left the room. Amy remained to ask various medical questions, some of which necessitated obtaining information regarding Janet's real father.

"Is that really necessary?" Barbara asked quietly.

"The more we understand of Janet's real father's medical history the better chance we have of maintaining Janet's health, post-op." Amy replied. But after all those years ago, Barbara could only provide scant details, since after what happened that night, actions she had regretted every single, remaining, day of her life, she had never seen the man again.

While Amy was obtaining as much medical data as she could, Henshaw had arranged for one of the crew to fetch Patrick. So, by the time Amy had finished her examination of Barbara, Patrick was allowed to be with his wife, while the two medical personnel walked across the jetty to the Augusta. Amy and Henshaw arrived in the War Room where Dennis and Ivan had written a timeline on the whiteboard. Jason and Mary were also there but they were to be literally '*flies on the wall*', silent observers. Jason attended in his capacity of being the commander of the two submarines, Mary because of her close friendship with Janet and some medical understanding. During the ensuing two hours the four-person medical team discussed the tasks that had to be completed for a successful transplant. The critical steps would be the transporting of the donated kidney from one submarine to the other. There were just not enough facilities to carry out two, almost simultaneous, operations on one submarine. It was agreed that Dennis and Ivan would operate on Barbara, beginning at 8:00 AM, to remove a kidney from her and Henshaw would assist. Amy would begin to prep. Janet and once the kidney was removed from Barbara, Dennis and Ivan would cross submarines to enter the Augusta's operating theatre and begin surgery on Janet, while Amy prepared the donor organ. Then, Amy would assist Dennis and Ivan with the transplant while Henshaw remained with Barbara. If there was any post-op. problem with Barbara during the transplant operation, Amy would be the one to return to the Connecticut to administer any treatment.

“It all sounds very simple,” Amy said, “but we all know it isn’t. Are we doing the right thing? We haven’t carried out all the cross-matches nor taken the appropriate risk evaluation.”

“You’re absolutely right Amy,” Dennis agreed, “but I think it is a sound calculated risk. If the donor had been a complete, stranger then I would not be going through with the procedure but it’s her mother. She is healthy and certainly well enough to withstand the operation and live with only one kidney. If we don’t provide Janet with a kidney, she dies, where’s the risk?” There was a silence in the room as the full force of the facts hit home.

“In view of your close relationship with Janet, do you think you are a suitable candidate to carry out this operation Dennis?” Amy asked candidly.

“Ivan will be taking the lead and yes, once the first incision is made, it will be just another operation on another patient. But thank you for your concern.” Dennis replied without a hint of compassion.

“Are you going to remove Janet’s kidneys?” Amy continued probing.

“It’s unlikely, we won’t know for certain until we open her up,” Ivan said, “but based on what we know from her blood tests it is more than likely they will have to be removed, so we are planning for the worst and hoping for the best."

"Henshaw, you're quiet, do you have any questions?" Ivan asked the medic, trying to lighten up the conversation a little.

"No sir." Henshaw replied with confidence, "my tasks are pretty straightforward."

"Well that's it then!" Dennis suddenly said as he placed his hands on his knees with a slap and rose from the conference table. If I don't see you before, have a good night's sleep and I'll see you all in the morning. For you two," Dennis said looking first at Henshaw and then Ivan, "that's 7:00 A.M. sharp in the Connecticut's sick-room. For you Amy, it will be when we see you, hopefully at approximately 10:00 A.M." Dennis left the room leaving behind a surprised group and Amy still a little unsure of Dennis' ability to treat this as just another operation.

"I have known Dennis a long time Amy." Jason began, "I know what you are thinking, trust me, he can do this."

"I hope you're right because we have two lives at risk here." Amy said.

Chapter 92

Transplant

Connecticut and Augusta

The next morning, Barbara was duly anesthetized then Ivan and Dennis began the procedure to remove one of her kidneys. The operation went smoothly without complication and once the kidney was removed it was placed into an ice-filled cooler and Dennis closed-up Barbara's torso. After one last look at Barbara's vital signs, Ivan nodded to Henshaw then the two surgeons left the room with the organ.

On board the Augusta, Amy had begun the pre-op. steps for Janet. Once Dennis and Ivan arrived, changed into clean medical garbs and sterilized their hands they began to work on Janet while Amy prepared the organ. It wasn't long before the team's worst fears were realized, Janet's kidneys had been badly infected and there was no hope of their recovery. Without the operation Janet may have had only weeks to live, maybe even days if another complication had arisen. The good news was, it was decided that the kidneys need not be removed, although, some repairs had to be carried out to portions of her tubes leading to and from the organs. Amy and Ivan had discussed Dennis' ability to assist in the operation and it had been agreed that she would jump in to assist if necessary. Amy was watching Dennis' eyes, as that was about all she could see with the medical mask on his face. But

Dennis did not appear to be troubled by what he was seeing, nor what he must have been feeling, at least, it certainly wasn't reflected in his work. The new kidney was attached but they did not immediately connect it to the urethra. They waited a few moments to ensure the new kidney was performing correctly and urine was being secreted. Satisfied that the kidney was functioning properly they continued with the attachment of the urethra to the bladder and closed up.

Because of the complications the surgeons encountered, the operation took a little longer than was expected, nevertheless, it appeared to have been a success. All the team could do now was to wait for Janet to come around then assess her condition. Amy left the two doctors with Janet to cross over to the Connecticut to check on Barbara. Amy arrived just as Barbara awoke groggily from the effects of the anesthesia. Henshaw was there with some ice chips, which Barbara gratefully accepted. Amy checked her vitals once more and touched her forehead for signs of a fever, fortunately, there wasn't any.

"I know you're not feeling great right now, but everything went well. We will know more when Janet comes around." Amy told Barbara, who just managed to mouth the words 'thank you' in return. Amy stood back from the patient and turned to Henshaw.

"She seems fine, you O.K.? Do you want to grab a coffee or something while I'm here?" Amy asked.

"No, I'm fine. I have a flask of the stuff here, thanks." Henshaw replied.

"I'll tell Patrick he can come and visit, and I'll be back later to relieve you to get some fresh air." Amy said.

"Thanks." Henshaw said. Amy left to return to the Augusta, but she saw Patrick waiting in the corridor and gave him an update on both patients then told him to go and see his wife.

Back onboard the Augusta everything was looking positive, not only was Janet's vitals at expected levels she was beginning to get a little color back in her face, a true test that her new kidney appeared to be functioning normally. Once Janet came around and the effects of the anesthesia wore off, Mary explained what had happened to her. Shortly afterwards, her father came in and tears of joy fell down her cheeks as she hugged him. It was a sign of emotion that none had ever seen in Janet, including her father.

Over the next few days, then weeks, Janet was being closely monitored but it appeared that the anti-rejection drugs were working, and the kidney was being accepted by her body. Janet was also behaving and doing what the medical team had told her to do. What with the near-death experience, the success of her project to bring livestock to the island and her unusual show of emotion maybe a new Janet was emerging. But Mary was soon to find out that the old Janet was still lurking.

Discussions about the Future

Coffee-Shop, St. Santia

Janet and Mary were sitting and enjoying a coffee in the peace and solitude of SBs. All around the island there was hustle and bustle but here it was quite tranquil, a perfect spot for Janet's recuperation after her operation. There wasn't a cloud in the sky, no breeze, no humidity just a warm sun and the gentle, sound of the waves lapping against the beach.

"This is beautiful." Mary said as she closed her eyes and felt the pleasure of the sun warming her face.

"Yes, it is," Janet replied, "imagine, we have a new generation of children growing up who have no racial bias, no religious differences and no gender intolerances. It's like a new Eden."

"But it's the gene pool. Do we have enough to sustain the human race?" Mary asked.

"Well, we have more now than we had a few months ago" Janet replied.

"True, and we have new relationships who will probably provide even more children, but will that be enough?" Mary countered.

"Of course, we can always add to the gene pool with fresh new children." Janet said with a mischievous smile on her face.

“How can we do that Janet?” Mary replied, then she opened her eyes to look at Janet. Mary saw her face and instantly knew what Janet was inferring.

“Noooo, Janet you can’t be serious!” Mary responded vehemently.

“Perfectly serious, Mary.” Janet replied, with the expression that Mary knew only too well. “After all, it is probably only your tubes that are damaged, not your ovaries, you’re a perfect candidate for artificial insemination.”

“Don’t be ridiculous Janet.” Mary scoffed.

“Why not?” Janet argued, “wouldn’t you want little ‘*Jasons*’ running around the island?”

“I’m sure Jason would never entertain the idea of artificial insemination.” Mary said stoically.

“Bet he would.” Janet taunted. “Have you even asked him?”

“Of course not, why would the topic have ever been raised?” Mary said belligerently.

“Well, ask him, we could do it you know.” Janet persevered. “I’m sure any man would enjoy the concept of fathering a new generation, especially under the circumstances we find ourselves in.” Janet was beginning to feel she was at least beating Mary down with her argument, bit by bit.

“I’ll give it some thought.” Mary merely replied.

“I think you should give it more than just some thought, I think you should discuss it with Jason to get his thoughts. Your clock’s ticking you know, tick tock, tick tock." Janet said as she moved her head from side to side, smiling and continuing her taunt.

"The truth is Janet, I would not be comfortable discussing things like that with Jason." Mary said demurely. Just at that moment Jason could be seen walking towards them from the Augusta.

"Oh, if that's the only problem, then I'll ask him for you." Janet decided.

"Good morning ladies, beautiful day." Jason said cheerily as he walked over to the table to pour himself a coffee. Mary gave him a smile and a small wave.

"Morning Jason." Janet said, "Jason, I've got something to ask you."

"Janet, no." Mary almost screamed at Janet, but Jason also knew that look on Janet's face and he wasn't looking forward to what she was about to say, even though he had no idea what it would be. Nevertheless, Jason smiled before he spoke.

"I'm glad to see you're feeling so much better Janet."

AVAILABLE SOON:

Ghost Marina on the Mississippi

Genesis Déjà vu – The Early Years (third book in the series)

To join the mailing list, email:

DEXTER-JAMES@OUTLOOK.COM

CPSIA information can be obtained
at www.ICGtesting.com
Printed in the USA
LVHW111414310319
612439LV00001B/6/P

9 781729 454077